THE VACATION

SAMANTHA M THOMAS

CONTENTS

Dedication: VI

Content Warning: 1

1. Chapter 1   2

2. Chapter 2   11

3. Chapter 3   19

4. Chapter 4   25

5. Chapter 5   33

6. Chapter 6   41

7. Chapter 7   50

8. Chapter 8   61

9. Chapter 9   71

10. Chapter 10   80

11. Chapter 11   88

12. Chapter 12   93

13. Chapter 13   102

14. Chapter 14   113

15.	Chapter 15	119
16.	Chapter 16	127
17.	Chapter 17	131
18.	Chapter 18	136
19.	Chapter 19	142
20.	Chapter 20	146
21.	Chapter 21	152
22.	Chapter 22	157
23.	Chapter 23	166
24.	Chapter 24	175
25.	Chapter 25	184
26.	Chapter 26	188
27.	Chapter 27	195
28.	Chapter 28	204
29.	Chapter 29	212
30.	Chapter 30	222
31.	Chapter 31	231
32.	Chapter 32	241
33.	Chapter 33	248
34.	Chapter 34	255
35.	Chapter 35	262
36.	Chapter 36	271

37. Chapter 37   283

38. Chapter 38   295

39. Epilogue   304

Acknowledgements   313

Also By   314

To my besties. This series is you. You are the inspiration, the support and I'm so damn proud to call each of you a friend.

To anyone struggling with grief.

There is no one way, there is no right way. Feel your feelings and take your time because there will be a time where it doesn't hurt so much. Where you can look back at memories and remember the happy times, not just the sad times.

Content Warning

This book depicts death of a loved one on page and the grief that follows. Please listen to yourself if you think this would be at all triggering and take care of yourself first.

Chapter 1

Jane

I walk off the plane, and the open air releases every ounce of tension built up over the last few months. When my shoulders physically drop, it's a relief. Teaching middle school English is no joke, and it seems to have caught up to me this year.

I'd never heard of the Northern Mariana Islands before, but according to Pen, it's a hidden paradise and still a US Territory that's perfect for her destination wedding. Pen and Andy are adorable together, and I couldn't be happier for them, but this means I'm the last one left.

Our little group has been going strong since freshman year of college. Bea, Pen, Larkin, and I had an ... *interesting* experience involving a guy who thought he could date us all at the same time. Joke was on him, because we became best friends instead and kicked him to the curb. We've been inseparable ever since. Well, until the last few years and that's only because we're all growing up and creating lives of our own. Bea found her love first. Riggs swept her off her feet on a road trip around Texas, and they haven't looked back. Pen was next, as Andy stormed into her life whether she was ready for him or not. And finally, Larkin not only found Theo, but sweet little Gavin who they've since adopted, too.

It's been amazing watching each of them fall head over heels for their men, but here we are, a few years later, and I'm still single as heck. It's ironic considering I'm the one they consider the romantic of the group. I live vicariously through romance books, and I've always wanted a storybook life. I just haven't been lucky enough to find my happily ever after yet.

I let out a heavy sigh. There's no point in dwelling on the fact I'm the lone single person at this wedding. We're in a literal paradise for a week of celebrations, so that should make me happy, but I just feel … worn out. This school year kicked my butt, and I swear I went on more terrible dates during that time than I have in the past five years combined. It's brutal out there.

But I still want to find my one—my soul mate.

Despite wanting to find my one true love, on the flight over here, I made a decision. I want to treat this week like my playground. I want to do a random hook up. I want to learn what turns me on, what will make me … *come* … and I want to experiment. Every boyfriend I've had has been *okay* in the bedroom, but I want—no, I *need*—fireworks. And the only way I'm going to get them is if I figure it out myself before I go on this quest to find my dream man.

My little pep talk gives me a sense of confidence I'm not used to, but I'm nothing if not determined.

"You okay, Jane?" Bea's voice pulls me out of my head.

"Of course! What's not to love? It's gorgeous here. I'm excited to see what the resort looks like."

Bea side eyes me, apparently seeing into the depths of my lying soul.

I breathe out, "I'm fine, I promise. I just need a day to really relax, I think."

"Mmhmm." Her mama bear voice comes out and she says, "You should take this week and really have fun. You know Pen, she isn't making us do a ton of wedding activities, so there is a lot of time to, you know, explore and look at the scenery." She wags her eyebrows at me.

"The scenery, sure." I snort. "You're a married woman, you know."

"Oh, I'll look, but they won't have shit on Riggs." She sighs dreamily.

I want that. I want what they have.

No, the goal for this week is to learn about myself, not find a husband. I barely contain my eyeroll at the thought. I sure as heck am not finding a boyfriend, much less a husband here, if the past year is anything to go by. There have been no sweet gestures, no men going above and beyond for me, and I don't think that's about to change anytime soon. No, this week is about figuring out what's next for me. I feel ... lost, completely lost in my life right now, and using this week to figure things out feels like a good step. Teaching has drained me beyond repair this year, and I'm honestly not sure if I want to stick with it. But the problem is, I have no clue what else to do. Everyone I surround myself with has their lives figured out, and it feels like I'm the last woman standing. I have a week to get myself in order and spend some time with *myself*. It's easy to distract yourself and spend time with people, but looking within yourself to figure out what you truly want is scary as all get out.

I follow behind everyone as we make our way to the waiting SUVs which will take us to The Vanstone. Pen spared no expense with this place and made sure none of us paid for anything—not that she cares about the money. Both Pen and Bea had a tech company for a long time, and it blew up when they launched a mental health app. They sold it to Google for an insane amount of money and opened up Phoenix House, a safe place for anyone struggling with mental health or who just need a little extra support. They've grown it over the years, and it still amazes me when I think about how much they've created.

I press my head against the window and watch the island pass us by as we drive. It's gorgeous here, soothing in a way I didn't know a place could be. There are breathtaking ocean views in every direction I look. I barely register pulling up to the resort, and it's not until my door opens that I realize we're here.

Awe. That's the only description I have. I'm in awe of The Vanstone. This place is exactly what I think of when I think *tropical luxury*. It's all high-end finishes while still keeping the island feel throughout the lobby. It's the perfect mixture, really. I vaguely hear the group heading to the check-in counter, but I'm too lost while looking at every single detail. This place makes me feel serene and laid-back in a way I haven't been in far too long.

This is a place I could get used to.

I start wandering in a large circle, trying to look at all the architectural details and finishes, lost in my own world.

"Jane!" Larkin says loudly, waving her hand in front of my face. I didn't even see her come over.

"What's up?" I ask.

"I checked you in, here's your key. It looks like they spread us out so we won't hear each other's shenanigans." She pauses to smirk. "You're on the north side. Just follow the walkway toward the back of the resort. They said it's easy to find." She hands me my key.

"We're not staying in the actual resort?" I'm confused, where are we staying if not in the place with all the rooms?

"Pen got villas for everyone." She gives me a knowing look. Within our group, Larkin and I have the normal, not so great paying jobs. We've talked about it a few times, and we've never felt like it was a divide in our group, but getting us all villas is extravagant to the max.

"Geez Louise, for the whole week?" I ask and Larkin nods back at me.

"Guess we better enjoy it, huh? Might be the only vacation we're getting for a while."

She's not wrong. Although I try to do random trips during my summer vacations every year, I'm never gone for more than a week so my getaways are always close to home. I volunteer at Phoenix House for most of the summer so it's not like I have a ton of free time even if I'm not teaching. I usually do summer school, but this year I forced myself to step back.

"Alright, I guess I'll go check out where I'm staying for the week." I grab my suitcase and wave goodbye to the group.

I need to get to my room and start psyching myself up for this one-night stand plan.

I find the walkway pretty easily—at least I hope this is the right one—and head north. There isn't a ton of foot traffic which makes me wonder where all the people are. This is a huge resort so there has to be a good number of people here, but it's quiet as I walk to my villa. I double check my room number as a couple of villas pop up along the path, and I realize I still have a ways to go if the numbers are anything to go by. I walk for another ten minutes before I finally find where I'm staying, and right before I turn down the walkway to my room, I lock eyes with the most vibrant green eyes I've ever seen in my life.

They hold my gaze, paralyzing me.

I blink, trying to snap myself out of my haze, and he continues walking as I hurry away. Once I reach my villa, I look back to see who the man was, but he's nowhere to be found. I'm alone on the walkway. Turning to the place I'll be staying for the next week, I tap my key and enter the large space.

Shutting the door behind me, I take a deep breath and try to slow my heartbeat down. I didn't even get a good look at the man, but those eyes are burned into my brain. If I'm able to find him again, maybe I'll try to convince the man to have one night of fun. If his eyes alone are able to have this much of an effect on me, it's worth a shot.

My attention turns to the spacious villa in front of me. It's nothing but open spaces and views for miles. The entire villa is bigger than my apartment; it has an open area housing the living room and dining room. There is an island in the kitchen which acts as a separator between the spaces, but even the kitchen is huge. The whole space is various shades of cream and keeps the feel neutral, so my eyes are drawn to the floor-to-ceiling windows spanning the back wall. Ocean as far as the eye can see with gorgeous, turquoise waters are the main focus of the villa, and I'm left speechless by its beauty.

I leave my luggage in the middle of the living room and race to the bedroom, hoping the view extends there. When I walk in and see the entire back wall is windows too, I squeal and jump onto the bed like a teenager. This place is beyond words, and I'm going to enjoy every second of this slice of paradise.

Flopping down onto my back, I let the smile overtake my face. This week is going to be just what I need to get out the funk I've been in.

⋯⋯◦◦⋯⋯

A knock at my door pulls me from my ocean-induced haze. I pull my phone out and see I've just been resting on my bed while looking at the soothing water for the last two hours.

I jump up and head over to the door before peering through the peephole. Seeing Larkin and Theo standing outside, dressed up for a night out, I swing the door open.

"You're not ready." Larkin looks me up and down with a disappointed look on her face.

"Ready? For what?" I'm confused.

"Where is your head at?" Larking pushes through my door, dragging Theo in behind her. He waves awkwardly at me, looking uncomfortable.

"You might as well get comfortable; we're going to be here a minute," Lark tells Theo.

"What am I missing here?"

"We're getting drinks and dinner. Pen texted everyone, like, an hour ago."

I take a peek at my phone again and see our group has text blown up. It's not unusual, so I didn't even bother to check it.

"Shoot, sorry. Okay, *fancy* dinner?" I rush to my bedroom, Larkin quick on my heels. I realize my suitcase is still in the living room, completely unopened right where I left it. I turn around to go back out and grab it but Larkin is already yanking it through my bedroom door. Tossing it up onto the bed, she wastes no time opening it up as I head to the bathroom to try and get my hair and face presentable. We've been friends for so long we don't have to communicate sometimes, we just know what needs to be done and we do it.

I brush out my short, straight, mousey-brown hair, not bothering to do anything with it. After dabbing on a smidge of powder to help take away some of the shine on my face, I grab my mascara and lip gloss from my makeup bag before turning back to see what Larkin pulled for me to wear.

"Absolutely not." I toss my makeup onto the bed and start rummaging around my suitcase to find something that covers my boobs.

"Jane, put on the damn dress. We're already late." She throws the dress at my face. I hold up the little black dress I usually wear a cardigan with. It's a good dress. It hugs my butt nicely, but the V-neckline is too low and shows too much of my boobs. I've never worn it by itself. I always have a cover-up of some sort.

This is your chance to throw caution to the wind. If you want to find a hook up, having the girls on display might not be a bad idea.

I'd be more annoyed with my inner voice but ... it's right. The whole point of being wild and free this week is to have a random hook up. Boobs sell, right? Might as well own it—even if I am a little uncomfortable.

I rip my shirt off and throw it onto the pile of clothes that are now strewn across my bed. Just as I go to grab the cleavage-baring dress, I hear a mumbled, "Oh shit, I'm sorry," before the door to the bedroom slams shut.

"For the love of God, please tell me your husband did not just see my boobs," I whisper to Lark.

"I mean, you're wearing a bra so technically he didn't see *all* of your boobs. Just some. It's totally fine," she brushes it off.

"You cannot be serious right now," I mumble as I strip out of the rest of my clothes and slide on the dress.

"It's fine, Jane. You know Theo, he's not going to make a whole big deal out of it. Hell, he's probably as red as a tomato now with how embarrassed he must be."

"That doesn't help," I whine.

"Okay, well this has been a great time. Put some shoes on so we can go," she says, ignoring me completely.

I find a pair of stilettos I never get to wear, because teaching middle school children is not glamorous, and put them on. They make me feel super sexy, and suddenly the little black dress seems like a great idea.

Walking out, albeit a little clumsily, I feel a confidence in my body that I haven't felt in forever. And then I see Theo's face and instantly feel embarrassed.

"I'm so sorry," I tell him.

"Definitely my fault. I know better with the four of you. Never interrupt shit going on in the bedroom. Ainsley just asked a question about Gavin, and I wanted to double check with Lark and didn't even think about it. I'm sorry."

"It's really a general rule babe. Even Gavin knows not to disturb us in the bedroom." Lark winks at him. "Is Gavin okay? What'd my sister say?"

"Jesus, starting early today, huh? Yeah, he's fine, Ains just wanted to know what level reading he was at so she could pick up some books, even though I told her we have plenty at home." Theo smirks as he walks over to her. The heat in their eyes makes jealousy flair in my gut.

"Okay, let's go eat before you two sully my room." I open the door, waiting for them to break apart from each other. When they finally do, Larkin's a little breathless and I'm a lot envious.

I'm surer than ever that discovering myself this week is the right move. Time for me to go on the hunt for my one-night stand.

Chapter 2

Pierce

Today has been a shit show. My meetings ran long, my general manager had a list of complaints longer than my dick, and the front desk messed up my reservation. You would think owning the fucking resort would give me an in on a place to stay, but my normal villa was rented out. I'm now staying in the villa on the edge of the property, the one we haven't updated yet, so I don't have a functioning kitchen, and the bathroom is barely serviceable.

It's not a huge deal, I'm not too posh to slum it, but add this on top of the ridiculous day I've had already and I'm on edge.

I'm weaving through the unruly brush we haven't taken care of yet this far out, mentally tallying what still needs to be done today, when I reach the maintained walkway. I hear someone walking nearby and realize it's the person who's renting out my villa. I stop in tracks, wanting to take a gander at who kicked me out of my cozy *home away from home* and am struck dumb.

A vision in loose, dark linen pants and a form-fitting cream tank top is looking down at something in her hand. She's all curves, and from what I can see from here, astonishingly beautiful. Medium-length silky brown hair distracts me until she looks up and our eyes lock. My entire body reacts. I'm hard as stone, my muscles are tense, and my breathing picks up. The instant pull I feel toward this woman is unnatural. It's as if we're frozen in time for hours instead of seconds. She blinks and the moment is broken.

I start walking and she hurries away, only looking back once in her haste to get away from me. As much as I try to look anywhere but at her, I feel that pull. The moment I glance back over in her direction, my stare finds her still hurrying away, that is, until she gets to her villa—*my* villa.

At least I know where she's staying.

All my plans for the rest of the day are put on the backburner. My new mission is to find out who this beauty is and put myself in her path. I've never had my body react to any woman like that in all of my forty-two years, and I'm not letting the chance to close in and fuck her get away.

While heading back to the villa I'm staying in, I call my assistant.

"Sydney, cancel the rest of my meetings. And get me the name of the guest staying in my villa." I hang up without waiting for her reply and try to figure out how to make an introduction.

It should be natural. I don't want things to feel forced. I can't have her disinterested before I even get a chance to put her beneath me. Maybe I'll just follow her this evening and see what opportunities arise. I'm a patient man, and by the looks of it, she just arrived at my resort; we've got time.

I make it back to my room right as my phone goes off with a text message from Sydney. At least she was punctual getting me a name.

Sydney: Jane Hatley.

Sydney also went above the call of duty and gave me some additional information. Jane is here for a wedding, along with three other couples. They've shared their itinerary with our resort, and they don't seem to have much on their agenda this week. She's supposed to be checking out in eight days, but if I have my way, she'll be begging to stay in my bed longer.

Opening up the laptop on the makeshift desk in the villa, I pull up my email and double check if there is anything that needs my attention right away. I have a couple of emails from general managers of other properties, but they look more like status updates as opposed to anything thing needing my immediate attention. I don't think I could handle any major problems or senseless bitching right now, not with my cock hard at just the thought of Jane. My focus is shot, and my patience is lower than its usual nonexistence with work so I'm glad things are running smoothly.

I send a quick text back to Sydney to run interference on my emails because I'll be indisposed for the rest of the day. At least, I hope I'll be indisposed. My goal is to be with a certain brunette shortly.

The clock reads just after four in the afternoon, and I decide to wander around the property to see if I can locate Jane. I just need an in, and then she won't be able to say no to what I have in mind.

I slowly make my way back toward her—my—villa, looking to see if she's still in her room. From what I can see she's not, which is mildly disappointing, but I carry on to the bar area. Just outside of our five-star restaurant is a large bar where guests tend to gravitate. If I'm lucky, this is exactly where she'll ended up.

I'm five minutes from the bar when an employee stops me.

"Good afternoon Mr. Vanstone, there's a problem with laundry—"

"Go talk to the GM." I continue walking past them without giving it a second thought.

I'm man on a mission, and nothing will get in my way ... not even incompetent employees who need to follow the chain of command.

Once I arrive at the bar, I try to stay hidden in the shadows in hopes I can observe Jane a little more, but also so my staff doesn't find me and think they can come and chat.

I sink into a bar stool at the very end of the bar. It's a decent spot because it's partially obstructed by some decorative trees. It gives me the opportunity to look around without being too noticed. It's pretty quiet in the bar this early but give it two hours and this place will be packed.

Looking over at the bartender on duty, I notice he's already made my usual drink, a Blood and Sand, and he's making his way over to me. Placing it down in front of me with a nod of his head, he wordlessly walks away. At least the bartenders know not to talk to me.

I bring the cocktail up to my lips and spin the barstool toward the open bar, savoring the smokey Scotch with a hint of cherry brandy and orange. My eyes scan every guest hoping one of them will be Jane. When I've finished casing the room, I'm disappointed she's not here, but I decide to wait it out until I least finish my drink. If she's not here by then, I'll take a lap around the resort again to find her.

I'm down to the last sip, two if I really make it stretch, when the atmosphere changes. *She's here.* I don't even see her yet, but I know she's here. The same pull I felt earlier flows through me, and I turn to the door searching her out. Unfortunately, all I see is a group of couples at the entrance, laughing and having a good time. The businessman in me is happy to see people enjoying themselves, but the man in me, well he's getting more impatient by the minute, too eager to see those luscious curves again.

The group parts, half heading to the bar, half heading to a corner booth, and that's when I see her. She's standing like a fucking goddess in a little black dress. My cock instantly hardens, and I clench the glass in my hand so hard I'm afraid it'll break, but she's here. *Fucking finally.*

She walks to the bar with one of the men, and I have to put my glass down. Sydney told me she was by herself. Was she bullshitting me? Is Jane actually taken? No, they were coupled up at the entrance, and she's by herself. I take a deep breath to sooth my racing heart at the thought of her being taken and think about how to get her into my bed tonight.

I turn back to the bar, careful not to draw attention to myself, and watch out of the corner of my eye as they order drinks for the table. There are a plethora of cocktails, but I'm only interested in what she's drinking. You can tell a lot about a woman by what she drinks, and I want the knowledge like I want my next business deal.

They finally get all their drinks and quickly realize they don't have enough hands. I was looking for an opportunity and here it is, handed to me on a cocktail covered tray. I stand up, buttoning my suit jacket as I do so, and walk the couple of steps to where Jane and the man stand.

"You need some help with those?" I put on my most charming smile.

"Oh, that would be great!" Jane exclaims, clearly relieved. Her eyes meet mine, and the jolt of recognition and heat in her brown eyes makes me smirk. So, she recognizes me and she's not unaffected. I hold her stare a moment longer before looking at her companion. The man with her gives me a side-eye, but it's not like he's staking his ground, it's more he's being protective of her. *Interesting.*

We all grab a couple glasses and head to the booth where the others in the party are waiting for them. The man drops his glasses off and heads back to the bar to grab the last drinks. I drop off the ones I'm holding, meet Jane's eye again as a pretty blush graces her cheeks, and then take my leave.

I need some time to observe the group, figure out the dynamics, and hopefully gleam some information about Jane from my hidden spot.

My mind keeps wandering to look in Jane's eyes when she saw me again, though. The pure lust in them has me daydreaming about what I want to do to her first. Maybe we won't even make it back to the villas, maybe I'll take her to the offices not far from here and fuck her on my desk. *No, I need the privacy of the villa.* I'll take her against the wall, in the shower, on every inch of countertop I can find. Deciding what to do first is the real challenge.

"Another Sir?" the bartender asks, holding my empty glass in his hand.

"Please." I nod.

Turning my attention back to Jane and her friends, I immediately notice how everyone, except her, is paired up. You can tell exactly who the couples are in the group just based on their body language. At least that's one obstacle definitively down. The next thing I see is the glass she presses against her lips. I watch her swallow as the liquid slides down her throat, and my cock twitches at the image. I can see her now, on her knees, taking my cock to the back of her throat and swallowing around my head. I clear my throat, trying to calm myself down. I'm getting ahead of myself.

She brings the martini glass back down to the table, and now I know I need to fuck her. Judging by the cloudiness and the olives in her glass she's drinking a dirty martini. Every woman I've fucked who's been a dirty martini drinker has been a proper shag. Dirty and fun and leaves without a fuss in the morning.

There seems to be a little dichotomy with her though, she's pulled her dress down three times since she got here, yet she's showing a fair amount of cleavage. Her drink suggests she's more sexual than she appears, and all of it adds up to her being even more intriguing.

I think I'm going to have to work for this one. And I definitely need to learn a little more about the fascinating Ms. Jane Hatley in order to figure out how to have her begging for my cock.

Her group of friends are all having a good time, she is too, she's just a little more subdued than the rest of the group. She laughs when appropriate, but there's something in her eyes. They're almost despondent. A pang hits my chest. I rub it wearily and continue to watch her.

She's fucking stunning with her curves, but now that I'm able to see her face clearly, it's equally so, if not more so than those fuckable curves. She has whiskey-colored eyes that immediately draw me in, and her shoulder-length brown hair has a shine to it which would look spectacular wrapped around my fist while I take her from behind.

The bartender interrupts my salacious thoughts, tipping his chin to my drink and asking if I want another.

"No thank you. But the table in the corner, charge their entire bill to my account please."

"Of course, Sir."

I look down at the dredges of my drink, contemplating my next move. The smart move would be to leave her alone for the night, well, at least appear to leave her alone. I'll most likely stick to the shadows and watch her to get any little piece of information I can. But making my move tonight could spook her, and I'm not willing to take the chance.

"Hey, can I get the bill for the corner table over there?" Her voice pulls me from my thoughts.

"Oh, it's already been taken care of, Miss."

"What? That can't be right. Did one of the others come over here first?"

"No ma'am. A gentleman already paid the bill." I can feel the uncertainty coming from the bartender. He's unsure if he should tell her I'm the one that paid for their drinks, but I'm more curious about how this will all play out to give him any direction. Call me an asshole, but I'm more focused on Jane's reactions than what he tells her.

"What?" The disbelief is palpable. Does she not think a man would buy her a drink?

"Umm, your bill is taken care of."

"By whom?" She huffs and puts her hands on her hips.

Feisty, I can work with that.

"Umm..."

"By me, Pierce Vanstone. Nice to meet you." I hold out my hand to her.

She looks so unsure, and displeasure from making her feel like that weaves its way into my chest.

"Nice to meet you too, I guess. I'm Jane. Thank you, but you didn't need to buy our drinks."

"I know."

"Wait, Vanstone? As in *The* Vanstone?"

"The one and only." Might as well be honest from the get-go.

"Holy shorts," she whispers and I'm sure I've misheard her.

"Well, thanks again." She abruptly turns and walks as fast as her fuck me heels allow until she gets back to her friends. The women start whispering, there are a few peeks over at me, but I just tip my chin in acknowledgment. I'm not hiding the fact I'm interested.

"Sir, I am so sorry. I didn't know if you wanted me to tell her it was you," the bartender nervously says.

"It's not your fault. I didn't specifically tell you not to. Thanks for the drinks tonight." I get off the stool and head to the entrance. Jane meets my eyes, and I throw her a wink.

Progress. This is definitely progress.

Chapter 3

*O*h god he has the hint of a British accent.

The second he introduced himself all I could focus on was the faint accent. Do I frequently binge British television shows purely to hear them talk? Absolutely. Hearing his subtle accent come through, no matter how faint, turned me on more than any man in the last three years had.

We were already seated for dinner by the time I got over the shock of him paying for our drink tab. His features flashed through my head like one of those old View-Master toys. Glossy, perfectly placed hair with a smattering of grey at the sides? *Check.* Angular face with a jaw cut from stone? *Check.* And those green eyes that caught my attention earlier in the day? *Double flippin' check.* And to find out he's the freaking owner of the resort was all too much for me. I didn't know how to act or respond to him. I've had guys hit on me before, but Pierce didn't just hit on me, it was somehow more elegant than that.

And then I walked away. Well, it was more of a sprint in heels, so basically the same effectiveness.

I'm so flustered at dinner that I'm barely listening to the conversation going on around me. Was he actually flirting with me, or was he just being nice because it's Pen's wedding?

Don't be ridiculous, he was just being nice because of the wedding.

I tune back into the conversation and hear all the happy couples talking about their plans.

The waiter comes to ask if we want another round, and we all agree enthusiastically.

"So, are we going to talk about why you're only drinking water?" Larkin asks Bea.

While we were at the bar, I didn't think anything of it because she was a little queasy on the flight over, but now it's all adding up.

"We wanted to wait until after the wedding," Bea mumbles.

My heart drops.

"Like hell! Spill, mama bear!" Pen smirks.

"We're pregnant!" Riggs almost shouts. His excitement is palpable and my heart aches in my chest.

When do I get my chance? How am I the last one left?

And know I'll feel like dog poop for the thought even crossing my mind later. I truly am so happy for my friends; I just feel a little left behind.

Heck, I can't even get an orgasm from a man, and all my closest friends are over here finding gems and getting married and having babies.

The cheers and tears break out around me as I come back to myself, and I join in the celebration. Now is not the time to wallow in self-pity.

All four of us girls get up and do a group hug. We all gush over the news and tell Bea how excited we are for her. It's been a long and hard road for Bea and Riggs. They've struggled, been to countless doctors, and Bea told us not long ago she had basically given up. Although selfishly, I'm upset, I honestly couldn't be happier for her and Riggs. She's the first one of us to get pregnant, and although Larkin and Theo have Gavin, this is a huge deal. We're all going to be the best auntie's for this little one, and I am *so* excited about it.

It takes the group a while to settle down, and we cheers to the happy parents-to-be before our food is served. The rest of dinner is spent talking about all things babies and weddings and eating some of the best food I've ever had in my life. I might gain ten pounds while I'm here, but it'll be worth it.

Pierce hasn't been far from my thoughts, though. He seems like a man who knows what he's doing, and he might be the perfect option for a hook up. If he was indeed flirting with me, that is.

We wrap up dinner, everyone deciding to call it a night early since we've had a long day of travel. I, on the other hand, head to the bar to see if the intriguing Mr. Vanstone is still there. It's unlikely, but maybe tonight is a good night to drink my problems away. A very healthy coping mechanism, if I do say so myself.

I scan the bar while standing just inside the entrance. There's no sign of the enigmatic resort owner, but I head to the bar anyway.

The same bartender greets me.

"Another dirty martini, Ma'am?"

Impressive. "Yes please, thank you very much." I sit down, making sure I adjust my dress to cover as much of my thigh as possible.

The bartender efficiently slides my drink over to me with a wink.

I can feel the blush take over my cheeks. Between the alcohol from dinner and trying to find the courage for this hook up, I feel out of sorts, so his wink, innocent or not, has me frazzled.

Two drinks later, and I'm feeling no pain. I'm having a lively conversation with the bartender. He's telling me all about his boyfriend and the new house they found on the beach. I listen, enraptured in his adorable life here on the island, when I suddenly feel a presence behind me. My new bartender friend, Leo, straightens up as the smile drops from his face.

"Mr. Vanstone, your usual?" he asks.

"I'm fine for now, thank you. Add hers to my account again please." His strong voice with the British lilt sends a shiver down my spine.

"We meet again. I don't think I caught your name," he says sitting down on the stool next to mine.

"Jane. Jane Hatley." I hold out my hand to his, just like he did to me earlier. My heart is pounding, but this is what I wanted, to find him and see if he's interested in hooking up while I'm on the island.

"Ms. Hatley, wonderful to formally meet you." He takes my hand and presses his lips to the top of it.

Oh, that's a good sign that he's interested, right?

"So, what brings you to the island?" I ask.

"Besides the fact I own the resort?" he asks with an amused smirk. "I try to round my properties a couple of times a year to ensure things are running smoothly."

"Of course, that was a dumb question." I chastise myself.

"Not at all, I could have been here to take a vacation."

"Is that something you do often? Take vacations to all your gorgeous properties?" *Holy moly, is this my idea of flirting?*

"Unfortunately, no. Running an empire leaves very little time for relaxation."

"What a shame. Everyone needs time to relax. How do you let loose?" I ask. I'm not sure if it's the alcohol or if I'm curious how he does it all. I don't run a luxury five-star hotel empire, and I can barely hold it all together.

He looks pensive for a moment, like he's genuinely thinking of a response. Then, he says, "I will admit it's been a while since I've had the time."

"Well, that's disappointing. I'm trying to use this trip as my time to relax. But I'll admit I'm pretty bad at it."

"Why do you say that?"

"Because I have a whole plan, but I don't think I can actually go through with it. And the whole point of the plan is to figure out myself ... and help myself relax ... and be exactly who I've always wanted to be." I sigh. Yep, I might be a little drunk.

"And who do you want to be, Jane?"

"Sexy, wanted, uninhibited," I say without thinking.

"You don't think you're sexy?" he asks.

I stare at the bar top contemplating my response.

"I think I'm average with an average love life, and I'm not quite sure how to break out of it." It's the sad truth, and I'm not sure why I'm spilling my troubles to this gorgeous stranger. Maybe these dirty martinis are extra special because we're at this fancy resort.

"You said you have a plan?"

"I do, but I'm not the kind of person who does the sort of thing I've planned out. It's very much outside of my comfort zone."

"Isn't the reason you go on vacation to do things you normally wouldn't? Be who you normally wouldn't be?" he pushes.

"It would seem so. That, and go to your best friend's wedding, I suppose." I smile over at him. Gosh, he really is gorgeous. The bartender slides another martini my way, and I happily down half of it without thinking.

Pierce watches me with keen eyes, and I decide to go for broke. *Thanks, martinis.*

"So, here's my plan," I say with intoxicated purpose. "I want to find a hook up. But not just any hook up, I need a man who knows what he's doing because I don't have a darn clue. I need a man who will show me how to ... do things and how to *relax* properly, you know?" I look over at him as I ramble. His eyes meet mine, and that dang shiver works its way down my back again.

He doesn't say anything for a few seconds but it feels like minutes go by, and I begin to realize what I just told him. Clinging to my drink, I chug the rest of it, hoping it will make me less awkward, or heck, even rewind the last ten minutes. A glass of water is placed in front of me, and I look up to see the bartender wink at me again. *What a life saver. It's too bad he's gay. I'm sure he would teach me some things.*

I chug half the glass and wearily turn my attention back to Pierce. He hasn't said anything, and I wouldn't be shocked if he just gets up and leaves.

"Answer me this, Miss Hatley, has a man every given you an orgasm?"

I freeze with my water glass halfway to my lips.

"Answer me." He turns to face me.

"No."

"Have you ever given yourself an orgasm?" His tone is unusually calm.

"No, I ... I can't, I've tried." My voice is shaky, and I'm unsure why I'm answering such insane questions.

He leans forward, his chest pressing against my shoulder. "You want a real man to show what true pleasure feels like? A real man to explore your needs with?" I can feel his breath against my ear. "I can teach you things you've never even heard of. I can show you pleasure you've never even dreamed of." He leans back. "But I need you to be a little more sober." He winks. "I'll be around. Think about it."

And then he's gone.

Chapter 4

Pierce

Walking away tested every ounce of my restraint, but I had to. I want her begging beneath me, and coherently sure I'm everything she needs in the exact moment. Right now isn't the time. She's been drinking, and although she spilled many secrets to me, I'm not a man to take advantage of a woman. She needs to feel safe, confident in herself, and most of all, she needs to understand I will give her everything she could ever desire when we're together. And she's not there yet.

I decide I need to walk around the property to calm not only my mind down, but my knob as well. It's been a while since I've taken a woman to my bed, mostly because I've been traveling from property to property, too busy to take an evening to enjoy myself, but I can already sense my fist won't get the job done this time.

I made the right decision.

While it may be true, it doesn't mean my balls are any less blue at the moment.

I make it fully around the property and see nothing amiss, so I head back toward my villa. Looking at my watch, I see it's been an hour since I left the shy, slightly tipsy, tempting woman, and I find myself wondering if she got back to the villa okay. I should have walked her back myself, but my control was barely hanging on. Not spending more time with her was the safest option until she's ready for me.

I'm almost to where she's staying, and I see the living room lights on. At least I know she made it back fine. Walking slowly down the path leading to the front door, I stand in front of the door wondering what the fuck I'm doing. I'm not usually a stalker, but something is pulling me to her. There's a gap in the window coverings, and I contemplate looking. It's an invasion of privacy, and I tell myself I'm just checking to make sure she's okay, but I know the truth. I'm hoping to get one last glimpse of her curves in the dress she was visibly uncomfortable in. Possibly a little more so I have vivid images in my head to yank with when I'm in the shower later tonight.

A muffled groan makes the decision for me, and with no control over my own body, I lean to the left to look through the sliver of an opening.

What I see stops my heart and has my cock painfully pressing against my zipper.

Jane's lying on the couch, facing away from me so I can't see her expression, but I don't need to see her expression to know what she's doing.

The strap of her dress has fallen off her shoulder, and I'm desperate to see if her pert nipple is exposed. One of her hands in between her thighs and from what I can see, she's working furiously to relieve the ache I left her with.

She lets out another groan but being so close this time I can hear it's not a groan of pleasure. *She's frustrated.*

When I asked her if she'd ever given herself an orgasm, I was unprepared for the answer and how much it would make me crave showing her what she's been missing. But to physically see it? And to hear the frustration in her voice? I don't have the willpower to stand by and let her be miserable. I gave her an hour, if she opens the door and is still tipsy I'll bow out, but if not ... She's mine.

Gently knocking on the door, I lean in close.

"Jane, it's Pierce. Let me in, love," I say in the gentlest voice I can manage.

I hear shuffling from behind the door before it opens to reveal a very rumpled and unsatisfied Jane. My god, she looks remarkable. Her hair is down and disheveled and one of the straps of her dress she attempted to hastily put back on is falling down her shoulder to reveal the porcelain skin.

"What are you doing here?" Her voice barely above a whisper.

"Showing you what you've been missing out on if you're ready." I trail my fingertips up her exposed arm and watch goosebumps appear. She looks up at me with such earnestness, such hope, it only reenforces my decision right now.

"Tell me how you're feeling."

"How I'm f-feeling?" she stutters out.

"I need to know you've at least thought this through and that you aren't too drunk to make the decision." God I might die of blue balls, but I will stand by my morals on this one.

"I ... I feel good, frustrated but good, not drunk. I want this if you're still willing." Her eyes are clear, and she looks at me with as much confidence as she can produce.

I crowd her in the doorway forcing her to step back into the villa. Once we're both inside, I kick the door shut, spin her around, and push her back against the door.

"What—"

I push the other strap of her dress off her shoulder and watch as her dress falls from her chest. She's bare underneath and I have to shift my dick in my pants to remind myself this is about her.

Her dress is caught on her sexy as fuck hips, and all thoughts of taking my time vanish. Hooking my thumbs in the sides of her dress, I slide the silky fabric down over her hips and watch it fall to the ground.

Standing in nothing but black silk panties, she looks like the ultimate temptation. I take a step back, trailing my eyes up and down her body. Her wide hips and dusky nipples have my cock throbbing in my slacks. I look up at her face and see she's unsure yet so turned on. Her breathing is fast, and she's pressing her hands against the door like it's a lifeline.

I slide off my suit jacket, tossing it on the entry table not far from us and begin to roll up my sleeves.

"Here's what's going to happen. You are going to stand there looking sexy as fuck, and I'm going to show you how a man takes care of a woman. Then I'm going to walk out of here and go back to my room." I don't give her an option; she doesn't need one. She needs an orgasm, and I'm damn sure going to be the one to give it to her.

The barely there nod of her head tells me she's hesitantly on board, but I need more.

"I need words, love. I won't touch you otherwise."

"Y-yes," she whispers. "Please." Her hands tighten into fists, and I know she's on edge.

My eyes follow her shallow breath and the clench of her thighs, trying to decide what I want to do. There are too many possibilities with this delectable woman.

"Pierce, please," she begs, and I stop thinking.

Dropping to my knees in front of her, I yank her hips toward me. I trail my nose against her panties, and her scent envelopes me.

"Fuck, you smell good," I murmur against her before nudging her clit with my nose.

Hooking my finger into the side of her panties, I slide them down her hips. Her hand reaches for me before abruptly pressing back to the door. I grab it, yanking it to my head and showing her I want her to use me.

Her fingers tangle in my hair as I lean forward burying my tongue in her cunt.

Fuck, she tastes sensational.

I sink into her, trailing her arousal up to her clit where she grips my hair tighter and bucks her hips. Smirking, I continue to explore and watch her reactions. If she's never had an orgasm before, I'm going to make damn sure this is not only the first but one of the best she'll ever have.

I circle her clit with my tongue, watching carefully for any reaction from her. When she whimpers, I repeat the motion over and over again before picking up her leg and putting it over my shoulder.

"Oh God," she cries out gripping my hair so tight it stings.

I rip my mouth from her, not saying anything until her eyes refocus on me.

"Call my name as you come. I need to hear my name on your lips." I stand my ground until she acknowledges my words. She frantically nods her head.

"Words, love."

"Okay. Just please... please go back to..." She waves her hand over her pussy, and I smirk.

"We'll work on that later." I don't give her time to ask me what I mean. I attack her gorgeous cunt picking up right where I left off.

"Pierce!" She gasps, putting both hands into my hair.

That's right, say my name love.

Her clit pulses against my lips, telling me she's close. I trace a circle around it, teasing the ever living fuck out of her judging by how hard she's grabbing my hair. Finally give in, I suck her clit in a pulsing pattern.

She screams as she falls apart and I let her grind against my face as she comes.

When she's released my hair from her punishing grip, I move my tongue to her pussy licking up every ounce of her orgasm.

"No more, please, no more." She pushes my head away from her, and I sit back on my heels dropping her leg from my shoulder.

I'm about to smugly ask her how it was, but her knees give out before I can. I catch her in my arms, then stand up and walk to the bedroom. She wraps her arms around my neck, burying her face into my neck. Her warm breath against me makes my balls tighten.

"Are you okay?" I ask her as I lay her naked body on the bed, my bed normally, and the vision she makes in it has my mind reeling. I won't push her any more tonight, but I'm damn sure not done with her.

"No wonder everyone goes crazy for sex. If it's like that, I get it," she says dreamily.

It's adorable she thinks what we just did was good sex. Don't get me wrong it was hot as shit, but that was just a taste, a tease, and I want so much more.

"There is more where that came from." I lean down pressing a kiss to her forehead.

"I just need a nap first," she murmurs.

Damn, she's charming, too.

She cuddles up under the blankets, closing her eyes before I have a chance to say anything else.

I watch her for a few minutes, trying to figure out why she has such an immediate hold over me. She's gorgeous, yes, but it's more than that. She's also different. She's so responsive yet this is the first time she's let herself relax enough to have an orgasm. It's something I want to explore and learn more about, but I can't push her too far or too fast.

I take one last look at her already sleeping soundly before I head out to the living area and to the desk which is usually fully stocked with everything I need to work.

I find a pad of paper and a pen and scribble down what I wanted to tell her before I left tonight. I reread it a few times, making sure it sends the right message, and leave it by the coffee pot in the kitchen.

I see her dress and panties on the ground as I make my way to the door, so I pick them up and fold them neatly before placing them on the ottoman in the living room.

I take one last look at her sleeping form before calling it a night and grabbing my jacket on the way out.

Walking back to my temporary lodging, my mind races and my dick is threatening to bust through my trousers.

Quickly unlocking my door and throwing my jacket on the beat-up couch, I immediately start stripping out of my clothes leaving a trail behind me as I walk to my room. I waste no time taking my cock in my hand when I lie down on the bed. I come embarrassingly fast because I'm so worked up. Seeing Jane have her first orgasm ... *feeling* it? I'm surprised I didn't come in my slacks. She was so fucking gorgeous, and I can't wait until I get to see her open up more and really embrace her sexuality.

She's here for another seven days, and if she'll have me, I'll be clearing my schedule to show her what her body can really do.

I'm unsure why I want her badly enough to even think about clearing my schedule, but there's something about her, something my both my cock and my brain want more of. I want to show her what she's capable of. It's not all altruistic, I want to fuck her desperately, but I want to watch her blossom under me. Bloom into a kinky little sex pot ready to take on the world.

I wasn't expecting Jane Hatley, but I'm damn sure going to enjoy her while I can.

Chapter 5

I stretch my arms over my head and quickly realize I'm naked.

What in the world?

Rubbing my eyes, I focus all my brain power on remembering what happened last night. It's not that I was super drunk; I just have a hard time functioning in the mornings and getting my mind to actually work—which is really fun when you are a teacher.

Pierce.

Everything comes rushing back and my face flames. I cannot believe I let him do that to me last night. What was I thinking?

You were thinking this was exactly what you need. He sure knew what he was doing so you might as well take advantage of it.

I fall back against the bed, more confused than ever. Yes, I wanted to find a hook up and figure out the whole orgasm thing, but Pierce is ... Pierce is way out of my league. I doubt I could handle him for anything more than what we did last night.

And not to mention he walked out of here with me not returning the favor. I've never been with a man who didn't expect something in return. I don't know how to handle a man who did what he did last night and then just walks away.

Was I bad? Was there something wrong with me?

Nope, insecurities will not get me down today. I'm on a dang mission, and I am going to see it through. If I happen to see Pierce again, I'll go for it, if I don't, I'll move on to someone else. Simple.

Nodding to myself, confident as hell, I get out of bed quickly. I make it to my suitcase and find a pair of lounge shorts and tank top to put on. I didn't grow up in a house where any type of nudity was acceptable, so I'm not used to waking up naked. I just finish pulling up my shorts when there is a knock at my door. It's probably the girls wanting to do something crazy.

I open the door without even thinking and see a staff member with a rolling cart standing in front of me. I instantly cross my arms over my chest hoping my nipples aren't visible to this poor, unsuspecting man.

"Umm, hi?"

"Good morning, Ma'am, just dropping off the room service you ordered." He nods to the cart.

"I didn't order anything." I'm confused. Maybe the girls ordered me room service? It seems like stretch.

"You're Ms. Hatley?"

"I am." I nod.

"Then this is yours. I believe there is a note in here too." He smiles like all issues are resolved.

I am hungry though, so who am I to turn down food? I move aside so he can bring it into the villa, and he places the trays on the table.

"Thank you very much." I realize quickly I don't know where my purse is to give him a tip.

He must read it on my face because he's already walking back out the door when he says, "It's all been taken care of Ma'am, enjoy your breakfast." And then he's gone.

Walking over to the table, I peek underneath one of the cloches and see a full plate of French toast, bacon, and fruit. My mouth starts watering, and my stomach lets out a loud gurgle letting me know I really am starving.

Yeah, a real mind-blowing orgasm will do that for you.

I plop into the chair, pull off the covering, and dive in. I have half the French toast and all of the bacon eaten before I remember the note.

I look around the plate and don't see anything, so I turn to the cart and see it's placed underneath one of the other cloches. I also find two other full plates of food I couldn't possibly eat, but it covers every breakfast food I could ever want.

An elegant cream-colored envelope with my name on it in sharp, block writing begs to be opened.

I grab it off the tray and start opening it like it has a bomb inside. I'm not sure why I'm so nervous, even *scared* of this little envelope, but the only way to get an answer is to open the dang thing.

Inside are three simple sentences, but their meaning makes my heart rate jump.

Jane-
I hope you enjoy the selection; I wasn't sure what you liked.
I'd like to see you again if you have time.
Call or text the phone number I left on the note by the coffee marker if you'd like to get together.
-P

He left another note. I abandon my delicious breakfast to go in search of the other note. I find it resting against a coffee cup sitting underneath the coffee pot. I read over his cell phone number and the words just below it.

Nothing is as exquisite as watching your face when I gave you the highest form of pleasure. I'd like to explore this more while you're on the island.

-P

Holy smokes. How is this possible? I'm just ... me, plain Jane just like I always have been, and this insanely attractive man not only gave me an orgasm, but also wants more? This is exactly what I wanted, but the fear keeps me cemented in place. The fear I'm not good enough, the fear last night was a one-time thing and I'll disappoint him. Heck, the fear this is all a joke and I'll get my hopes up only to have them crushed.

It wouldn't be the first time.

I pace around the kitchen for a couple of minutes before I realize some outside opinions might be good.

Me: SOS, I need help and I have food as bribery.

Bea: I can be there in five minutes, you okay?

Me: I'm not totally sure. Bring Riggs too if he doesn't have anything going on with Andy. I have a ton of food that needs to be eaten.

Bea: Got it, we'll be over in a few.

I have an issue with wasted food so this kills two birds with one stone.

True to her word, Bea and Riggs are at my door exactly five minutes later.

"What's up?" Bea asks as she beelines to the table with the food. She lifts up all the cloches before deciding on an Italian omelet. Riggs sits down next to her and takes the last plate with a full American breakfast on it.

"I met someone."

Bea's fork clatters to the plate and Riggs is looking at me like a proud older brother.

"When? Where?" Bea asks.

"I met him last night at the bar before dinner. He paid for all our drinks. I went back after dinner to see if he was still there and ... I might have brought him back here." It's not totally the truth, but they don't need to know what actually happened.

Bea chokes on the bite she just took.

"Did you get down and dirty?" she asks incredulously.

"No, you know me better than that," I say sharply ignoring the fact that I'm lying through my teeth. I'm not mad at her for asking, it's just a gut reaction to doing something so far outside of my comfort zone.

"Okay, so what's the issue?"

"Ugh, I don't even know. He's way out of my league. He can't possibly want someone like me." I throw my hands up. I'm also not sure why I'm keeping who he is to myself, but I'm not quite ready to tell them he owns the entire dang resort.

"Are you serious right now?" Bea asks, exasperated.

Shrugging, I don't respond. I don't have an answer she's going to like so I keep my mouth shut.

"Babe, no one is out of your league. If anything, you're out of his league. If you don't want to tell me details, that's fine, but remember, you don't have to settle. And that goes for hook ups too." She winks at me.

I can feel my face turn bright red as I sneak a peek at Riggs.

"Sorry for the girl talk," I say to him.

"Oh, don't mind me, if I hear anything potentially leading to girl talk, I tune out and think about rugby shit, or work."

Bea shoves him hard.

"What? I'm sure Jane wants privacy; I thought it was a good thing to do!" He looks so confused, and it really is adorable how they are together.

My parents have never been this way. They essentially tolerate each other, and my relationship with both of them is strained at best. I don't have the best example of what a good relationship looks like. Not like Bea and Riggs, or heck the rest of the girls too.

Bea grins at him before turning her attention back to me.

"We're hitting up the pool with Larkin and Theo if you want to join us, if not ... Have a lovely time and tell us all about it later." She wags her eyebrows at me.

Rolling my eyes, I watch as Riggs stacks up all the plates on top of each other, putting them back on the cart and pushes it toward the front door.

"I might join you later, but I'm just going to try and relax for a little bit. And thanks for taking the cart out, Riggs!" I yell toward him as he puts it outside the front door.

He waves me off as Bea comes to give me a hug.

"If you like this guy, go for it. You're here for a week so have some fun, enjoy him, and then go home and never see him again." She walks over to join Riggs. "I'm sure Lark will have her phone on her so call her if you need anything. Otherwise, we'll see you later!"

Both disappear as they close the front door, and I'm still stuck at the dining room table trying to figure out what to do.

I came here wanting to do something out of the norm, so why am I hesitating? Pierce has already proven he knows what he's doing, so this is my chance. I doubt I'll have another opportunity handed to me like this.

Getting up, I walk to the note with Pierce's phone number on it and pull up a new text message. I may have decided to do this, but a text seems like the much safer way to initiate this. If he decides he doesn't want me then I can act like it never happened.

I stare at the blank text for entirely too long before I say screw it and go for it.

Me: Hey, it's Jane. From last night. I got your note, well notes, and if you aren't busy today, I'd love to get together. If you are, that's okay too. No worries.

Me: Oh! And thank you so much for breakfast, it was delicious.

I re-read what I sent and cringe at my awkwardness. Why am I like this? I teach middle schoolers every single day, and I'm never this awkward or unsure of myself. I don't understand why my brain shuts down when a hot guy enters the picture. Heck, they don't even have to be that hot, just interested in me and I completely forget how to function.

My phone chimes and my anxiety rachets up to ten. This is going to be an absolute disaster and I'm going to be crushed that the first guy to give me an orgasm wants nothing more to do with me.

Pierce: Good morning love. You're very welcome. Did I order something you liked? I can be free in about an hour if the timing works for you.

Oh my gosh! He actually wants to hang out!

Me: Everything looked delicious, but I decided on the French toast. An hour would be perfect. Do you want to do anything in particular?
Pierce: You.

My heart stops.
Take the chance Jane. You're never going to have this opportunity again.

Me: When and where?

Did I really just ask that? I'm in way over my head here. I can feel my breath picking up, and I'm very much overwhelmed.

Pierce: I'll pick you up in an hour. Let me worry about the details.
Me: See you in an hour.

The planner in me is freaking out. I like plans, heck, I *love* plans, and not knowing anything is already nerve-racking. But I know I need to treat this week like I'm not … me. I want to do things that scare me, that are out of character.

So, in an hour, the new and improved Jane is going to shine. I'm going to be ready for anything, go with the flow, and hopefully get at least a couple more mind-blowing orgasms while we're at it.

The time to let go of everything I'm used to is right now, I just hope I can handle it.

Chapter 6
Pierce

T here was a man in her villa.

I wasn't spying, per se, but I happened to be walking by when a man was wheeling out her room service cart. It took everything in me not to burst into her room and figure out what the fuck was going on. It isn't my place, but I will be finding out who he is today. I ordered her room service to be courteous and to make sure she ate, not to feed some overgrown boy.

When she texted me twenty minutes later, I'll admit I fully expected her to tell me to get lost. The fact she still wants to get together gives me hope that maybe I'm just mistaken about the huge ass dude who was in her room. I mean, I could probably take him, but I'd prefer not to make a scene at my resort.

Now, I'm running through my emails after talking to my assistant. She's clearing my whole day of meetings and letting everyone know I'll only be available in case of emergency. I also had her arrange for us to have lunch at our five-star restaurant. We have a chef's table which should give us the privacy I crave while also showing her the more lavish side of my life.

I may only want to enjoy her company while she's here, but there's no excuse not to spoil her in the process. And if it happens to make her want me just as much, I definitely won't complain. Nothing is going to distract me from fucking Jane now that I've had a taste.

Last night was probably out of the norm for Jane, so I want to ease her into it, give her time to get used to my more ... forward approach to things. Because make no mistake, she'll be under me before the night is over, and I'm going to enjoy every second of it.

My dick twitches in my slacks, and I have to will myself to focus. I need to get a couple emails out of the way before I pick up Jane.

The next thing I know, my work is done, and I'm walking the path to Jane's.

She opens the door after I knock, and I'm blown away but just how lovely she is. She's wearing a white sundress that highlights her pale skin and glossy chestnut hair. She's wringing her hands together, and I realize I've been standing here with my mouth gaping.

"Hello love," I say quietly.

"Hi. I wasn't sure if you were coming, and I didn't know what to wear. Is this okay? I can change quickly." She says it all in one breath and the nerves are written over every inch of her body.

"Hey." I reach out and take her hand to try and relieve the tension. "What you're wearing is perfect. We're just going for lunch at one of the restaurants here. Is that okay?"

"Yes, let me just grab my bag." Turning around, she grabs a handbag on the table of the foyer and heads back toward me. I have to shift my eyes off of her ass quickly. Now's not the time to make her uncomfortable.

"Ready?" I ask, holding my arm out for her. She takes it warily, looking down at the ground as we walk to the restaurant.

"How are you liking the island so far?"

Her eyes meet mine. "It's gorgeous but I haven't had a ton of time to explore it yet. The resort is really beautiful, and the villas are unlike anything I've ever stayed in before. You've got a really nice place here, Pierce," she says with a shy smile.

Fuck, her innocence is going to kill me. I want to undress her shyness and her clothes all at the same time. Unleash the little vixen I know is simmering just below the surface.

"Thank you. I have a particular soft spot for this one, as it was the first major resort I opened. We've recently been giving it a pretty major facelift so it's nice to see it almost completely finished."

"How many do you have all together?"

"I now have ten resorts, thirty singular hotels, and a plethora of other real estate." Saying it all out loud makes me realize how much my empire has grown, and how much I've hit a wall in my professional life. How many more properties will I collect? How many more resorts do I need to open to feel like I've done enough in my life? But those are questions for another time.

"That's impressive. I can't imagine organizing and running all of that. I can barely manage my middle schoolers." Her tinkling laugh makes my cock come to attention.

Clearing my throat, I attempt to distract myself—and my dick.

"I couldn't handle middle schoolers in any number, so you've got me there." I grin at her.

"It's not for everyone, that's for sure."

We round the corner and walk into Le Papillion, bypassing the hostess stand and heading straight back to the kitchen, where the chef's table is. The restaurant is fully booked, which is always good to see, but it also means every man within the space is eye fucking Jane.

I steer her quickly to the private room, pulling out her chair and making sure she's sitting before pushing it in. Taking my seat, I turn my focus back onto Jane instead of the assholes checking her out.

She looks around the space and I follow her eyes, trying to see it from her view. I've held countless business meetings here, as well as many women in a thinly veiled attempt to get them back to my bed. Usually, women eat up the special attention, but as I'm quickly finding out, Jane isn't most women. She appears highly uncomfortable. Her eyes are darting around and she's ringing her fingers together again.

The waiter stops by our table with my usual bottle of wine, and I wave him off immediately.

"We're actually heading out, my apologies." I scoot my chair back, holding my hand out to Jane.

"What are you doing?" she asks in a confused voice.

"We're going somewhere else. I'm sorry this made you uncomfortable. Let's get out of here."

She stares at me like I've lost my mind, but what she doesn't realize is I'll do anything to ensure she's comfortable. My thoughts stutter in my head. I'm not sure why I need this—her— so much, but all I know is I need her in my bed more than I need to show off some bullshit achievements she doesn't care about.

I practically drag her out of the restaurant and back toward her villa.

"Where are we going?" The panic in her voice makes me stop and turn toward her.

I want to take her somewhere regular guests don't get the opportunity to see. Somewhere quiet where she'll have a better time. There's a hidden beach on the island where only the locals go but considering its peek tourist season it should be empty. Plus, I made sure there was a little secluded cabana installed when I built the resort here so I could have a little privacy whenever I needed it, not that I've really used it.

"You're going to need to grab a swimsuit."

"A swimsuit?" Her eyes are comically large, and I would laugh if she didn't look scared out of her mind.

"It's going to be just us, I promise. Do you want to bring one with you and change there, or put one on under your dress?" I try to keep my voice as gentle as possible. She's definitely less confident than she was last night thanks to a couple of drinks, but it doesn't make me want her any less. If anything, it's intriguing and very different from the women I'm usually with. We arrive at her villa, and she opens the door.

"Right. I'll change here if we have time. Have a seat and I'll be back in a second." She spins on her heels and books it to her room, well, my room technically.

Would it be strange to make the housekeeper keep the sheets on when she leaves? Just so I can keep her scent on them?

Shaking my head, I take a seat on the sofa. Not going to lie, I miss this place. I set it up specifically for my needs, so the half done shithole I'm in right now is less than ideal. But if anyone took over my villa, I'm damn glad it was Jane.

The door to the bedroom opens, and I couldn't look away if I tried. She still has on the white sundress, but this time there is a navy-blue strap around her neck. In my mind, it's a skimpy bikini, but I have a feeling she's more modest than a bikini would allow.

God, I can't wait to see her undone. See her come completely out of her shell as I fuck her and show her just how sexy she is.

"Ready?" Her hesitant voice has me standing up quickly. I wordlessly walk up to her, cupping her jaw in my hands and placing a soft kiss to her lips.

She lets out a shaky breath. "What was that for?" she whispers.

"Just wanted to get you out of your head for a minute. We're going to go somewhere secluded to have a fun, and hopefully stimulating, day."

I smirk at my double meaning. "I don't want you stressed out about anything. I want you as relaxed as I can possibly get you." I let go of her jaw and slide my hand down her arm to her hand. Intertwining our hands, I make sure I have her full attention.

"Don't think about the possibilities, just enjoy the day, okay?"

She nods and I squeeze her hand.

"I need to run to my room quickly to change, are you okay waiting here?" I don't really want to bring her to a half-done villa, and I should have done this while she was changing, but I didn't want to miss anything.

"Oh, um sure. That's fine." The nervousness is back on her face, and I'm annoyed I didn't plan things better.

"I'll be five minutes." I rush out the door before she can say anything else. The quicker I can get her to the beach, the quicker I can get her to relax.

As promised, I'm back at her door in five minutes.

"Ready?" I ask, already pulling her out the door. She's quiet as I practically haul her to the front entrance where my car is waiting for us. I need to get her on the beach and see what's under her dress. I need to see her curvy body, roam every inch with my hands just to get my fix. And I need to be the one who takes all the anxiety she's broadcasting and throws it in the ocean.

We finally make it to my car; one I keep here so I don't have to deal with renting or using one of the resort vehicles. Walking her around to the passenger side, I open the door for her.

She's looking at the car with curious eyes.

"I'll admit, I don't know much about cars but this one's really cute. What is it?"

Cute? She thinks my two hundred- and fifty-thousand-dollar car is cute? Who is this woman?

"It's an Aston Martin DB-11," I inform her, still amused by her statement.

"Oh! Like *James Bond*. That seems fitting considering your accent." She climbs into the car, and I grin at how adorable she is.

Walking around to the driver side, I pull my sunglasses from where they're clipped on my shirt and put them on as I climb in.

"So where are you from anyway?" she asks, finally releasing some of the tension in her body.

"You didn't look me up?" It's a genuine question. It's rare for women to not know who I am let alone not look me up after they find out.

"No, should I have?" she asks with the tilt of her head.

"I'd prefer if you didn't. You can ask me anything and I'll be truthful. The tabloids are awful at getting stories correct so I try to avoid them at all costs."

"Huh." She has a thoughtful look on her face.

"Technically, I'm from Leeds," I answer her earlier question. "I was born there but moved to the States shortly after. My father is English, and my mother was American. I spent time in both countries, hence the subtle accent." It's more than I tell most people about my family, but in my mind, if I open up maybe she will too.

"You must have spent a decent amount of time abroad to keep even a little hint of accent," she observes.

"I would spend summers with my father, and then I opened up my company in London, so I've been stationed there for a while." What I don't tell her is the only reason I opened my main office in London was to try to get closer to my father. In the almost twenty years I've been there, I've learned not to expect much from him. I'll never be good enough or what he wants in a son because of my mother, so I've moved on with my life.

"How interesting. This is the farthest I've been from away from the continental US. I can't imagine traveling that much from such a young age."

I shrug because it's all I've ever known. I've enjoyed it over my forty-two years, and it's made me very successful.

A little voice in my head reminds me of how bored I am of this so-called life I've created. Adding more money to my extensive wealth is dull and all of my properties run like well-oiled machines now. So, what's left?

The question hangs in my mind as Jane keeps talking.

"You know, I like this dressed down look of yours. You look like a completely different person."

"You like the suits better?"

"I think I like them both equally for very different reasons." Her blush takes over her cheeks and floats down her chest.

I look down at myself and try to see it from her viewpoint. I'm in boardshorts and a long-sleeved linen shirt rolled up to my elbows. It is drastically different from my everyday attire and most people don't get to see me dressed down, but I couldn't very well wear my suit to the beach.

"You'll have to tell me those reasons sometime." I grip the wheel tighter. Hopefully while I'm balls deep inside of her.

Her flush deepens, and I fight the grin threatening to break free.

"So, when is your friend's wedding?"

"Oh um, it's on Saturday. She wanted everyone to have a fun week not related to the wedding and have it on the last full day everyone is here. They're staying here an extra week to celebrate their honeymoon," she says.

I make a mental note to remember to send some champagne to their room and comp their room for the honeymoon.

"They sound like good friends," I comment while internally realizing the closest thing I have to a friend is my assistant, Sydney, and I'm pretty sure she hates me.

"The very best," she whispers.

We pull into the beach's parking area, and I stare at her for a moment. She's more than gorgeous, she's *real,* and I have a hard time believing she's really here with me. I'm so used to vapid, self-absorbed women this is all brand new to me, and I fucking *like it.*

"We're here," I say gently, motioning to the beach ahead of us.

She startles and rips her eyes away from mine to look at where we are. The entire drive, she was giving me her full attention and didn't even look at the views we passed.

"Oh my gosh, this is beautiful," she says in awe.

"Yes, it is," I tell her, keeping my eyes one hundred percent directed on her.

"Let's go, love," I climb out of the car and round the hood to open her door.

She jumps out of car and gives me a big hug. She tries to release me, but I hold her tight, looking into her eyes.

"Thank you for bringing me here," she whispers before gently pulling away from me. I let her go, watching as she takes off her shoes and wiggles her toes in the sand.

I might be in trouble with this one.

Chapter 7

Jane

I have never seen anything as beautiful as this beach. It's secluded, the sand is almost white, it's so soft, and the ocean is a glittering turquoise. I breathe a sigh of relief at the calm just standing here gives me.

Although the fancy lunch was probably something women fall over all the time, I was a ball of anxiety. I wasn't dressed right; I couldn't figure out the place settings and there was no menu. I'm not a big fan of eating the unknown. I like to know what's in it before I commit to eating it.

I must have broadcasted my feelings because Pierce didn't bat an eye before dragging me out of there, and now, I'm standing on possibly the best place on earth with a man who makes me want to be someone new. *No, not someone new, just a better version of me.*

When Pierce came back to get me after he changed, I had half a mind to say screw it and jump him right there. But I was entirely too curious about where he was going to take me dressed like he was. I get the feeling he is rarely in anything other than a suit. The thought sparked the idea I'm somehow special enough to see him dressed down.

You aren't special. You're a boring, slightly overweight middle school teacher.

Well, thank goodness my self-doubt has kicked in. God forbid a little positivity sneaks its way in.

I feel Pierce step behind me, the warmth of his body inches away from my back makes me shiver.

"Don't thank me for bringing you here, love," he whispers next to my ear. "A woman such as you deserves to be confident in her surroundings. I apologize for lunch."

Gosh, his voice is commanding yet sweet at the same time, and I swear my swimsuit bottoms melt. And his words are inching their way into my heart. It's weird for me to have such a visceral reaction to a man. Usually, I'm looking for companionship, someone I can grow old with, and sex doesn't necessarily become a huge factor. It's not like I don't want good sex, I just haven't ever ... gotten it. And I sure as heck haven't prioritized it.

Well, that changes today.

I slowly turn around to face Pierce, scared to break whatever tension is running through us. But when I look up into his eyes, I see nothing but heat, no *want,* and I'm shocked it's directed at me.

"Tell me to stop and I will," he says, his voice almost haunting.

"I don't want to stop, but..."

"But what?"

"But I don't think I'm very good at any of this, and I don't want to disappoint you." My eyes shift to down the white sand at my feet.

The only way I change and become more secure in myself, and in the bedroom, is to put it all out there. It's just scary as all get out to do it with a man like Pierce.

"First"—his hand moves to grip my hip—"there is no way in hell you are bad at anything. What you've been with in the past are boys. It's on them for not showing you what you're capable of."

My breath catches in my throat. "And second?"

"Second, this is all on your terms. We move at your pace, and if any time you decide you don't want this, want me, then we move on. No hurt feelings, no harm done."

He says it so simply. But I guess with his status he's probably used to short hook ups with no commitment.

He puts his finger under my chin and lifts it up so I'm looking in his eyes. I see only truth in them.

This is what I want. This is my chance to figure out what gets me going and explore new things. Explore myself.

I stop thinking and take the step into uncertainty.

Raising up on my tip toes, I grip his shoulders pulling him down to me at the same time I surge up.

Our lips crush together in a bruising kiss, catching him off guard. But he's only frozen for a second before he takes control. His other hand tangles in my hair at the base of my neck, gripping it hard and moving my head where he wants it.

He rips his lips from mine, trailing them across my cheek to my ear. His breath sends goosebumps down my entire body.

"This may be on your terms, Jane, but make no mistake I'm in charge," he growls in my ear before nipping just below it at the pulse point.

A moan releases from my throat as his grip tightens, and his other hand moves to my butt.

Lifting me one handed, I wrap my legs around his waist and cling to his shoulders, so I don't fall.

"Oh my gosh, I'm too heavy! What are you thinking?" I lean back to look in his eyes like he's lost his dang mind.

"Get that shit out of your head right now. You are not heavy. Period." He goes back to the spot by my ear, trailing his lips down my neck to the area where it connects to my shoulder. His teeth clench down harder this time causing me to arch my hips forward begging for the friction.

"That's right love, find what feels good," he says as his lips move to my collarbone, down to the swell of my breasts.

The hand tilting my head moves to my butt and holds me up against him, helping me grind against him, but it's not enough.

"I need more," I whimper. "Put me down." I pant, frustrated with need.

He gently slides me down his body where I feel his very prominent erection. My feet finally hit the sand, and I immediately start stripping my dress off then freeze with it barely over my hips.

"Get out of your head, Jane. Tell me what you need, and I'll do it." He stands there like he has all the time in the world while I'm losing my mind with lust and a voice in my mind screaming about where we are.

"I ... I can't. We're literally on a public beach!" *What am I doing!* Oh my gosh, I was about to get off on a public beach. I shake my head, eyes focused on the sand I'm standing on.

Pierce places his knuckle under my chin, drawing my eyes up to his.

"Do you trust me?"

Such a loaded question.

The logical part of my brain says no, absolutely not. I barely know him, and I was just about dry hump him to death on a freaking beach. But there is something in my head that says *yes*. There's something about him, something unequivocally honest, and it's endearing in a way. It sure makes me want to go along with anything he wants. Yes, he's cocky but it only draws me more to him.

So far, he's treated my friends and I to some very expensive drinks, gave me a mind-blowing orgasm, ordered me an impressive room service spread, and he saw I was feeling out of place at out fancy lunch and immediately changed plans. He hasn't done anything to make me question why I'm standing on this beach with him, other than not wanting to get caught by anyone walking on the beach.

"Yes," I whisper. For better or worse, I'm jumping in. This is the week I learn about myself, what I like, and Pierce is the man to help me do it.

His eyes flicker back and forth between mine; I assume he's checking if I'm sure, but I've honestly never felt more sure in my life.

Dropping his knuckle from my chin, he grabs my hand and pulls me toward an alcove of rocks. Now that we're closer I see a fairly large cabana I completely missed. To be fair, I was highly distracted by the gorgeous beach and the even more gorgeous man by my side.

"What is this place?"

"It's a little getaway I set up here for myself. It's hard to get away from the resort sometimes, so I wanted this place as a type of escape. The locals know about it, but guests and most of my seasonal employees don't so it keeps the entire area quiet."

We walk into the curtained off cabana, and I can't help but whistle.

"This is quite the cabana. I don't even think you can call it that honestly." I laugh. It looks like one of those fancy spas where they have an outside massage area—it's expensive and unnecessary.

"Money has its benefits I suppose," I says as he pulls me closer in, facing me toward him.

He drops my hand as he starts to unbutton his shirt, and I stand frozen in place. Every inch of skin he reveals is sexier and sexier. His muscled pecs are dusted with dark hair and lead to his equally impressive abs. My eyes continue scanning downward, and I see his happy trail leading directly to the promised land. I'm so lost in ogling his body I don't notice when he steps forward and gently pushes me so I lose my balance and land on the fluffy bed behind me with a squeak.

"Now tell me what you need, love." His silky-smooth voice coats my skin, and the arousal I thought was long forgotten after my freak out is back with a vengeance.

I swallow hard before taking a deep breath and take the leap with this new, improved me.

"I want you to get me off."

"How? With my fingers? Tongue? Or maybe my cock? Be more specific."

Oh my goodness, how am I going to do this?

"I liked what you did with your tongue yesterday. Can we start there?"

The smirk on his face is purely wicked and I feel wholly unprepared for what's coming my way.

"Yeah, love, we can start there." He stalks toward me, softly trailing his fingertips along my swimsuit, shoving my dress up as he does. "I pegged you for a more modest suit, but I have to say this is a very pleasant surprise."

He's not wrong. I packed this bikini as a way of forcing myself out of my comfort zone. I would usually be in a one piece that covers as much of my butt and boobs as possible.

"Sit up." He holds his hand out to help me up as he slides my dress over my head, tossing it aside before pressing me back to the bed.

I shiver as his fingertips move over the swell of my breast and down my stomach. He hooks his finger into my bikini bottom and moves it back and forth against my skin. My back arches involuntarily, and he doesn't waste another second.

He moves his thumbs into the sides of my bikini bottoms, yanks them down my legs, and throws them off to the side. He drops to his knees and grabs ahold of my right leg and kisses up my leg, taking his sweet time making his way up to where I really want him while I squirm trying to get him to hurry up.

"Patience, or I'll take even longer. I will give you what you need but you need to trust me to get you there." His stern tone stills me immediately, but I can hear myself panting. I'm so worked up I don't know if I can be patient, but I have no doubt the man knows exactly what to do to give me pleasure I've only ever read about.

"Good girl," he whispers right up against my exposed area.

"Hurry up, please for the love of everything, hurry up," I whine.

His dark chuckle reaches my ears, and I swear the sound alone could make me orgasm.

I can't believe how easy it is for this man to get me off. I couldn't even get myself off and here he is playing me like a dang fiddle.

He seals his mouth over my clit, and I almost fly off the bed.

"Pierce!"

He starts up a rhythm alternating sucking and licking my clit, and I'm quickly against the edge of orgasm and trying to hold on.

"Oh crud, I'm so close!"

His laugh reaches my ears as he pulls back from me.

"Do you ever relax enough to really let loose? You never curse and it's making me want to do everything in my power to turn that sexy little mouth of yours into something dirty. I want you talking absolute filth to me, and only me." His eyes twinkle up at me from between my legs, and I can't help the blush that sweeps down my chest at his words.

"I stopped cursing when I started teaching. It was easier to stop completely so I didn't accidentally say something bad at school," I rush out, desperate to have his mouth back on me.

"Yeah, I can understand that. But you know it's now my mission to turn you into a dirty girl, right?" His tongue swirls around my clit, "And

I always get what I want, love." His lips suction around my clit and suck hard and I immediately fall apart. My entire body clenches up tight and I bite my tongue to keep from cursing. It may be his mission, but I'm not going to make it easy on him.

I feel like my orgasm lasts for hours, but when I finally come down from it, I look up to see Pierce staring at me with fire in his eyes. His hand is gripping his dick through his board shorts, and I can't wait to see what he's packing.

"Take them off," I tell him.

My gosh, who am I right now? He's turned me into Larkin.

He doesn't respond, just unties his board shorts and lets them drop before stepping out of them.

My jaw drops.

I've read a ton of romance novels, and you get many variations of penis descriptions, but I have never, in all my thirty years, seen a more perfect one. Usually, I could take it or leave it. I mean, no one I've been with before could get the job done so I don't have high hopes for any man at this point. But Pierce just proved me wrong in every sense of the word.

He's definitely longer than average, but not obnoxiously so. He's also thick, thicker than anyone I've been with before, and I'm a little on edge about how this is all going to work.

"Don't look so scared Jane, I promise you'll enjoy this." His devilish smirk does not ease my hesitation in the least.

"Take your top off for me, love," he says in a gentler tone.

I move like I'm a robot reacting to a voice command, and before I know it, my top is joining my bikini bottoms on the floor.

"Now, show me what you like."

"What ... What I like?"

"I know you haven't gotten yourself off before." *Screw tipsy me, I swear.* "Just show me what you usually do."

I tentatively move my fingers to my clit.

"Stop."

I freeze.

"Touch your breasts first. Get yourself warmed up before you move onto the most sensitive area."

I follow his directions, bringing both my hands up to my breasts. I knead them a little bit, then squeeze them.

"Stop. You're not kneading bread dough; you want to be gentle to start. Pluck at your nipples if you need more stimulation."

I nod and follow his direction in a daze. After a couple minutes I start squirming and want more. I move one hand down to my clit and start slow circles around it as my other hand stays on my breast.

"Good girl."

I whimper just hearing his voice, and it heightens all my senses. My orgasm is barreling down on me, but I'm still just a little bit too far away.

"Look at me," I hear Pierce say. I refocus my attention on him and see him stroking himself.

Seeing his large hand around his even larger dick and seeing how turned he is because of me sets me off. I free fall into my orgasm and can barely catch my breath.

I feel his hand on mine in between my thighs as he joins me on the bed. Grabbing my hand, he pulls it up to his lips where he licks them clean, moaning at my taste.

I have never been so turned on in my life and this is after two orgasms already.

He snags a condom off the side of the bed where he must have stashed it while I was distracted and rolls it on. I spread my legs in a silent ask of where I want him to be.

"You want my cock, love? You're going to have to ask for it." He smirks.

Time to go for broke.

"Oh Pierce, please let me have your dick." I smirk back, my sarcasm making a rare appearance.

"I'll give you this one pass, brat. But make no mistake, the next time you'll be paying for a comment like that," he growls as he rolls over me. He wedges himself between my legs using his hands to shove my legs apart more.

"God, you look phenomenal. Spread out and dripping for me." He pumps his fist twice before lining himself up with me.

I expect him to just push in, but Pierce is anything but predictable. He takes himself in his hand and teases the ever-living heck out of my already over sensitive clit. I try to pull away, but his other hand holds me in place.

"Please. Please, I need you in me now. It's too much." I'm thrashing around, trying to get away or get more, who's to say but I can't focus on anything other than his dick swirling around my clit.

"Love to hear you beg," he growls before moving his dick away and replacing it with his fingers. I feel two enter me immediately, and I arch my back. He feels so good, everything he does turns me on and turns me into a completely different person. He scissors his fingers a little, before tapping that spot only he seems to know, and I know he's trying to prepare me for his thickness a little more.

I open my mouth to beg some more, but he removes his fingers and replaces is with what I really want.

He pushes in gently, just an inch and stays still.

"Move, dear god move, Pierce," I whimper, not caring about anything but feeling him completely inside of me.

"I'm trying not to hurt you," he says through gritted teeth.

I hook my heels around his butt and pull him into me. The stretch as he slides in is unreal. I've never understood the phrase until now, but it's incredible. I feel so full and hypersensitive, but when I look up at him, I lose it completely. His eyes are closed, and his head is tilted back. The veins in his neck are bulging with his restraint. The sight makes me want to break his control just like he's done to me. I arch my back and pump my hips trying to get some friction.

It seems to pull him from himself as he grips my hips and thrusts hard. I scream from how good it feels, forgetting everything except where we're connected.

He sets a steady pace, and out of nowhere, I'm on edge again.

"Oh my god, I'm close," I whimper. I don't think I can handle more.

"I know I can feel you. Come on my cock, love."

I shatter around him, completely oblivious to everything except the high of my release. I have never felt this good. Never felt as free as I do right now.

"Fuck Jane," Pierce says right before he thrusts into the hilt and holds it there as he comes. I open my eyes to take in his release. His face is pure pleasure, and my heart skips a beat knowing I'm the one who put that look on his face.

My body feels like jelly as my muscles unclench, but I already know I'm going to do everything in my power to keep him in my bed all week.

Chapter 8
Pierce

I knew there was a wild cat under that prim, albeit sexy, exterior.

I'm at a loss for words, and that's a rare occurrence indeed. I wasn't expecting to take it this far this soon, in spite of being prepared if it did.

"Wow," her whispered wonderment pulls me out of my stupor.

Looking over at her, I see the relaxation written all over her face and a sense of pride fills my chest. Her eyes are closed, her hair fanned out behind her, and she has a small smile on her face.

I did that. I fucked her so good she's actually content.

I know I'm good in bed, but I don't think I've ever felt as accomplished as I do right now. Seeing Jane satisfied sends a thrill down my spine I'm not used to. I do, however, know I'll be doing everything in my power to do that many more times.

"Round two?" I ask on a laugh.

"Oh my gosh, no! I can barely move." She groans happily.

"Then I'll call this afternoon a success."

Her carefree giggle is new and the goal for the rest of the day is to hear it more often.

"Are you hungry?" I ask, already rolling over and reaching for my phone.

"I could definitely eat," she says as her stomach growls. Her cheeks heat as she giggles again, and I'm already addicted to the sound.

Sending a quick text to my assistant, I tell her to bring a large variety of food and drinks out here without being seen or heard. Throwing my phone on the bed I turn back to Jane. If she replies, it will be with a "yes sir" so I don't need to wait for her answer. Sydney will make it happen.

"Okay, that's done. You want to check out the beach?"

I feel happy, carefree for the first time in far too long. Jane's quickly making me see I've been hung up on building my business for the majority of my life and I'm starting to question why.

"Umm, sure?"

"Food will be here momentarily," I tell her, realizing she's not used to the way I work.

"Oh, okay. So, the beach then?" she says unsure, her eyes firmly focused on the bed.

"Jane," I wait until she looks up, "We're here to relax, to enjoy the quiet. Whatever you want to do while were here with, I'm good for. If you want to just lay here and open the curtains, we can. You want to go swim in the ocean? Done."

"What about the food?" she asks meekly, and it kills me. I want her confident like she was ten minutes ago.

"It'll come to us, love." I try to make my voice gentler, hoping to make her more relaxed.

"Umm, okay. I'm definitely not used to that. Can we go swim in the ocean then?"

I don't answer her, I just grab her hand, pull her up, and hand her the long-forgotten swimsuit. Dragging my board shorts over my still semi-hard dick poses a bit of challenge, but I manage it fast enough to turn my full attention to the beauty before me.

She pulls her bikini bottoms up over her plump ass, shifting clumsily to cover it. Shaky hands grab her top as she puts it back on and tries to tie it.

"May I?"

Nodding, she turns around and presents her back to me.

She's so fucking sexy and she has no clue. It's a travesty.

I carefully tie the back of her suit together before wrapping my arm around her stomach and pulling her back to me. I press a kiss to her neck, breathing in the scent of her. She smells like fresh air and freedom I didn't know I was missing.

"Let's go swim," I whisper and watch a shiver trail down her spine as I let her go.

I pat her on the ass, causing her to squeak and rush out of the cabana. I don't suppress my chuckle watching her flee. She's so fucking adorable and nothing like I expected, but I couldn't be happier about that.

She's halfway down the beach by the time I step out of the cabana, running and yelling with excitement and kid-like joy and it's fucking infectious.

If I'm honest with myself, I haven't been to this beach in at least five years. The sad fact has never been more prominent in my head than it is right now as I watch Jane wade through the ocean.

She's so carefree right now, and excited about something as simple as a beach and I want to bottle it up.

I stand just outside of the cabana, watching her and feeling this intense want in my chest. Not sexual, although I wouldn't say no to a round two, but this overwhelming feeling like I've been missing out on life, and I want to enjoy it like Jane is currently. *With Jane.*

So why am I just standing here watching her?

I walk down the white sands to join her and by the time I reach the water the excitement of relaxing with Jane has reached its peak. I feel fifteen years younger wading into the ocean splashing Jane as I go.

Her screams of fake outrage fuel my need for her. And as we play in the ocean like lust fueled college kids, I feel a lightness I haven't felt in two decades.

I see Sydney scurrying back to her car, letting me know the cabana is now packed with food for us, and just in time because I'm starving.

"I think our food is here, you want to head over?" Before I finish my question, she's already nodding and wading out of the thigh-deep water.

I'll gladly follow behind her, taking in the view of her plump ass in that sorry excuse for a bikini. Although I'm not complaining, far from it, I'm just glad we're alone on the beach so I don't have to kill anyone for seeing this much of her.

When we enter the cabana, even I'm surprised at the spread Sydney set out. A full selection of gourmet sandwiches, a large charcuterie board, and an extensive selection of drinks, among other things, lay before us.

"How on earth did you manage to get all of this here so quickly?" she asks, and from the look on her face it appears she's not abundantly happy at the notion.

"Perks of being rich, I suppose," I mutter. This woman looks at everything I have, everything I can do, and isn't impressed in the least. I've never been with a woman who wasn't impressed with my wealth in some form or another.

"So, what happens when we don't eat all of this?"

"What?" I ask, confused why she's asking.

"What happens when we eat a tenth of the food here and then leave? What happens to the left-over food?"

"I'm not entirely sure. I usually just call Sydney and have her deal with it." I shrug, unconcerned with mundane things like this.

"And Sydney is?"

"My assistant," I clarify.

"And you don't know what she does with all the extra food?" Her tone heavy with annoyance and disbelief.

"I do not, but I can ask her." Honestly, I'll do anything to get this look off her face and turn her back into the carefree woman who was just in the ocean with me.

She lets out a huge sigh. "I'm sorry. I just don't like the idea that all of this will get thrown out. If your assistant doesn't already, you should look at donating it to local schools or shelters."

"I will make sure she does from here on out," I reassure her.

"Thank you." She sounds genuinely relieved I took her request to heart, which makes me wonder what kind of man she's used to.

"Can we eat now?" I try to inflect a little humor in my voice, and it works because she doesn't hesitate to grab a sandwich and take a huge bite.

I can't help but laugh at how unabashed she is right now.

"What?" she mumbles around her bite as slowly lowers the sandwich back to her plate. She instantly looks hesitant and withdrawn.

Shit, what did I do?

"Nothing, I just like the fact you're enjoying the food this much," I reply, hoping she sees the truth of my statement.

"Oh, okay." She picks her sandwich back up and continues as if nothing happened.

We quietly eat the rest of our food until we're both overfull. I discreetly send a text to Sydney, letting her know we're finished and to donate the left-over food somewhere like Oceanview.

"So, what's next?" she asks.

"What do you want next?" I offer, this is her vacation after all.

"I want to go back to the villa," she says shyly.

"Right, of course. I'm sure you have plans with your friends." The insecurity in my voice is obvious and I hate it. I'm never insecure. What is this woman turning me into?

"I was actually hoping you could come with me," she says meekly.

"Are you ready now?" I ask, entirely too eager.

Her laugh tinkles around in my head and makes my black heart a little lighter.

"I think I am. Do we need to do anything to clean up?"

"We do not." Apparently, the perks of being with a billionaire are still a little cloudy for her.

"Right, duh." She shakes her head as I hold out my hand to help her back out to the car.

Taking it willingly, we walk to the car after taking a quick shower in the cabana and throwing our clothes back on.

The drive back to The Vanstone is fairly quiet, mostly Jane is looking around the islands scenery while I think of all the things I want to do to her when we finally get back to the villa. There are too many options, too much I want to do with her, yet I don't think she's ready for me to completely let loose on her. I know she isn't ready for all the depraved things I'd really like to do to her, but I can give her a little taste.

She's quiet as she opens the door, and I can feel the nervousness radiating off her.

"Strip and go lie on the bed." There's no question in my tone, either she does what I say, or we'll see how far I can really push her.

Her back straightens, her eyes wide in shock. I stand my ground, seeing what she decides to do.

I wait ... thirty seconds, a minute ...and she finally turns on her heel and quickly walks to the bedroom.

I have to hold back my groan and palm my cock because I honestly was not expecting her to obey but fuck if it doesn't get me as hard as stone and *excited* for the possibilities.

I wait a couple minutes, thinking of everything from investment properties to my father, trying to get my cock to calm down a little before I come in my slacks.

She was so nervous walking in here, and I want her to be the confident woman she was on the beach. So, a split-second decision means I'll be coming in my hand tonight in the barely functional villa I currently reside in. I want her to see herself like I do. I want her to see how fucking gorgeous she is. No, I want her to *feel* how gorgeous she is.

I count to five in my head, squeezing the tip of my cock to make sure I keep the focus on her and not lose all the control I've carefully curated over the years.

Walking into the bedroom, I'm instantly taken back by the sight of her on my bed. Her shapely legs are crossed, shielding herself from me. Her arms are fidgety, but they aren't crossed in front of her breasts, so I'll count it as a small win.

I walk to the closet without speaking to her. I know I'm making her nervous, but if I talk to her before I grab what I need, she'll be scared shitless and won't give this a chance. I grab the full-length mirror leaning against one of the walls and returning to the bedroom, placing it on a clear wall off to the side. Next, I grab the chair from the corner and place it in front of the mirror.

Taking a deep breath, I turn to face the woman who has me on the edge of my control.

"Come here, love." She looks at the mirror like it will attack her.

"I want to try something, but at any point you can stop it. I want to push you, but I don't want to break you. Does that make sense?" I ask, genuinely trying to get her to understand she's the one in control, even if it feels like she isn't.

Her nod and the scramble off the bed are my only answer.

"I need words, Jane. This is very important to me. I need explicit answers when I ask you something while we're together like this."

"Yes, I understand," she says standing fully in front of me.

I take a seat in the oversized chair, motioning her to follow me. Turning her hips so she's facing mirror, I pull her down onto my lap.

"What—"

"Shh, let me play," I whisper in her ear.

Trailing my fingertips down her arms, I lace our fingers together.

"I want you to see yourself. I need you to really see just how beautiful you are. You're going to sit here and let me lead us in your pleasure while you watch. You're not to close your eyes. Do you understand?"

"Y-yes. I understand," she stutters out.

Moving one of our combined hands, I feather our fingertips up her stomach to her full breasts. Her breathing picks up, her skin pebbled with goosebumps when we circle her nipple lightly. Our other hand rests on her lower stomach while we explore more.

We ease into the nipple play, circling gently, light pinches until both nipples are beaded and hard. Then I start kneading her breasts one at a time until she squirms in my lap.

"Pierce," she moans and tilt her head back.

"Watch," I growl, nipping at her neck.

She jolts her head up as I continue our ministrations. I take our other hand and move it down to her dripping pussy. I dip our fingers into her before moving them up to her clit and getting it nice and wet.

"You're dripping for me, love. Do you see how wet you are?" Her eyes go to her pussy and widen at the blatant show of arousal.

Tapping her clit a couple times while I continue to tweak her nipples, her hips start to grind against me. It takes everything in me not to tilt my hips and take advantage of the motion, but I promised this was about her, and I won't go back on that.

We circle her clit harder as I watch her eyes hyper focus on her fingers. Her chest is flush, there's a trickle of sweat falling between her breasts. She's fucking intoxicating and she has no idea.

"Do you see how fucking sexy you are? How turned on you are?"

"Yes," she pants out.

"See how wet you are? See how fucking beautiful your body is?"

Her back arches as she moans out in agreement, and I know she's getting close.

"Keep your fingers on your clit for me," I tell her before taking our other hands and wrapping it around her torso just under her breasts before I move my other hand to her pussy. As she stimulates her clit, I press two fingers inside of her.

"Oh God!" she screams.

Her hips have a mind of their own at this point, trying to get my fingers deeper and at a faster pace. All it's doing is making me damn sure I'm about to come in my pants like a fucking teenager, and I couldn't care less.

I curl my fingers as I piston them in and out of her, feeling the clench of her inner walls.

"Let go, Jane. See what a fucking goddess you are." I moan into her ear, barely controlling myself.

She explodes on a silent scream, squeezing my fingers so tight I can't move them. Her orgasm is so powerful her entire body is locked up for several seconds before it finally releases her from its grasps. She's gasping for breath as I arch my hips up and come in my trousers on a groan.

I don't even care. It feels like the biggest win I've ever had in my life.

Her eyes refocus on her body in the mirror, flushed and satisfied. A giant smile overtakes her face, and she starts to giggle.

"Oh my god! Oh my god! Did you see that? Did you see how hard I came?" she asks in happy bewilderment.

"Do you see yourself now?" I ask against her neck, breathing in her scent.

"I don't think this will be an overnight change in thinking, but yeah, I think I do." She sighs wistfully. "Thank you, Pierce."

She's bewitched me by simply taking a hold of her life, and for some reason, I don't want to get left behind.

Chapter 9

Waking up alone in bed this morning was not something I thought would make me a sad, but here we are.

Last night was ... Last night was something I didn't know I needed. Pierce showed me a side of myself I had no idea existed. Forcing yourself to see yourself orgasm is empowering as all get out, and I felt like a whole new woman.

And then he left me for the night.

I understand on principle why he left. He even said he wanted me to sleep, relax, and think about what just happened without him there. He wanted me to get my head together before we talked about what happened I guess. I've never been with a man who wanted to talk about a sexual experience and how I feel about it. It's a level of thoughtfulness I never knew I wanted.

I just had no idea him leaving last night would put this melancholy blanket over me.

My phone chimes from the nightstand and I jump to grab it, hoping it's Pierce.

Pen: Brunch today! Meet at the little restaurant by the spa at ten.

Disappointment hits my chest and I have to physically stop the reaction. Pierce doesn't owe me anything. He's given me more than I thought possible with just a couple interactions, sexy interactions but still. Exactly what I wanted. *I just can't help but wish for more. Wish for the romance novels I read to turn into real life.*

Me: I'll be there.

Bea: God yes, why didn't we do this sooner?

Larkin: We've been here like two days ... chill. I'll be there. See y'all later.

I sink back down into the bed, not feeling like engaging in our usual banter. My mood is all over the place. I'm going to have to work up to brunch, and I have exactly two hours to get there.

Questions rapid fire through my head.

Do I want to spend more time with Pierce? Do I want to sleep with Pierce again? Do I tell the rest of the girls about him?

The answer to all of those questions should be yes, but I'm leery about telling the girls. I just want to stay in this little bubble with Pierce and not have them pop it with their logic.

And what's the etiquette with Pierce? Do I text him? Call him? Wait for him to contact me? Gah, I don't know the rules with a man like this. I'm used to extra needy boys who need more attention than the kids I teach.

The spark of confidence I had yesterday is nowhere to be found this morning, so I guess I'll play the waiting game and see if I hear from him.

I finally roll out of bed and head to the bathroom to take a shower before getting ready for brunch. I quickly scrub everything, washing off what remains from last night.

How can I be that girl every day? How do I keep the confidence?

I finish up my shower and throw on a sundress. I'm still left with no more answers than I had this morning, but at least I can distract myself with brunch.

Packing all the essentials in a little crossbody bag, I put on my sandals and head out the door to meet the girls. I decide to leave my phone here because the temptation to check it every ten seconds would be too telling for the girls. If, by the time I get back he's gotten touch, I'll have some answers at least.

These past couple year has been weird in terms of our little group. We've gained some amazing men into our group, but I feel like a third wheel, well seventh wheel, really. And as much as I love our group, and as much as they try to include me, sometimes it's just exhausting to put on a happy face when we get together. It's not always that way, but it's hard to have always been the hopeful one in the group and then be the last one left to find love.

Following the path to the restaurant my mind drifts to Pierce again. I know this week is about Pen and Andy, but dang, I just want to hang out with Pierce more. And I know he's probably ridiculously busy so I shouldn't get my hopes up, but here I am … getting my hopes up.

I make it to the restaurant entirely too fast and realize I'm the first one here. The hostess walks me to our table, and I order a spiked coffee in hopes it will pull me out of my head a little.

By the time my drink arrives, the girls start trickling in.

"What's up stranger? Haven't seen you in a minute." Bea grins as she sits down.

"Is that because you've been locked in your room with Riggs?" I snark back.

"Mostly, but we did happen to drop by your room yesterday, but you weren't there." She quirks a knowing eyebrow in question. I just know she's trying to get me to tell the girls, but she'll respect my boundary if I choose not to.

"I went to the beach yesterday." *Do I sound believable? Technically it's not a lie.*

Her critical eye stares me down and I turn my gaze to my drink in an attempt to not give anything away. Lucky for me, Larkin and Pen show up.

"How are we doing ladies? Did we order drinks?" Pen looks around the table. "Just Jane?"

"The waiters on his way, you won't have to play catch up." I roll my eyes playfully.

"Oh good! So how is everyone liking the place?" Pen asks. Her excitement is infectious, and I decide to keep Pierce close to my chest. We're here for her wedding so it should be the focus, not me hooking up with the sexy owner of the resort.

"It's fucking amazing! I don't know how you found this place but I'm freaking stoked. If there was a place to make me feel less guilty for leaving Gavin, this is it," Larkin says opening her menu.

"Andy found it." Pen chuckles at our shocked faces. "I know right! Insane, but I might just have to have him pick vacation locations more often."

"Riggs and I are enjoying the relaxation. This is far and away less adventurous than our usual road trips. I kind of love the change of pace." Bea laughs.

"And what about you?" Larkin says turning to me. The rest follow suit and my mind freezes. *How much am I telling them?*

"It's gorgeous here. I went and explored the beach yesterday and it was picture perfect."

There, technically not a lie.

Why am I not telling the girls about Pierce? Lord knows I could use the advice on what comes next.

"Oh, good to hear. Andy said he wants to hit it up later if anyone wants to join." Pen sucks down half her mimosa the second it hits the table.

We all nod noncommittally. When Pen said she wanted to do this for her wedding, she made it clear we were all on our separate vacations and are just coming together at the end of the week for her wedding, so we haven't made any plans to really hang out, outside of our impromptu brunch. But this is what we do. Brunch is almost always a weekly thing for us, so gotta keep the tradition going.

We order a plethora of dishes from the menu as well as another round before conversation turns back to me.

"So, who was the guy at the bar?" Larkin asks.

Lovely, exactly what I was hoping to avoid.

"Umm, just a guy trying to buy us drinks. You know I can't turn down free drinks for the group." I laugh, attempting to play it off.

Bea's hard stare meets mine and I just know she wondering why I'm lying. Out of the corner of my eye I see Larkin smirk, and Pen sitting with her chin on her fists like she's a teenager listen to all the good gossip.

"And was this man hot?" Bea asks giving me another change to come clean.

"You know, I didn't even see. It was dark and I was in hurry to join you guys at the table for dinner, and I wasn't thinking about if he was hot or not," I ramble knowing I just gave away everything.

"So, he was hot and bought our entire group drinks in order to get to you. This is very interesting," Larkin sums up oh so helpfully.

"Can we not just talk about Pen's wedding?" I ask.

"Absolutely not. You're a terrible liar and just told us he's super-hot, and the fact you lied about it tells me there is much more to it. Did you happen to go to the beach with said hottie yesterday?" Pen chimes in.

"You guys are the worst." I sigh. "I may have gone to the beach with him yesterday. We had a good time; I just don't know if we're going to do anything else together," I concede. Maybe if I just give them a little crumb I won't have to talk about the fact he's given me multiple orgasms.

Bea stares at me again, trying to see into my soul, and I give her a look pleading with her to not push this. I'm not ready to delve into things about Pierce, especially when I haven't talked to him or attempting to figure it out for myself first.

"Are we ready for our food ladies?" the waiter asks, drawing everyone's attention away from me.

I breathe a sigh of relief as the girls jump into the multiple plates set before is, grabbing a little of everything before turning back to our conversation.

"So, are you ready for Friday?" Bea asks Pen.

"So fucking ready. It makes me wonder why we waited so long."

"Because you made poor Andy wait that long." Larkin laughs. "Not that we blame you, you had good reasons."

"I know. Everything is just so perfect and I'm so damn happy. It's weird to be this happy right?" Pen looks around the table.

Bea and Larkin shake their heads, but all I can think of is when it's my turn? Am I ever going to be as happy as my best friends? Is it even possible to be that happy? *You were happy last night with Pierce.*

"Enjoy the happy. Enjoy your wedding and just ... soak it all in because it only happens once," Larkin says happily.

My heart clenches painfully in my chest. I'm not closer to any of this than I was a week ago. Pierce is abundantly fun and I feel more like me than I have in a long time, but he's still just a vacation hook up. He doesn't want anything more from this. *Does he?*

My thoughts continue their torrential down slide along with my mood while the girls talk all things wedding. I make sure to chime in randomly, so they don't focus on me at all.

We finish what's left of our brunch and sit back full and happy.

The waiter comes over to start cleaning up the plates and Pen asks for the check, much to the chagrin of the rest of us.

"It's actually already been taken care of," the waiter explains.

Pen raises her eyebrow. "By whom?"

"Oh, umm, by Mr. Vanstone," he says completely oblivious.

I sink lower into my chair in an attempt to hide, but all three sets of eyes turn to me.

"Mr. Vanstone huh? I think you have some explaining to do," Larkin says.

Pen turns back to the waiter. "Is there any way to add a tip onto one of our rooms? I don't have cash on me."

"That's been taken care of as well, thank you so much though miss." He bows out, clearly sensing the third degree I'm about to get.

I make a split second decision I know won't really do me any good later, but I need to leave ... now.

My chair scrapes back as I throw up my hand. "See you guys later, I forgot I had to call ... someone. I'll talk to you later!" I yell over my shoulder, knowing they may give me a reprieve now, but it won't last long.

I can hear them laughing as I speed walk out of the restaurant, but I'll deal with them later. I need to figure out my own head right now more than anything.

I can't believe he paid for the entire group, again. Who is he trying to impress here? His money is probably my least favorite thing about him at the moment.

I follow the walkway down to my villa, rounding the corner to the hidden space I so desperately need right now. Using the key card to unlock the door, I rush in and lean against the door once I close it. I'm breathing heavy, trying to come up with a game plan for the day to avoid not only the girls, but Pierce too. I need to figure out my emotions and where I want to stand with him before we talk about everything that's happened with us.

"How was brunch?" The baritone voice scares me so much I scream. My eyes zero in on Pierce standing in the living room while I clutch my chest.

"What in the ever-living HECK are you doing here?" I yell.

"You weren't answering your phone, so I got worried. I don't like to worry. So imagine what happened when I found your phone here, but not you." He holds up my phone making me remember I left it here, so I wasn't obsessing over him contacting me.

"That doesn't mean you can just break into my room!" I'm grasping at straws right now because the lust and excitement running through my body is starting to take over my brain power.

He came to look for me. He broke into my room because he was worried, and it's making me feel all sorts of things about this man.

"We need to talk, love."

"You're right, we do." His commanding tone may have me wetter than an ocean, but my last remaining brain cell remembers he paid for brunch and the anger returns with a vengeance.

Chapter 10

Pierce

S he went from scared shitless to pissed off in the blink of an eye, and it turns me on more than I care to admit.

I wanted to give her time to process, some time to herself, and I needed to wrap up a couple things that couldn't be moved at work. But when I tried to get a hold of her and got nothing, I panicked. At first, I thought she was just ignoring me, but after a couple phone calls, I got very worried and went to check on her. When I "broke in" and found her phone, my worry skyrocketed, and I sent out a message to security to find her.

Imagine my surprise when security found her within ten minutes at brunch with her friends. To say my temper flared would be an understatement. It's irrational, of course she's out with her friends, but my heart was pounding so hard I couldn't calm down. The worry that something happened to her hit me so hard it made me realize just how much more time I want with her. How much more of her I want.

I did the only thing I could think of without actually going and dragging her ass back her; I paid for brunch and told the restaurant to let the table know it was me. Regardless of if she's told her friends anything, I knew me paying for brunch would get her hot under the collar. Her abhorrence to my money is something unfamiliar to me. But the thing she doesn't realize is even if she protests, if I want to spoil her, I will. She'll learn to enjoy it eventually. *Hopefully.*

"Why didn't you have your phone on you?" I ask, attempting to minimize the frustration in my voice. I have no real ground here, she doesn't owe me an answer, but damn if I can get that through my head at the moment.

"I didn't want distractions at brunch." She crosses her arms over her chest in defiance. *Fuck she's gorgeous.*

"I don't like not being able to get in contact with you," I grit out.

"Well, I'm not sure why you would even want to seeing as you left at some point last night while I was asleep." She huffs.

So, she's upset I left her last night. I can work with that.

"Shall we sit down while we continue this conversation?" I ask, gesturing to the couch, calming down enough to start thinking rationally.

Her shoulder slump and she leads the way to the living room.

"You shouldn't have paid for brunch."

"Yes, I should have. You girls were having a good time, and I wanted to treat you to a delicious meal with your friends. There's nothing wrong with that."

"We aren't dating. Heck, I don't even know what we're doing, but it's not your place to take care of me like that." She throws her hands up, exasperated.

I move faster than my head has time to catch up with. Grabbing her arm, a lay her out over my lap. Her stomach presses delectably against my thighs and I'm hard in a second. I pin her upper back down and swing my leg over the outside of hers to keep her still.

"What are you doing?" she yells, wiggling all over the place to get away. All it does is make my already stiff cock hard as granite.

"Showing you what we are." I flip her dress over her ass and spank her lightly. The slight sting in my hand has me closing my eyes and reigning myself in so I don't go in too hard, too fast with Jane. She has no idea about what I'm truly capable of.

What I want to do to her.

"Pierce!"

"Shh. You don't get to talk right now. I'm talking, and you're going to listen."

She wiggles her ass on my lap, and I growl.

"Stop." I press on her lower back to halt her movements. She freezes when she feels my erection.

"Yes, I'm going to talk. I have a proposition for you." Hopefully by phrasing it this way, it won't immediately turn her against the idea since this is what she wanted in the beginning. "I want to spend the time you're here ... exploring. Seeing what you like, pushing your limits, but we're exclusive during that time."

The silence is deafening.

"What do you think, Jane?"

"Oh, I'm allowed to talk now?" The attitude in her voice is so fucking hot. When she owns who she is and her shyness melts away, God, she's unstoppable. She doesn't even realize how deep I already am.

I swat her lightly again and hear the slightest intake of breath.

Fuck yes, she's liking it.

"I think it sounds okay," she finally says.

"Okay?"

"Yes, okay," she huffs out, clearly annoyed.

"Here's what's going to happen. We're going to explore something today. You're going to drop the attitude, and then after, we'll talk about why you're really mad at me."

"I'm not mad at—"

"Hush, we'll talk after, that's the deal. Now, for the attitude and for arguing about me paying for brunch, you need to be punished." I can hear my voice drop an octave just thinking about what's next.

"Punished? I'm not a child!"

"I'll make it two." Her silence is my cue she's listening.

"I want to explore what I just did to you." I run my hand over her plump ass as I explain more. "Did you like it when I spanked you?"

She nods.

"Words, love."

"Yes, I think I liked it," she whispers.

"Good. Would you like to explore it more?"

I feel her take a deep breath before speaking, "I do, but it makes me nervous."

"Okay, what makes you nervous about it?"

"What if you do it too hard and it's too much?" She tilts her head so she can look at me.

"First, I want to push you, push your boundaries, yes, but I don't want to do anything you don't like. My goal is and will always be to bring you as much pleasure as possible. Second, I'm not against using a safe word if it makes you more comfortable. I will be one hundred percent attentive to your body's reactions, but the added layer of control may help you relax into it more."

Her eyes are like big pools of blind trust as she looks up at me, and my heart jolts painfully in my chest. I don't know what the hell is going on with me and this woman, but I don't want it to end anytime soon contrary to the deal we just made.

"Grapefruit," she says with a surprisingly strong voice.

I blink, confused.

"Grapefruit?"

"My safe word. Grapefruit."

This woman is so ... intriguing.

"Grapefruit it is. We're going to the count of two, then we'll see how you feel." I give her no time to get prepared. We've discussed now it's time for action.

The first spank is harder than the earlier ones, my hand has a pleasant sting and her ass, God her ass is a lovely shade of pink.

She gasps out after the initial impact but doesn't jolt or cry out in pain. Placing my hand on her freshly pinked skin, I rub the heat and barely hold in my groan.

Her body relaxes again, and I spank her other cheek, this time she moans and all control I thought I had disintegrates.

My leg holding her down drops to the floor and my hips arch up begging to get closer. Moving my hand to the seam of her panties, I circle the wet spot on them and throw my head back on a groan. *God damn, I won't survive her.*

"You're wet for me love. You liked me spanking your delectable ass?"

"God yes," she moans out.

"You want more?" I ask, although I don't know if I can endure more.

"No, no I want you. I want you now."

Usually, I would tease her for such a demand, but I'm barely hanging on and all I did was swat her tight little ass twice. No, I need to fuck her now. Jane has a hold on me no other woman has managed. I'm flying blind and I can't even be upset about it.

I haul her up against me, forcing her to straddle me. She instantly starts rocking her hips looking for the friction, but I grip her hips and slide her back a couple of inches. I unbutton my pants and tug down my boxer briefs just enough that my cock springs free. Snagging the condom from my front pocket, I quickly sheath up before turning my attention back to Jane.

"Sit on my cock." I grip her hips and help her position over me as I move her panties to the side. She's just as wound up as I am because she sinks down with zero hesitation.

"Oh fuck." I grip her hips so hard, I know they'll bruise but apparently, she brings out the caveman in me because it makes me feel absolutely feral knowing my mark will be on her.

We match each other thrust for thrust, moan for moan.

Trailing one hand to her clit, I start a circling it the way I know she likes, and she goes off like a rocket. Her pussy squeezes me so tight the tingle in my back turns into a full-blown orgasm. Plastering her to me, I cup her jaw and kiss her like it's the last time I ever will.

She moans into my mouth as she falls limp against me.

Breaking the kiss, I take a second to really look at her, into her whiskey colored eyes, and make sure she really is okay. What I see makes me feel like my actual net worth. She's completely blissed out with the brightest smile on her face.

"So, we like some spanking," I murmur against her neck, pressing a gentle kiss there.

Her giggle is infectious, but her answer has me wanting a round two.

"God, yes. That was ... intense and different but I want to see how much further I can go, you know?"

"With just spanking?" We can definitely test her boundaries with spanking, but if she's this interested there are a few other things I want to try.

"I honestly think I'm open to more," she says with confidence.

I grip her ass in both hands, standing up from the couch and heading to the bedroom still inside of her.

"What are you doing Pierce?" she says on a gasp as I pick her up.

"Getting us cleaned up so we can get dirty again."

Her hips arch into mine, and I have to swat her again.

"We're getting clean first, love."

"God you're annoying when you're bossy." She huffs with a laugh.

"You seem to like it when I'm bossy." I turn on the hot water as I finally set her down. Pulling off the condom is comical since I'm still just as hard as before I came.

"How?" Jane asks, staring at my cock in amazement.

"You really have no idea how alluring you are, do you?" I ask, pulling her into the shower with me.

"You don't need to flatter me." She laughs, but I'm not having it.

"You are fucking stunning, Jane." I pin her to the wall by her hips and drop to my knees.

"I will continue to show you until you believe it." I waste no time licking her pussy with enthusiasm. Her gasps and moans fuel the need to show her exactly what I think of her. I don't let up until her knees give out and she sinks down onto the shower floor, I hold her to me, wrapping her legs around my waist.

"We're supposed to me getting clean!" She laughs. I don't miss how she ignores my comment about showing her until she believes it.

"Reach up on that shelf and grab the soap. I'll clean you right here." She does as I say and hands me the body wash. I squeeze some into my hand and am filled with the scent of peonies, of Jane.

I rub every inch of her and let her do the same to me. It's hell on my restraint to not fuck her again, but not only do I not have a condom on me, I don't think she can handle another round right now. Judging by the heaviness of her eyes, she's about to crash. I quickly grab the shampoo and conditioner as well, making sure every part of her is clean.

"Let's get you dry love," I pick her up and walk us out of the shower, grabbing a heated towel as I sit her on the counter. I dry every inch of her sexy body, and quickly dry mine as well. I grab the brush sitting on the counter and start brushing through her strands.

"You don't have to do that," she says sleepily, grabbing my hand.

"Yes, I do. You're mine to take care of today," I want to tell her it's not just today. I'll take care of her for as long as she'll let me.

"Stay with me," her whisper hits my ear.

"Of course, love." I lean in pressing a kiss to the corner of her mouth.

Finally finished with everything, I carry her to the bed, pulling the sheets back before placing her inside. I walk around to the other side, crawling in next to her and pulling her to me.

It's a good thing I've cancelled all my meetings today because as long as we're in this bed together. I'm not going anywhere. Hell, even out of the bed my sole focus is on this woman today.

Chapter 11

Pierce

P enelope's wedding is in two days, and it feels like it's come too soon.

Jane and I are currently lying in bed catching our breath after a rather exhaustive spanking session, and my mind is starting to wander. Her small, soft hand glides across my chest as she curls up to my side.

"What has you so in your head?"

The fact that she can tell that should be worrying since I never let anyone in, but somehow it just feels *right*.

"I'm thinking about how much time you have left on the island." I feel her stiffen beside me, and I can't tell if it's because I brought it up, or if she's ready to be done with me.

God, I hope it's not because she's done with me.

"Tell me why you got into hotels? Or resorts, whatever you call this." She chuckles, waving her hands around.

I allow the change in subject purely because she's asking questions about me, about my past.

"This is technically a resort, but I own hotels too. I got into it purely for the clout, as shallow as that sounds. Real estate was something I was interested in and once I dipped a toe in, I found I was actually damn good at it too. I wanted to build an empire ... to be proud of." What I don't tell her is a huge reason I've amassed such wealth was to pander to my father. A stupid reason, sure, but pride makes a man do some stupid things.

"And you just took a leap of faith? Jumped in with both feet?"

"Yeah, I guess I did. I'm not usually one to second guess things."

"I wish I could be that way," she sighs out. "That was the whole point of this week, I guess. To not second guess things and go after what I want."

"I'd say you did a pretty good job of that." I smirk as I trail my hand over her shoulder.

She snorts out a laugh. "That's because you've only seen one version of me."

"I'd like to see more then. I'd like to get to know all the versions of Jane." I want to know every version this woman would let me see, but I get the feeling I'll be working hard for it. For some reason she doesn't want to discuss what happens next.

Her silence kills me, but I decide to keep the questions going.

"What do you do for fun when you aren't saving the youth of America?"

She laughs at that. "I hardly save anyone. Talk to the girls if that's what you think. All three of them actually save people, I just ... force kids to learn things for tests that don't really matter. But when I do have free time, I like to read."

"Lovely, what do you read in particular?" She tries to pull away when I ask, but I hold her to me, planting my hand on top of hers on my chest so she can feel the way my heart beats for her.

"I read romance. The girls used to make fun of me for my choice in books, but then Andy joined the group and got Pen reading them so apparently our whole group reads them now. They've always said I'm the romantic of the group—the dreamer. I'm not sure how accurate that is, though."

"Why do you say that?"

"I've always been the person who does what they're supposed to. This is the most rebellion I've ever experienced, and I wouldn't even really call it that. I've always been the one who dreams of the fairytale life, the prince charming, and yet I'm the last one in our group left single." She lets out a self-deprecating laugh and I start to understand her a lot more.

When she tipsily told me her plan for the week, I didn't really think about how out of character something like that would be. But everything she's told me leads me to believe a short hook up, a one-night stand, was never in the cards for her.

Good because I don't think it was ever in the cards for me.

Contrary to my usual escapades, after that first night I was too taken with this woman. She's been different from every woman I've been with. I've never thought twice about any of them but there is something about this dichotomous woman that leaves me wanting more.

"Do you still believe that?" I ask, not sure what I hope the answer to be.

She thinks on it for a moment.

"I think I do, but it's scary you know? Putting yourself out there, going after what you want. It's something I've been thinking about a lot lately, and this entire trip has felt like the first step for me."

"You know, I don't have it all figured out either. Having all of this"—I gesture to the gorgeous ocean beyond the windows—"is great, but I travel most of the year. I'm a horrible micromanager, but I haven't really had anything else in my life that's made me stop and take a break. Lately it's just been … exhausting. Traveling doesn't have the same shine, new resorts and buildings don't have the same high as they used to."

I'm not sure when I started feeling that way, but this time with Jane has put it all in sharp focus.

"I get that, although I don't know that anything I've done has been particularly enthralling. My mom always put a ton of pressure on me throughout school. I needed to pick a sustainable career choice, something suitable for a woman so I just followed her lead. I don't think I ever stopped and thought about what *I* wanted, you know? It's weird being this age and feeling like a teenager again." She laughs.

"Do you talk to your family a lot?" I ask, curious.

"We do the standard every other week call, well my mom and I do, my dad is more of a seen and not heard kind of man. It's ... not the best relationship."

This relaxed and open Jane is breathtaking. The fact she's letting me in right now, even if it's because of a post sexual haze makes me even more sure I want to keep her around longer.

An idea forms and I mentally file it away to work on once she falls asleep, for now I want my full attention on the woman who just may have changed everything for me.

"My mother passed away when I was younger, and my father and I are on very tumultuous terms." I want to share more, but my story isn't clean cut. It's messy and my father is not someone to bring into a conversation like this. I want to keep the lightness, the vulnerability, not crush it with the weight of too much pressure.

"I'm sorry to hear that." She rubs a little circle over my heart.

For the first time tonight, we're both silent, lost in too many thoughts and too many feelings, at least for me.

Every little piece of mundane information she's shared tonight feels like a nugget of gold. One that shines so brightly it's become addicting, and I want to continue digging.

Jane Hatley doesn't know it yet, but our week together is not nearly enough time together. I'm going to do everything in my very vast amount of power to make it so we have more time together.

Chapter 12

It's officially Pen's wedding day, and I'm standing in front of the full-length mirror in nothing but my lingerie.

It's incredible what a couple days of exploring what good sex looks like does for your overall perception of yourself.

This week has been ... honestly, I don't know if I could put it into words. It's not just what I've learned about myself; it's Pierce. I don't think I could do this with anyone else. We've delved a little more into the world of kink, and it's been insanely fun.

Now, I'm standing in front of the mirror hyping myself up to go to Pen's room so we can all get ready together, and all I want to do is go find Pierce to let out some of the stress.

But I can't because I didn't invite him. Because I'm a coward who was unsure about the implications of inviting him. We're not technically together, we're just ... screwing. As much as I want the possibility of more, nothing has been said between the two of us to think it's anything else.

The bigger problem is I'm starting to like him ... A lot. And I'm scared that he doesn't feel the same way, that this is all in my head and I'm jumping into a proverbial pool that's shallow, and I'm going to break my neck.

Woah, that escalated.

The truth is, I can see the fairytale with Pierce. I've dated a lot. I've seen what's out there and from where I'm standing, none of them can touch Pierce with a ten-foot pole. He's just so ... freeing. He makes me feel free to be myself, free to figure out just what that means, and I don't think I've ever had a man make me feel that way about myself.

I roll my eyes at myself and throw on a tank top and lounge shorts. Triple checking my dress and shoes, I grab everything and head out the door to go meet the girls.

The long walk only gives me more time with my thoughts, and if anything makes me more confused about the situation with Pierce. We both know I'm leaving tomorrow, both agreed to meet after the wedding, but nothing else. The conversation we had a couple nights ago was so domestic; it gave me hope. It gave me too many thoughts of what could be, but we haven't talked about anything past this week. The pang in my chest tells me I should probably ghost him tonight. I'm too caught up in him and how I feel around him, but nothing will happen after I leave. We don't even live on the same continent for goodness' sake.

I'm standing in front of Pen's villa before I have a chance to come up with any answers, and the second the door swings open, Larkin is yanking me inside.

"About time you showed up." She puts a champagne glass in my hand and slams the door shut behind me.

"Look who finally decided to take a breath from her sexcation."

Lovely, even Pen's upcoming nuptials aren't going to distract this group.

I down the champagne, placing my empty glass on the table as I take in the scene.

The girls are wearing matching robes, drinks in hand, and all giving me the same "spill it" look.

"What?" I ask innocently.

"Spill it now! It's my wedding day, and I demand a play-by-play of what the silver fox hunk has been doing to you!" And Pen's already tipsy, but she also has this look in her eyes like she knows something I don't.

"I'm not giving you a play-by-play. Where's my robe?" I ask hoping for a little bit of a distraction.

Bea throws a robe, and I'm caught off guard as it hits me in the face.

"Thanks." The sarcasm is thick in my voice.

"Anytime! So, how's the dick?"

"How's his stamina? I mean I know he's not super old, but I am curious." Pen taps her lips with her pointer finger in thought.

"I need another drink," I say under my breath, already feeling claustrophobic with all the questions.

Larkin hands me my champagne glass already refilled with a wink. "You're not getting out of talking about it, Jane. We've barely seen you all week and we want to hear all the dirty details."

My head drops back on an exhale, trying to channel the patience I usually reserve for the kids I teach.

"We're not talking about this. Today is about Pen's wedding and my focus is going to be making sure every detail is exactly the way you want it." I pointedly look at Pen, daring her to disagree.

All three of their shoulders slump in defeat, knowing I'm not going to cave.

Conversation turns to hair and makeup plans as my mind drifts to the last couple of days.

The things I've let Pierce to do my body are things I've never even thought about asking a boyfriend for. We've delved a little deeper into spanking, which I can easily say I desperately want more of. We've had sex in every room of my villa and tried positions I've never even heard of. And all the while I'm actually having orgasms. Real ones, one's that shake me to my very core about what I thought was normal.

One particular time a couple of days ago stands out in my head and plays on repeat.

A knock at the door has me hoping it's Pierce and not one of the girls, which makes me feel like a terrible friend. But Pierce is taking me on a wild ride I don't want to get off of, and I'm desperate for more. More sex, more exploration, and shockingly more conversation with this surprising man.

Walking to the door, I steel my face just in case it's one of the girls. I don't need them to read the disappointment all over my face if it's not Pierce.

I'm in luck though, because his gorgeous face with the salt and pepper scruff on his jaw greets me when I open the door.

"Disappointed, love?"

"Definitely not." I pull the door open to let him in.

He wraps his arms around my waist, kicking the door shut as he draws his nose up the side of my neck.

"God, you smell good," he whispers against my skin as goosebumps break out across my body.

He presses open mouth kisses to my pulse point and I'm practically a puddle in his arms.

"I want to try something different." He pulls back and looks me in the eye.

"Okay," I whisper hesitantly. It's not that I don't trust him, because I do, I just like knowing what I'm getting myself into.

"How do you feel about delayed gratification?" he asks with a mischievous twinkle in his eye.

"I think it sounds interesting." Knowing what I know about Pierce, this is no doubt something designed to torture me and make me absolutely love it in the process.

Gripping my butt in his large palm, he pulls me to him letting me know just how excited he is for this new adventure.

"Interesting? Guess I'll have to show you how interesting it can be." His devilish smirk makes my skin heat and my panties wet.

He picks me up as I wrap my legs around his hips. He continues kissing my throat and collar bone while he walks us to the bedroom.

Tossing me on the bed and stripping me in a matter of seconds has my thighs rubbing together trying to ease the throb in between my legs.

"Oh yeah, this is going to be fun," he says, kneeling on the ground fully clothes and dragging me to the edge of the bed.

He brings me right up to the edge of orgasm then leans back and watches me struggle to get more friction.

"You'll come when I say, not sooner. If you come without my permission, there will be consequences."

My thoughts are pulled from my memories by Pen's voice.

"Speaking of wedding plans, Andy and I got upgraded for the honeymoon," Pen says with a twinkle in her eye. My curiosity is peaked, even though my body is still back in the past with Pierce taking my body to the edge over and over again before finally showing how powerful an orgasm can really be.

"How much more upgraded can you get?" I ask.

"We're going to a completely different resort. The general manager flagged us down while we were walking through the lobby and gave us an entirely new itinerary at this resort not too far away. It's on a small island and the resort is just bungalows on the water, all secluded with everything you could ever want brought to you." She's smiling so big I have to force myself to be cheerful for her.

This has Pierce written all over it again, and I told him to stop interfering.

But he's also being thoughtful and my head and my heart, and my vagina can't reconcile all the different versions of him. The romantic in me wants to find a way to make a real relationship work with him, but my logical brain knows he doesn't want that, and even if he did how in the world would we even make it happen? We don't even live on the same continent. Nope, I can't even go there thinking it's a possibility. It's not, we're just hooking up and enjoying the limited time we have together.

Limited time, only tonight since I'm leaving tomorrow. My heart lurches in my chest knowing our time's almost up.

"Oh, girl! I bet the place is gorgeous! Take all the pictures so we can see it when you get back," Bea says excitedly right as a knock at the door sounds.

I instantly think it's Pierce before I realize it's probably something for the wedding. I open the door and sure enough it's the hair and makeup people here to get us all dolled up for later.

Bea jumps up, ready to take charge as usual and directs everyone into chairs and make sure everyone has snacks and drinks before the team gets started on us.

As I'm sitting there, the urge to text Pierce is so strong I have sit on my phone to stop myself. I feel needy and dependent on his company, and I need the separation to ensure I'm not attached to this man I can't have in the real world.

"So, Jane, have you spent all week with the man? Or have you just been avoiding us to get some quiet time?" Larkin asks. I meet her stare in the mirror and see her gleefulness at calling me out when I thought I had beat the third degree from them.

"A little of both," I tell them deciding to give them something, even if it's a half truth, in order to feed their insatiable nosiness.

"Oh, so she finally admits it!" Pen claps excitedly.

I'll give them credit though; they aren't explicitly saying his name now that some of his staff is in here with us. I'm grateful to not be a part of the rumor mill even if I'm leaving tomorrow. And I'm sure Pierce doesn't want his business broadcasted to his employees.

"I admit it's been a fun week but that's all you're getting out of me." I stick my tongue out at them.

They all pout in return, but Bea seems to realize I don't want to delve into it right now and veers the conversation back to wedding stuff. The look she gives me though, says I can't run away from this forever.

Before I know it, hair and makeup are done and I'm staring at a brand-new woman.

It seems fitting, to not recognize myself in the mirror after this week. I feel like this is who I'm meant to be. The last few years have been challenging and I've felt more lost than when I was two years younger than everyone my freshman year in college. I've never felt like I've found myself, I've just jumped into the next big thing I'm supposed to be doing. The things my mom said I should be doing. Sure, I've found an amazing group of friends in the process, but they all are so secure in who they are, what they're doing.

Somehow, over the last week, with the help of Pierce, I feel more like *me* than I ever have before. And now I have to come to grips with the fact I'll never see him again after tonight. *If I even see him again tonight.*

Flashes of Pierce enter my mind. The laugh lines around his eyes you can only see when he smiles. The mischievous smirk when he gets a crazy idea in his head. The caring in his eyes when he's pushing me past a limit I thought I had, always making sure I'm one hundred percent okay.

A shoulder bumps against mine and hands me my dress.

"Thanks," I tell Larkin absentmindedly.

I'm in too deep.

"It's almost time how are you feeling?" Bea asks Pen.

And I'm the worst friend ever. It's my best friend's wedding day and I'm too caught up in a man I can never really have.

"I'm so fucking excited! Is everyone ready? I want to go now. I don't know why I waited so long for this!" Her excitement is infectious, and I'm so dang happy for everything she's overcome to get to this point in her life.

All of us agreed when her and Andy decided on a destination wedding, we wanted to get her something special from the three of us, and it looks like it's finally time to give it to her.

"We have something for you," I tell Pen.

She tilts her head questioningly.

"We wanted to make sure you have a little tradition on your wedding day," Bea continues. "I got you something blue." Bea hands her the jewelry box with a sapphire pendant in it.

"Oh Bea ..."

"I got you something new," I tell her, holding out the small gift bag.

She opens it, pulling out a white lacy pair of panties with Mrs. Becker embroidered on the butt.

"You guys ..." Pen's voice is watery.

"I have borrowed and old," Larkin says handing her a flat box a little bigger than her palm. Pen opens it up and sees it's the birdcage veil Larkin wore to her wedding.

Bea is frantically waving her hands in front of Pen's face. "We should have done this prior to getting our makeup done."

"Oh my god, you guys! This is the most thoughtful, amazingly perfect present ever," Pen chokes out.

We hug each other, relishing in our found family.

"Let's go get your ass married!" Bea happily yells. We all laugh while wiping our tears and we get Pen adorned in her newly added attire before head out to the beach to join the men.

The set-up is as simple as it is beautiful, but it fits Pen and Andy perfectly. I'm about to take my seat when a hand grabs my elbow.

"May I join you, love?"

Pierce.

Chapter 13

Pierce

D id I ask Penelope if it was okay to join Jane as her date for the wedding? Yes. Did I also expect Jane to be happy to see me? Also, yes.

But the woman is an anomaly as always, so when she pulls her arm away from me, it shouldn't really be a shock.

"What are you doing here?" she asks in an angry whisper.

"I'm your date to the wedding."

"No, you aren't. Pierce, you can't just barge your way into things."

It's usually what I do, but I don't' dare tell her that while she's looking at me with real aggravation in her eyes.

"If everyone could take their seats!" the Justice of the Peace calls out, and I get a blessed reprieve from a very unhappy Jane.

It's the exact opposite of what I wanted, but there will be time later to talk about all of it. And discuss my rather brilliant plan as well.

In the meantime, I take in Jane. She's wearing forest green silk dress that hugs her every curve even though everything is covered. She looks fucking brilliant and I can barely take my eyes off of her.

The wedding is beautiful, and as I look around at the small group, I see how involved everyone is. The group of women are all crying as Penelope says her vows, and the men are all grinning at Andy with nothing but pure elation for him.

I don't think I've ever had people authentically happy for me in any accomplishment as these people are about their friend getting married, outside of my mother when she was alive.

The thought has me sitting back with shock.

How is that possible?

This week with Jane has made me realize a lot of things. Like my love for my business isn't quite enough to feel fulfilled anymore. I was already feeling a little restless, questioning what's next and how much more money I really need in my life. And I've never really gotten over the face my father genuinely doesn't care about me or my accomplishments. It's all hitting a breaking point right when I met Jane, a coincidence, yes, but something to think about. And how if there is the slightest chance of continuing things with Jane, I'm willing to do whatever it takes to make it happen.

She makes me feel alive, and free, and hell, young again. The last week has been filled with not only the best sex of my life, but it's shown me the glimpses of what life could be like. What a different kind of life would look like, one where work isn't my number one priority. One where Jane pulls me out of my seriousness and opens my eyes to new things. She thinks I've been teaching her things all week, but it certainly feels like the other way around from where I stand. My callus and short attitude suddenly doesn't feel good. I've made it a point to be less of a dick to Sydney and not ask stupid shit from her at all hours of the day. Being here at her best friend's wedding, witnessing the love and the support here makes me realize how much time I've really wasted. Sure, the money's nice, but it sure as hell isn't making me happier than Jane is at the moment.

There is a lot I need to reevaluate in my life, but first, I need to Jane to agree to my plan. She'll no doubt tell me I'm going overboard and I'm crazy, but I don't care. What use is having all these damn resources if I can't spoil the person I want to the most?

I want her to stay here with me for at least an extra week. I already shipped off Penelope and Andy to one of my more exclusive resorts not terribly far from here so we will have complete privacy.

If she agrees.

That will undoubtedly be the hard part if her reaction to me showing up to the wedding is anything to go by.

The thing is, she briefly mentioned that she was the only one not coupled up for the wedding. The look in her eyes was far more telling than her words. I knew the second she said it, I wanted to be the one who shows up for her. This impulse to just be here for her was more powerful than I could stop.

So, she can be mad at me for now, but I know she didn't want to be alone for this. And I'll make it up to her later anyways.

"You may kiss the bride" The officiant pulls me from my head. The cheers, catcalls, and tearful laughs surround me, and I feel truly honored to have witnessed this level of love among not only the couple, but among their friends as well.

Jane leans into my shoulder for a second as she regains control over her emotions and wipes her eyes.

And in that moment, I know I'm done for. I'm irrevocably changed thanks to this woman.

The reception, if you want to call it that, is in full swing. It's basically just a fancy dinner, but it took a while for the group to stop hugging and laughing and just being who they are with each other. I quietly observed

Jane and could see her happiness for her friends, but I could also see the despondency on her face. She wants this, wants the fairytale life with her prince and the exact life she's always dreamed of.

I've never been the man who wanted any of that, let alone felt like I was missing out on anything. But somehow, Jane is making me rethink everything.

It's not just about our chemistry in the bedroom either. She's a fascinating woman from what I've gleamed so far, and I am desperate to know more about her.

This is why I want the extra week. I need more time with her, more time to really get to know her before I start making even more drastic plans like the ones already circling in my head.

I take my seat next to Jane and lean in close to her.

"Are you going to pretend you're still mad at me?"

"I am mad at you, there's no pretending involved." She huffs.

"Do you want to tell me exactly why you're mad at me?"

"Not at the moment, thanks." She looks up at me with a bratty smirk on her face and I know I'll be taking it out on her later.

"You're going to talk to me eventually."

"I don't know. You haven't really given me any reason to want to talk to you." The champagne she's been sipping is making her bold and I fucking love this side of her.

"I can change that," I say simply. If she wants a reason, I'll gladly give her several. But for now, I'll let her stew a little while we enjoy the rest of the reception.

She gives me the side eye, probably wondering what I have in mind, but she'll have to wait.

Waiters come and serve the main course, a beef wellington with truffle mashed potatoes and roasted vegetables. Pride hits my chest at the lovely spread we put out and at watching people enjoy what I've created here at the resort.

Is this enough? Is this feeling and pride enough to fulfill me for the next thirty years?

Who knew crashing a wedding would make my ass reevaluate his life.

It's not the wedding, it's Jane.

It is Jane and it should scare the hell out of me, but it doesn't. If anything, it makes me more obsessed with the woman.

Looking around everyone is enjoying their meal, but when I look at the men in the group and see them all checking in on their wives, being attentive with a look of blatant love on their faces, I start to wonder what my face looks like when I look at Jane, because it sure as feels like adoration at the very least.

People start finishing up their meals as the waiters takes plates off the table. The music in the background gets a little louder, but everyone is properly full from dinner.

Content. That's how I would describe almost everyone in this group. Except Jane.

Jane looks happy but worn down. She has a sweet smile on her face, but it's her eyes that give her away.

A song starts and the four friends perk up and jump out of their seats immediately. They all run to the center of the room and break out in a dance they all seem to know.

My eyes are instantly drawn to Jane. She's having fun, she's letting loose, and it isn't from an orgasm I gave her. It's amazing to witness and I don't try to hold back the smile on my face. I don't remember the last time I smiled this much in general, let alone because of a woman.

The dance finishes before I'm ready, wishing I could watch more of this uninhibited version of her with the people she loves most.

She ambles her way over to me, laughing at something one of the women said, plops down in her chair, and smiles over at me. I lean forward, putting my hand on the back of her chair.

"Does this mean you're not mad at me anymore?" Trailing my nose of the side of her neck, I can't resist a little taste.

"It means my focus isn't on you and it's on enjoying my best friend's wedding." The twinkle in her eyes tells me show knows exactly what she's doing, and I can't wait to show precisely what I think about it later.

"I think you want to see how far you can push me. I don't think you really are mad at me."

"You think you know me so well, huh?" She turns to face me.

"I think I don't know you nearly as much as I want to."

Her eyes search mine as the smile slowly falls from her face.

"Pierce, I'm leaving in the morning." Her voice is barely above a whisper.

"How about we just enjoy the rest of the wedding reception, and we'll talk about it later tonight." I want to tell her my entire plan, but now is not the time to do it. I refuse to be the person to take any attention from these lovely people Jane calls family.

We spend a couple more hours dancing, laughing, and celebrating Penelope and Andy's nuptials before Jane pulls me to the side.

"Everyone's getting ready to call it a night. We aren't really the group that parties all night, you know?" She laughs.

God she's fucking gorgeous.

"Do you, maybe, want to come back to the villa with me?" she asks hesitantly.

"Absolutely. Let's say goodbye to everyone first."

We make the rounds; all the women tell Jane to text them later and the men make pleasantries with me while also giving wordless warnings with their handshakes. Their strong holds tell me all I need to know. Break Jane's heart and I answer to all of them, not just the women.

What they don't realize is my heart is probably more on the line. I would never intentionally hurt Jane and if I did, I would gladly lay myself bare for the beating they threaten.

Jane grabs my hand, dragging me to the door as she waves goodbye to everyone. Catcalls greet us turning Jane's cheeks a lovely shade of pink with her blush.

She doesn't slow down or talk until we reach the villa, quickly shutting the door behind us.

"Jane—"

"Why did you come tonight?" She interrupts me.

"I wanted to see you, spend more time with you."

"No. Tonight was different. Tonight was my best friend's wedding, and you don't just crash that because you want to spend more time with me. Heck, you could have just come over here after if that was the reason because that was our plan initially."

She wraps her arms around her torso, a physical move to protect herself.

"Will you come and sit with me," I offer instead of an answer.

She follows me to the couch where we sit, and I take a moment to gather my thoughts. I have to get this right because I'll either get her to stay or force her farther away from me.

"I came tonight because I didn't want you to be alone at the wedding. I came because I couldn't stay away no matter how hard I tried." She looks over at me with curiosity in her eyes, so I take it as a good sign to continue.

"I want to ask you something, but I need to you to really think about it, not dismiss it instantly."

Her nod urges me on.

"I want you to stay here, with me, for another week."

"That wasn't a question." The spark in her eyes and the smirk she's trying to hide tell me more than the snark of her response.

"Please, love, stay here with me for another week."

"How do you know I don't have to be back in Austin for work?" she asks.

"I don't, but I have an abundance of hope—being that it's summer—that you don't have anything pressing to do," I admit, suddenly annoyed with myself for not having the forethought to even ask what her plans for the summer were. I know she teaches middle school, but nothing specific. I've done a piss poor job of learning anything about her outside of what makes her back arch in pleasure, except for the other night, and that's why I want her to stay. Because I need to know more about her.

"If I say yes, is this purely for sex?"

"I won't lie and say it's not a motivating factor, but it's not the only reason. I'm not nearly done with you yet and I'd like to get to know you better." It's better to keep it light, otherwise I know I'll scare her off.

"And this is why you are sending Pen and Andy on that fancy honeymoon?" She raises her eyebrows at me.

"Truthfully? Yes, but I was going to comp their room either way." I shrug.

"Pierce!"

"What?"

"You can't just pay for my best friend's honeymoon to get in my pants! That's not how real life works."

"I did it so they could be somewhere really special because they mean a lot to you. I did it so on the off chance you say yes to staying, you aren't worried about what Penelope is doing, so you both could enjoy a peaceful week. And I would never pay for something just to get in your pants, love. I've already proved I can get in them just fine all on my own." I wink.

"You're annoying sometimes you know?" She laughs.

"I know, but it made you laugh so it was worth it." I smile at her. She really has no clue how much power she has over my right now.

"If I choose to stay, am I staying here still? In this villa? Or would I be switching into a room? And I'd have to change my flight, like now." She starts rambling and I know I have her. I feel ten pounds lighter.

"I'll handle your flight, well my assistant will, and you will be staying here." I'd give her the villa forever if it gets her to say yes.

"If I say yes, I want to do more than just stay in bed the whole time," she says pointedly.

A belly laugh bursts out of me. "I promise I will show you more than the four walls of the bedroom."

Her eyes shift between mine for a minute. Debating her options, her wants, and I see the second she decides.

"Okay, I'll stay. But I need to let the girls know because we're supposed to be all flying out tomorrow." She immediately turns her attention to her phone, but I'm still hung up on the fact she said yes.

I get one more week with this intriguing woman. One more week to figure out just how far we can take this. And I'm fucking ecstatic.

She puts her phone down on the table and I swoop in to cup her jaw and bring it to me.

"Thank you," I whisper. "I'll make this the best week you've ever had." And then I kiss her.

I kiss her like I've never kissed anyone before. So soft, so gentle, a promise to make this week more than worth it for her. And a hope it turns into more.

I deepen the kiss, pulling her closer to me.

Sitting through the wedding and not being able to touch her the way I wanted to is quickly dissolving my resolve to go slow.

Her phone buzzes on the table causing me to pull back and look at it.

"Leave it. There blowing it up because they want details on why I'm staying. I'll talk to them later," she pants.

When Jane swings her leg over to straddle my lap, all sense of propriety is over. I keep my grip wrapped around her jaw as the other palms her ass. She grinds down on me on a moan, and I lose it.

Standing up, her legs wrap around my waist as I head to the bedroom.

She's got half my shirt unbuttoned by the time we make it there and I toss her onto the bed.

I throw off my suit jacket and finish unbuttoning my shirt as she watches me from her position.

"Strip," I command.

She slides the zipper on the side of her green dress all the way down to her hip, carefully sliding the straps off of her shoulders before she stands up and it drops to the ground.

My cock twitches painfully at what I find underneath.

Pale green lacy lingerie greets me and I nearly drop to my knees at the sight, ready to worship the body the lace touches.

She goes to reach behind her to take her bra off.

"Stop. Leave it on, I want to unwrap you like the best present I've ever gotten." Because she is, there's no doubt about that.

I slowly take off my shirt and move to my trousers, watching her reactions as I strip for her. Her fists clench tight at her sides when I finally stand before her in nothing but my boxer briefs.

Neither of us move, sucked into the vortex of sexual tension.

I want her so bad I can barely move. Right as I'm about to take a step toward her, a pounding at the door jolts us both.

"Mother of all that is holy, you've got to be kidding me." Jane exhales in exasperation.

She moves around me, walking to the bathroom and grabs the robe hanging on the door. She wraps it around her body tightly before heading to the door.

"Wait here and don't come out. I'll deal with them."

And then she leaves me nearly naked with an erection to end all other erections and slams the door shut behind her.

Chapter 14

Jane

I should have freaking known the girls wouldn't let it rest. I knew they would blow up the group text when I told them I wouldn't be flying home with them, but I really should have expected this.

I stomp to the front door of the villa, pissed off and horny as heck. Throwing the door open I stare at Bea and Larkin, both who have their fists up ready to pound on the door again.

"What?" I throw my hands up at them

They both silently look me up and down.

"Well, this is interesting," Larkin observes.

"That I'm changing?" I ask, deflecting any other ideas they have.

"Can we come in and talk?" Bea asks, giving Larkin the *shut the hell up* look.

"By all means." I roll my eyes as I let them in.

We all sit on the couch, and I wait for them to grill me about what a terrible idea it is to stay here for another week.

"Can I just say, your villa is fucking beautiful. And like, twice the size of the rest of ours," Larkin says while looking all around the living area.

"Really?" I tilt my head. "I thought they were all the same size."

"Not even close." Bea chuckles.

Huh, that's weird.

"Anyways, back on topic. You can't just send a group text saying you won't be on the plane tomorrow and you're staying an extra week. Did you expect us to say, 'Oh, cool Jane. I hope you have a blast, and we aren't worried about you at all!'" Larkin gives me a hard stare.

"Obviously I didn't think you would just let it go without more of an explanation, but I was going to get some sleep and then explain more in the morning. Like I told you I would in the text."

"Okay, we're not arguing semantics right now. What happened? Why are you staying another week? Can you afford to stay? I can totally pay for you," Bea adds. I know she doesn't mean it the way it sounds, but man for once I wish I wasn't the poor woman in our group.

I tip my head back on the couch, taking a deep breath to not lose my cool on my best friends.

"I was asked, by Pierce, to stay and after some consideration I decided to say yes. If you're worried about the classes I'll miss at Phoenix House, I'll get them covered."

"We're not worried about your damn classes, Jane! We're worried about you! You're spontaneously deciding to stay another week on a secluded island with a man you literally just met." Bea looks at me like I've lost my mind.

The thing is, I don't think I have. I think I've finally decided to take my life into my own hands, and they're concerned because it's out of character for me. They aren't wrong, but isn't that what I wanted from this trip? To figure out what I really want in my life? I'm at a crossroads and deciding to stay here feels like the first right choice I've made in far too long. I want the fairytale romance, I want a guy that will sweep me off my feet and there literally isn't anyone that's done that. Not until Pierce. And maybe taking advantage of being away from everyone will be good too. Maybe I just need a break from everything, including my best friends.

"Can I be honest?" I ask, looking at my two best friends. I know they truly only want the best for me, but I feel claustrophobic with their constant analysis of everything wrong with my love life.

They both nod. Keeping eye contact even though their phones are buzzing on the table.

"I love you guys, and that will never change, but I think I need space."

"From us?" Larkin asks with nothing but concern in her eyes.

"From everything. Work has been so stressful. All three of you have found the love of your lives and I am so, so happy for you. But I feel like the extra, the lonely friend who needs looking after because she's alone and bad at picking men. I've felt more like myself here, in the last week, than I have in a really long time."

I've often felt left out in my life because I was always the young one. Graduating early and going to college at sixteen will have that effect on you plus having what turned out to be a pretty toxic relationship with my mother didn't help. But I've never felt like this with my girls. I've always been included and with them paired off now, I feel lost and distancing myself from them feels like the safe option.

I look and see Bea looks heartbroken, and Larkin looks thoughtful. The social worker in her is no doubt trying to analyze everything I just said.

"I don't say that to make you feel bad. I just ... need this week, and I really don't want the endless questions that usually accompany my decisions involving the male species." I sigh.

"Okay." Larkin nods. "Okay, I'm sorry and we'll definitely make more of an effort going forward."

This is why I didn't want to have this conversation. Now they're going to be tiptoeing around me.

"It's fine really." I brush it off. Right now is not the time to have this conversation, not with Pierce probably eavesdropping from the bedroom.

"So how much do you know about Pierce? And I'm not asking because I'm judging your taste in men, I'm asking to make sure you're safe," Bea says.

"I know enough to know that if at any point I feel uncomfortable or want to stop, he'll bow out no questions asked and send me home whenever I ask." I may not know a lot about him, but I know he would really listen to me if I wanted out of whatever we're doing with each other.

I should probably figure that out.

Larkin grabs her phone from the table.

"Pen wants to know how good the sex is. And how big his dick is." She laughs.

"Is she not supposed to be having hot wedding night sex right now?" I laugh.

"She may not have come with us, but you knew she would want to know what's going on. I just didn't realize her mind would be so focused on sex." Bea cracks up.

"So, I'm going to tell her the sex is phenomenal, and his dick is like ten inches, yeah?" Larkin looks up as she's texting a message to Pen.

"Oh my God! Do not send that to her! I don't need her sending me inappropriate memes about ten-inch penises every chance she gets." We all burst out laughing at the accuracy of it.

"I swear Andy finds all that shit," Bea wheezes out.

"No!!" Larkin and I gasp at the same time.

"Oh yeah. I saw him scrolling on his phone one time when he was at Phoenix House, and he literally scrolls them and saves any good ones in the hopes either him or Pen can use them," Bea adds.

"The two of them are ridiculous." I sigh out.

"I'm just glad she finally put him out of his misery. I swear if he came over one more time to talk to Riggs about proposal plans, or if he should just scrap the whole idea, I was going to stage an intervention." Bea says.

"It was gorgeous though," Larkin says dreamily.

"It really was."

We sit in comfortable silence for a few minutes.

"You're really going to be okay here?" Bea tilts her head to me.

"I will absolutely be okay. Probably better than okay honestly. And if I need anything I promise to call one of you two. I refuse to bug Pen on her honeymoon," I say with a smile.

"We'll keep bugging you in the group chat, but don't feel the need to keep us updated every hour." Larkin winks.

"I really do love you guys. You're the greatest best friends anyone could ever ask for."

"Love you too, Jane," they both say.

"Well, we'll leave you to it. We're all leaving here at noon so if you need anything in the morning, let us know, please." Bea gets up and Larkin follows.

I stand up and walk them to the door.

"I promise I will call you if I need anything or on the off chance I change my mind." I smirk.

"Be safe and have fun, okay?" Larkin says, leaning in for a big hug.

"I will."

"And keep us updated please," Bea says as she switches out with Larkin.

"Yes, mom." I smirk.

"Oh my gosh you really are a mama now," Larkin gushes.

"We're growing up ladies," Bea says as she opens the front door.

"Let me know when you get home," I say as I wave them off and shut the door behind them. Leaning my back against the door, I take a deep breath.

"Well that certainly was enlightening," Pierce's voice reaches my ears.

"We're not going to talk about what you just overheard."

"Done. Shall we take a hot bath?" he asks with real concern in his eyes. I'm shocked he's not trying to pick up where we left off, but I'm relieved he's surprising me with his attentiveness.

"That sounds perfect." I take his hand and follow him to the bathroom.

Chapter 15

Pierce

How did I find myself almost naked in a woman's bedroom while she chats with her best friends in the living room?

I became utterly smitten with Jane Hatley, that's how.

I pull out my phone and send a text to Sydney telling her to cancel the next week for me. I can't think of a better reason to shirk off work for another week than spending it with Jane.

Sydney texts me back saying she'll handle it but asks me if I'm okay. Reassuring her I'm fine, I toss my phone on the nightstand when I hear raised voices.

It's almost impossible not to overhear them, but I was trying to be respectful. Now, I don't care. If they're yelling at Jane, I will step in.

"We're not worried about your damn classes, Jane! We're worried about you! You're spontaneously deciding to stay another week on a secluded island with a man you literally just met," one of her friends yells.

I'm about three seconds from barging out there until I hear Jane's reply. Her voice is so sad and worn down. If I can make the week something really special, let her really let loose and just be then I think I'll be happy.

And then I hear the question about my dick and I have to cover my mouth to suppress my laugh. These women are unlike any I've ever met, and I envy the friendship they have with each other.

I don't think I've ever had one close friend like they do, let alone three.

I continue to listen in, hearing their concerns and making a mental note to do something to ease their worries some time in the next week. I'm not trying to make enemies of the people closest to Jane.

I hear the front door open and close so I make my way to the living room.

"Well that certainly was enlightening," I tell her before I see her face.

When she turns around all I want to do it hold her and sooth her and take the exhausted look off her face.

"We're not going to talk about what you just overheard."

"Done. Shall we take a hot bath?" I'd agree to just about anything she wanted right now.

She agrees and I take her hand, leading her to the main bathroom.

Picking her up, I set her on the counter while I dig around in the cabinet to find some bath oils. I turn on the water and set the temperate to just on the verge of too hot before turning back to Jane.

"How are we doing, love?" I ask, gently caging her in.

She leans forward, putting her head on my chest before taking a deep breath and answering.

"I'm good. Sorry you had to hear all of that." She lets out a self-deprecating laugh.

"Nothing to be sorry about. Is jasmine okay?" I hold up the bath oils. She doesn't want to talk about it, then we don't talk about it.

"It's perfect." She's looking at me with confusion in her eyes, and I'm not sure I understand why. I'm just listening to what she wants.

I pour a little into the almost full bath and walk back over to Jane, pulling the string on her robe. The light green lingerie set greets me once again and I have to remind myself now is not the time to jump into sex. I push the robe off her shoulders and watch it fall to the counter.

Holding her gaze to make sure she's okay with everything, I slide my hand around her back and unhook her bra. The intensity of her stare hits something deep inside of me, and I have to push it away to focus back on her.

Slipping the straps of her bra down her arms, she shivers, and goose-bumps follow my fingers as they trail down her arms.

Tossing her bra on the ground, I move my hands to her hips. Stroking the edge of her panties, I watch for any sign she wants me to stop. I see nothing but desire radiating from her as she scoots her hips closer to the edge.

The connection between us is so intense, it rivals everything I knew about getting close to a person. Nothing we're doing right now is ex-plicitly sexual, yet I feel closer to her than I've ever felt before.

I hook my fingers into her panties, waiting to see is she's okay with it, when her hips lift ever so slightly off the counter allowing me to slide them down her legs.

"I think there's enough water," she says as she breaks our gaze to see the water almost overflowing.

I quickly step back and shut the water off as Jane jumps off the counter.

"Join me?" she asks hesitantly.

"Of course."

She steps into the steamy bath, signing with relief as she sinks in up to her neck. I strip off my boxer briefs and toss them in our growing pile of underwear before stepping in behind her.

She leans back, resting her head on my chest before her body finally starts to release the tension it's holding.

I wrap my arms around her stomach, letting her breathing soothe an inner turmoil I didn't realize was taking such a toll on me.

"My friends, they mean well," she whispers. "I'm the baby of the group. I graduated high school two years early and was barely seventeen when we all met in college. Sometimes it feels like I'm the little sister they're forced to take of even though I know it's not their intention."

My thumb starts a melodic rhythm against the skin of her stomach as she continues to talk.

"And now they have these wonderful partners and I'm just ... left behind. I don't want to feel this way though. There's no logical reason for me to feel like I do. The girls have never done anything to leave me out or not include me."

"It doesn't negate the way you feel," I encourage her. We haven't done a lot of talking this past week and I want to keep her talking.

She sinks deeper into me as she sighs.

"I just don't understand it."

"Understand what, love?"

"In the past two years, they've all found their perfect soulmates. I think I've been on more dates them all of them combined, and I feel ... never mind."

Tensing up when she mentions dating other men. My gut reaction is to find them all and teach them a lesson about how to treat women. But I force my body to relax as I think about what she said.

I debate whether I should push her or not. I'm so fucking curious about what she was going to say, but I have a feeling if I push, she'll go back into her shell and that's the exact opposite of what I want. I decide to go with honesty.

"I want to push you to finish that, but I also don't want to push you away. Just know that I really do want to know everything you're willing to let me in on. If you want to just relax in here and not talk about things, I will gladly do that too."

I can guess about the direction she was going anyways. She wants what her friends have. She wants the whole fairytale, a house in the suburbs, white picket fence and two point five kids.

I've never been the man who's anyone's knight in shining armor. I've never kept anyone around long enough to even think about it. How can I even think about it with Jane when I'm the last person she should consider?

Because you're already changing. This is already different than any other woman you've been with.

Before I can really analyze my thoughts, Jane sits up a little before turning toward me and straddling me hips.

"I like the tub," she says with a smirk as she grinds down on me, all thoughts of deeper conversation lost.

"*Fuck.*" Tipping my head back, I exhale hoping to regain some of my control.

And then she circles her hips.

I grip her hips hard, controlling her movements.

"I think you like something else, too," I growl.

I didn't intend for this to turn into sex, but if she wants the distraction who am I to tell her no.

"It's decent." She smirks.

"Decent? Did you just say my cock is decent?" I lean back utterly shocked at the nerve of this woman.

She shrugs, barely containing the smile on her face.

"I'll show you decent." I slide her pussy along my length. She tilts her head back in pleasure.

God, I want to slip inside of her so fucking back but I don't have a condom close by. And I'm not about to interrupt the look on her face right now. I'll give her one hell of an orgasm and pray I can hold my shit together in the process. Although, it wouldn't be the first time this woman undoes me.

I pull her upper body closer to mine, leaving no space between us as I continue to slide her hips. This new angle allows me to wrap one of my hands around her ass and have access to pussy as her clit drags along the ridge of my cock.

I circle her opening with my finger, teasing her before I hear the breathy, "Oh God," from her lips. Her head is buried in my neck, her hot pants send waves of arousal down my spine.

I shove two fingers into her and watch her body soar.

Pumping them in and out of her, I marvel at just how fucking responsive she is to me. If she hadn't have told me she'd never had an orgasm before I would never have guessed.

Her hips match my rhythm and her gorgeous cunt pulses. She's getting close, and I want to see how far I can take her.

I shift my hand a little, keeping my fingers thrusting, and move my thumb to tap on her ass. I circle it around and hear her gasp with pleasure.

Holy fuck, I don't think she could get any more perfect.

"I'm so close," she whines out as she presses a kiss to my neck.

She instinctually presses back against my finger, so I go for it. I press against her, just barely getting the tip in before she explodes. Her entire body flexes so hard, I have to fight to keep my fingers inside of her. But I have to feel her orgasm. It's as necessary as eating a breathing for me right now.

She clenches against my fingers so hard at the same time she bites down on my shoulder.

"Next time you want to say my cock is decent, you won't be getting off so lightly."

She slumps against me as I pull my fingers out of her, trailing my hand up and down her back.

"Holy shit, I didn't know it could feel like that," she breathes out.

"So, ass play is what made you break." I chuckle.

"What?" She sits up giving me a confused look.

"You just said 'holy shit.' So, all it took was a little ass play to turn you into the dirty girl." I smirk.

Her cheeks instantly heat.

"I didn't mean to, it just came out." Her embarrassment is so damn endearing.

"I won't tell anyone, love. I'll just enjoy the fact I'm the one that made you come so hard you broke your no cursing rule."

"Shut up." She buries her head back into my neck and I laugh.

We lie like that for another few minutes before she bolts up.

"You didn't get off," she accuses.

"I don't need to get off every time, love."

"Yes, you do, let me take care of you." She starts to scoot back and grips my dick in her hand, but I cover it with my own.

"Who the fuck made you think you had to get a man off no matter what?" I lift her up putting her back on my lap.

"Umm ..."

"Let me make one thing very clear. If I want to make you come, I will. If I want you to suck my cock, I will ask very nicely while pushing you to your knees. If I want to fuck you, I will make sure we're on the same page before I make you scream my name. No part of that means you have to get me off every single time. It is never a requirement that I have an orgasm. Am I clear?"

She nods.

"Words. This is important. I need your words so I can make sure you never think this is an equal exchange. With you and me it will never be equal. I need at least three of your orgasms to my one, at a bare minimum. Is that clear?"

"Very clear."

"Good. Because I'm not nearly done with you." I stand up from the tub, holding her ass in both of my hands.

She shrieks, gripping my shoulders for dear life.

"You are going to fall! Put me down."

"I won't fall. I'd never put such precious and sexy cargo in jeopardy." I smirk.

"You're insane." She huffs out on a laugh.

I just might be, but there's something about Jane, and it's turning me into a whole new man.

Chapter 16
Jane

*S*unday

When we woke up this morning, Pierce asked me what I wanted to do today. I took my time, thinking about all the things we could do, including more sex, hanging out in the villa, or maybe touring the island some more, and then I decided to just go for it.

So now, we're parasailing.

And it's the most incredible thing I've ever done in my life.

Pierce is next to me as we glide over the ocean, and I don't think I've stopped smiling yet.

"You know, I've never done this," Pierce says to me as I watch the waves coming in.

I turn to him, "You've never parasailed? How is that possible?"

He shrugs. "I've never really had the time to. I've been busy building my empire." He says it with a crooked smile, infusing a little sarcasm in his voice, but I see the truth there.

"Okay. If you had to pick one thing you've always wanted to do, but never had time for, what would it be?" Although this week is supposed to be about exploring all the things I want to, his words not mine, I feel the need to do the same for him. I may have been sheltered because of my age for a lot of my life, okay very sheltered thanks to my mom, but his is self-imposed and I want to break him of it just as badly as he wants to do the same for me.

"I think I'd like to have a normal day, or what most would consider a normal day. Maybe go see a movie in the middle of the day, go find a little hole in the wall to eat at and go walk in a park." He looks over at me. "Sounds boring, right?" He sighs.

"Doesn't sound boring at all. Sounds peaceful."

My heart breaks a little bit hearing the one thing he's wanted to do is to just have a normal day. He's been so focused on growing his business he's never stopped to enjoy it.

"My mother used to take me on walks around the park when I was a kid. We did it all the way up until I went to college, and it was something we did to take a break from the fast-paced life we lived. I'm not sure why I ever stopped."

Oh, Pierce.

"She died while I was away at college. Never told me she was sick, just called me one day and said her goodbyes. I didn't know that's what it was at the time, but when doctors called me about a week later to tell me she had passed, I realized she was saying her goodbyes without putting me through the trauma of seeing her wither away."

"I'm sorry," I whisper just loud enough to be heard over the waves below us.

"I was mad at her for a long time." He looks over at me with a sad smile on his face. "I was mad she took away my chance at closure. It took me a long time to realize you don't really get closure from something like that. Nothing can make the grief better, or easier to deal with."

I grab his hand, squeezing it. I don't know what I could possibly say in response to his words, but I want him to know I'm here for him.

This is the first time I've really learned anything of deep substance from him and my already smitten heart is pounding. There is so much more to this man than what he shows people.

"Anyways, this has been an unexpected surprise. I never thought you'd want to do something like this," he says.

"You expected me to want to stay in and bone you every day this week?" I smirk.

His booming laugh is something to behold indeed. Even when he's asleep I don't think I've seen him this carefree.

"Something like that. But I'm glad you picked this. Getting out of your comfort zone is almost therapeutic." He tips his head back and closes his eyes taking a deep breath of the salty air.

It is therapeutic, so I decide to share a little bit of me as well.

"So, you know I went to college super young. All my life I was pushed to be the best academically. My parents, well my mom, figured out pretty early that I was smarter than an average toddler, so they ran with it. I can't say I blame them. I've worked with kids long enough to know sometimes even the best intentions with parents aren't always what's best for the kids. It was so hard to be two years younger than everyone in every single class I was in, from kindergarten to college. I don't know if you noticed, but I'm quite socially awkward." I chuckle.

"I was at a developmental stage completely different from my peers, and I didn't understand why I didn't really fit in. My parents did what they thought was best, but they pushed me to be smart and not take any chances. I picked a safe major in college. I never partied until I met the girls." I smirk over at him. "But even then, I was the extra cautious one. The safe one."

He squeezes my hand.

"I've never really done things just for me. That's why this trip is important to me. I don't want to be the cautious one. I don't want to hide what I truly want behind an average life."

"You are anything but average, Jane."

I smile sadly over at him. "This me you've met, isn't the real me. I really wish it was though."

"I don't believe that for a second, and neither do you. Hell, you got me to go parasailing and I'm scared of heights!"

"You are not!" I gasp. "Why didn't you say something?" I shove him the best I can under the circumstances.

"Simple. Because it made you happy."

Chapter 17
Pierce

*M*onday

I walk up behind Jane, who's staring out the floor-to-ceiling windows in the living room, as the sun sits high in the sky. Pulling her flush against me, it's impossible to resist her.

"You smell good," I murmur against her skin.

"Well, I'm glad you like it. Your resort supplied it." She giggles.

"You smell like me," I growl.

"Because you're using the stuff in the shower too."

"Because this is my villa and you're using my body wash." I bite her shoulder where it connects to her neck.

"What?" She spins around so fast we almost knock heads.

"This is my villa. It's usually kept open at all times in case I need to come here on a whim, but they overbooked and gave it away," I explain. I don't think I realized she didn't know this yet.

"So, I've been staying in the freaking owner's villa this whole time! You could have kicked me out and moved me somewhere else!" She's so worked up over nothing, it's kind of adorable.

"I would never kick you out, that's just bad business." I smirk.

She smacks my chest. "Shut up, you know what I mean. We can trade places so you can have your place back," she offers.

"I had just planned to stay with you this whole week." I trail my hand down her back to grip her ass firmly.

"That could work."

"You know what else could work?"

"What?"

"You with my cock down your throat."

She says nothing but drops to her knees. I drop my head back trying to calm my racing pulse. She's teased me a little bit but has never fully done this with me yet. I've always been too impatient to fuck her.

She pulls down my joggers releasing my cock.

"Commando. I like." She has a wicked smirk on her face. When her sassy side gets going, she's unstoppable. And I'm helpless to resist.

"Seemed counterproductive to put on another layer."

She doesn't respond with words, but she does grip the base of my dick and lick the tip.

Her moan reaches my ears as she takes my head into her mouth. I flex, pushing deeper into her mouth as she opens up to take me.

Fuck, I can't believe I stopped her from doing this all week. She feels phenomenal and we've just started.

"That's it, take me deep love." I grunt when she pushes herself further down me and hollows out her cheeks.

She reaches up and cups my balls, and everything in me clenches up tight. I'm not going to last long at this rate.

I meet her gaze as she pulls back, leaving only the tip on her delectable mouth.

"I need you to take a deep breath for me, okay? I want in that pretty throat of yours, but we'll work our way up." My voice is deep, and I'm barely hanging on by a thread, but I want her to deep throat me so fucking bad.

She releases me completely, leaving her hand to stroke me while she catches her breath. Then she attacks me with enthusiasm and before I can say anything else, I feel the back of her throat around the head of my cock.

"Fuck," I hiss.

She bobs a little before pushing all the way down. Her nose touches my pelvis and I involuntarily thrust my hips. We keep a rhythm, she deep throats me for a minute then comes up for air before I thrust back into her mouth for a few minutes before I start to feel the tingle in my balls.

"Jane, I'm coming." I breathe out just as she sucks so hard, I swear she pulls out my soul through my dick.

I collapse against the window, my hands holding me up as I try to catch my breath.

"Holy shit love, you're going to kill me."

"I've wanted to do that since we met," she says brushing her lips with her fingers.

I don't speak, I just rip her up off the floor and strip her naked. Spinning her to face the windows, I press against her back.

"And I've wanted to do this." I push on her upper back making sure her tits are pressed against the cold glass.

I can hear her panting and I'm already hard again. This fucking woman makes me feel like I'm twenty-five again.

I grab her hips with both hands, pulling them away from the window putting her at the perfect angle for what I'm about to do.

"Do not move from that window. If you don't like something, tell me and we'll stop and discuss it, but I want to try something okay? You liked it the last time I explored your ass, is that still the case?"

"Yes," she moans out, jutting out her hips more.

"Good." I spank her ass lightly before stepping away from her.

I quickly go to the bedroom where I have my travel bag and grab the little bottle of lube I keep there before going back out to the living room.

I slide my hand up her back, gripping her neck in a strong hold and toss the little bottle next to us.

"This is going to be a little rough, but I think you'll enjoy it," I tell her at the same time I try to calm myself down a little, so this doesn't end too fast.

I kick open her legs and bring my hand up to her already dripping pussy.

"Did sucking my cock make you this wet, love? Or is it the anticipation of what's next?"

"Oh God, both."

I don't give her a warmup; she's so turned on she doesn't need one. I pump two fingers into her a couple of times as her back arches, then I add a third. I pull them out and trail them up her crack, circling her hole as she pushes her hips back against me.

She wants more, and I'm about to give it to her.

I keep my fingers circling as I lean down and grab a condom. I make quick work of rolling it down my dick and then pick up the bottle of lube. I pop open the bottle and the sound draws her attention.

"Eyes on the ocean," I command.

She refocuses her attention just as I notch my cock at her pussy. I put a little bit of lube directly on her ass hole before closing the cap and tossing the bottle aside.

I circle one finger against her as I push into her cunt.

"*Fuuuccckkkk*" She's already pulsing against me, and it feels like the best place on earth.

I press a little harder against her ass as I set a leisurely pace.

"Oh my god," she breathes out. She's pressed up against the glass and I can see her eyes are closed in the reflection. Nothing but pure pleasure is on her face so I take it as my cue for more.

"Push against my finger, love," I tell her softly as I apply more pressure. When my finger slips into the first knuckle her pussy clenches around me hard.

I test her a little, not wanting to push her too hard too fast. I pull out of her ass a little before thrusting in a little more of my finger. She whimpers and my eyes flicker to her face.

Her mouth is gaping open, and I look at her eyes to see if she's in any pain.

Our gazes meet and it's like lightening through my entire body. She nods once and it's all I need.

I pick up my pace, fucking her hard and I shove my finger into her ass.

"Oh fuck." She slaps her hand against the window. I smirk, knowing I'm the only man who gets to see her like this.

I feel her start to pulse more, and I know she's close.

Her orgasm catches her off guard and the surprise on her face makes my balls constrict up as my orgasm takes hold.

I gently pull out my finger from her ass and slump forward on her.

"I think you broke me," she mutters.

"I think you fixed me," I say without thought, pressing a kiss to her back.

Chapter 18
Jane

*T*uesday

Pierce said he had a little work to do this afternoon, so I decided I wanted to cook for him.

I've always loved cooking and anything to do with food, but I rarely get to do it for anyone one except myself.

I called down to the front desk and asked if it was possible to get some groceries delivered and they had everything on my doorstep within fifteen minutes of the call.

Perks to being associated with Pierce, or staying in his villa, I guess.

Now I'm prepping everything for when he decides to come out the office.

"Smells good already. What are you making," He slides up behind me, wrapping one arm around my waist before placing a kiss to the side of my head.

I think I'm in big trouble with this man. I only have four more days here and I'm falling for him faster than I can catch my breath. He's so much different than I thought he'd be. And everything has felt so effortlessly domesticated.

"Tonight, we're having roasted chicken and vegetables with risotto."

"Damn. Do I need to hire you for one of my restaurants?" He chuckles.

"I'm not that good, I promise." I can feel the heat rising to my cheeks.

When I decided to cook Pierce dinner, I didn't think about how personal it would feel. The only people that know about how much I love food and cooking are the girls, so this feels like I'm sharing too much of myself to a man who won't care when I leave in a few days.

What am I doing? About to be drowning in heartbreak by the end of the week if he isn't feeling the way I am.

"Hey, you okay?" he asks as he steps back.

"Yeah, totally fine," I say too brightly.

"Jane ..."

"I'm good, really. I just need to get this chicken in the oven if we're going to eat anytime soon."

"How can I help?" he asks moving around to the side and rolling up his sleeves. I must say, it's comical he wears dress pants and a button-down shirt, even on a day off.

"If you want to grab the veggies from the fridge, we can cut those up after I put the chicken in."

He moves gracefully, grabbing every vegetable available in the refrigerator. "So, tell me something surprising about you," he says as he grabs a knife from the butcher block on the counter.

"I think you know far too many surprising things about me already." I huff out a laugh.

"I think I don't know nearly enough about you, honestly."

"Well, what would you like to know?"

"You're a teacher, is that what you always wanted to do with your life? I know you said you picked a safe major, but is it genuinely what you wanted to do with your life?"

Somehow, with one question he manages to hit on the one thing with a chokehold over me. This is the problem about learning more about each other, I'll end up getting too attached and he will send me on my way when Saturday comes and not think twice about it. No matter how many nice things he says.

"I wanted to help people, in any way I could. I took a lot of time to narrow down my focus to teaching in college because I knew I wanted to do something that could potentially help the most. Teaching sounded like something I could have the biggest impact with. I mean, teaching the next generation everything from life skills to English to how to be a functioning member of society. It seemed like a no brainer."

"And now?"

"You're very astute, you know that?"

"I just listen when you talk, Jane. You've told me all about teaching in the past tense, so I figure it's not all you thought it would be."

I didn't even realize I did that.

"Now ... It feels like I have zero control over my classroom and what I'm able to teach. It feels like I don't make any difference to the kids I teach and it's disheartening. They are all just there for the grade, but they don't really care. And administration only cares about test scores and politics."

I've talked with the girls a little about how I've been feeling lately, but everyone's been busy, and my dramatic career crisis isn't really high on the importance scale in the grand scheme of things. I get it, and honestly, I understand it. It's not a huge deal. I just need to figure out if I actually want to keep teaching or not. That was a huge reason I decided to stay the extra week. More time in paradise means more time with Pierce as my only distraction to figure out where I go from here. What I *really* want out of my life.

Way easier said than done, but maybe this trip will gain me some clarity.

"It's a thankless job," Pierce mutters.

"When I first started, people in the field used to tell me the same thing, but I used to brush it aside. I didn't need the thanks, I just wanted to be the difference maker regardless of recognition. But the longer I teach, the more I feel ... discouraged. It's not even about the recognition," I say as I slather the chicken in butter and spices. "It's not being able to actually do my job."

I look up at him and see he's nodding in sympathy, and I wonder how this conversation got so derailed.

"So, tell me something surprising about you." I move around him to put the chicken in the over, then move to the vegetables.

"The last time I had a real relationship was college."

My head jerks up to meet his eyes. I'm not sure why my knee jerk reaction is a sharp pain in my chest when I was never promised anything by him, but I feel crushed.

"Well, you were busy with your company. It makes sense," I turn my attention back to chopping vegetables, ignoring the hurt I feel.

"I think when my mother died, and I really understood what my parents' relationship, or lack thereof really, was like, I decided I didn't want to go down that path. I wanted to carve my own way, create my business, and thrive that way."

And the knife to the heart deepens. I was so stupid to think this was anything other than what it is ... a vacation hookup. Darn my overly romantic heart for a man like Pierce could really fall for plain old me. My life is not a romance book.

"Hey, what just happened?" He grabs my shoulder, turning me toward him.

"Nothing, just want to make sure I get these in the oven on time." I can tell he doesn't believe me, but I'm not about to discuss how my stupid, gullible heart made me believe there was something more here. No. I'm old enough to be mature and take the rest of the week as it comes and still enjoy the heck out of what he does to my body. But that's all it can be, and I need to remember that when my heart tries to get involved again.

I grab another sheet pan and toss the already seasoned vegetables on it and toss them in the over with the chicken.

"What's next?" Pierce asks.

"Next, we wait for everything to cook for a while then I'll start the risotto."

"How much time do we have?" The smirk on his face telling me exactly what he's thinking.

"About a half hour," I counter with as much sass as I can. Fight sex with sex and call it a fun time.

I squeal when he lifts me up onto the counter, stepping in between my legs.

I instantly forget all about my naïve little heart when his dick presses against me sending sparks against my clit.

"You should stay in just my shirts the rest of the week," he murmurs against my ear as he slides his hands up my hips to grip my panties.

"I can make that happen." I gasp out as he kisses that sensitive spot below my ear.

"Good. So, a half an hour? Let's see how many times I can make you come." He drops to his knees, taking my panties with him.

Leaning back on his heels, he slides his shirt up my hips, exposing me to him.

"I'm thinking four, over or under, love?" He looks up at me with a devilish smirk.

I can push my feelings aside for this. I can deal with the fallout when I go back home. If he continues to do this all week, it'll be the perfect distraction.

"Over." I meet his eyes, challenging him.

Chapter 19

Pierce

*W*ednesday

I kick my flippers, trying to follow the school of fish underneath me. Jane is next to me trying to keep up, but I've been keeping an eye on her.

I've only been snorkeling once in my life—when I was a couple years out of college. I had taken a trip to Australia and checked out the Great Barrier Reef the best way you can.

My life's been decidedly less exciting in the years that have followed, but it all seems to be changing now.

Except I fucked up last night. I saw the light Jane usually carries dim the second I told her I haven't had a relationship since college.

My intention was to show her just how fucking special she is, and how my whole mindset has changed because of her, but I failed miserably. She saw the statement as the complete opposite. So I did the only thing I knew to do, gave her endless orgasm. I should have just fucking talked to her about it, made her tell me how she was feeling, but I chickened out. I didn't want to put a damper on the week.

I know I'll have to talk to her about it soon, but I need to get my plans together first.

It's what I was doing while I was "working" yesterday. I had called Sydney to start the process of looking for a home base in Austin, both to live in and for the office. I know I can't live in London if I want a real relationship with her, so this is my solution. It'll take a little time to get things set up, so I didn't want to tell Jane about it until more was finalized. I don't want to get both our hopes up only for something to pop up and it take longer for me to come to her. Feeling stagnant in my profession has had me thinking of different options. And getting away from my father is a huge plus to this all, but Jane made the location decision for me.

For now, we're enjoying exploring the vast ocean and all of its sea life and ignoring what happened last night. It really is beautiful and freeing. Not having the constant worry about every little thing happening at all my properties. Or the latest drama my father incites.

I've learned quickly over the last week and half I've been micromanaging a lot of my business. I've got a great team at each hotel and resort, but I tend to not let them do their job. It's another change I'll be implementing along with moving my main office.

I'm pulled from my musings by a gentle tap on my shoulder. I move upright, wading in the water and come face to face with a very gorgeous Jane.

Removing the snorkel from my mouth, I can't help the smile that takes over my face.

"How's it going, love?"

"So freaking good! Did you see the turtle back there!" Her excitement is contagious.

"I did. Did you see the volcano we passed? I know the guide said there were somewhere around sixty of them in the area, but I didn't expect to actually be able to see them."

"It's so crazy! I'm so glad we did this!"

This smile, the one she's wearing right now? I want to put it on her face every single day she'll let me.

She puts her face back in the water before I can say anything else and is off chasing more fish.

We took the boat I keep here out today and I bribed one of the guides at The Vanstone to take us out privately, so we can stay out her all day if she wishes. The boat is fully stocked with everything we could possibly need.

Along with snorkeling today, I want the day to be relaxing. Yes, I want to fuck Jane every single time I see her, but I want her to see there is more to me, more to us, than the sex. So today, we aren't having sex.

I woke up feeling disheartened by my careless words last night. And because I don't want to let Jane in on my plan just yet because I want more of a solid plan before getting either of our hopes up, I think showing her there's more to me might help ease her mind.

We stay in the water, talking, laughing and just having a good time for a couple more hours before we get back on the boat.

"Oh my gosh, I'm starving," Jane says as she lies on a lounge chair on deck, throwing her arm over her eyes.

She looks stunning right now. Her hair wavy from the salt water, the smallest amount of freckles coming out to play on her nose and shoulders, and her body in a bikini is testing every ounce of control I have.

"I'll run below deck and grab us some food." She nods as I linger for a moment just committing this moment to memory.

When I finally come back with food, I drag a small table over and place a plate of meats, cheeses and fruit on it along with a couple bottles of water.

"This was one of the most perfect days ever." Jane sighs as she sits up and digs into the food.

"What's next for the day?" she asks after taking a sip of water.

"That's entirely up to you. We can send the guide back to the island and stay on the boat tonight—"

"You really need to stop calling this a boat, Pierce. It's a freaking yacht and you know it." She shakes her head, exasperated.

"We can send the guide back on the dinghy," I continue. "We can spend the night here, or we can head back and go eat at one of other restaurants. Whatever you want to do, Jane, I'll make it happen."

She stares at me for a long second, and I wonder what's going on in her head.

She abruptly stands up and makes her way over to me before sitting in my lap and wrapping her arms around my neck.

"You need to stop being so sweet to me," she says with conflict in her eyes.

"Never."

She presses her lips to mine, soft and gentle at first. Full of emotion and intent.

God, I hope she can feel how much she already fucking means to me. Feel how much I need to keep her in my life long after her vacation is over. With any luck, I won't completely fuck this up, and I'll be able to tell her exactly how I feel when all my plans fall into place.

Chapter 20
Jane

Thursday

Waking up on a freaking yacht this morning is something out of one of the romance books I read. Things like this don't happen to me, and I just know the other shoe will drop at some point.

It feels like it already has, because although we had the yacht to ourselves all night, Pierce didn't put the moves on me once.

Did I mess up? Can he tell I'm in too deep and he wants an escape plan? I don't know anymore.

There are times I see this look of deep adoration on his face, when he looks at me like I mean something. But then we haven't talked about what's next, or if he even wants something more. But my heart feels too tied up with him to be the bigger person and breech the topic. I'm not sure I want to know if he sees this as only a hook up anymore. I'd rather wait until I'm about to get on a plane so I can cry into my carry-on.

My gut reaction is to call the girls and have them point out all the red flags, all the things I'm conveniently overlooking so when I leave, it won't be so hard. But outside of sending an *I'm okay* message in the group chat periodically, I've been staying true to my need for space. If I always need their help figuring out if a man is bad for me, am I ever really figuring it out for myself?

This vacation and being with Pierce feel like my chance to prove to myself I can spot a man who isn't good for me. And to prove that I can really think about what I want to do with the rest of my life in general. Keeping that in the back of my mind will be key if this all goes south the way I think it will.

He's been upfront from the start about what he wants, and I need to listen to what he's telling me and not makeup some fantasy about how he'll turn into the love of my life overnight. He hasn't said anything to lead me to believe he sees this as more than that.

"What are you thinking so hard about over there?" Pierce's gravelly morning voice hits me right between the thighs.

Be bold. Take control of what you want and keep your overwhelming emotions out of it. Lean into the lust—nothing more until we have a conversation.

"I was just thinking about how I missed your dick last night." I turn to face him and trail my fingertips from his collarbone down to this hip.

"Well, what are you going to do about it then?"

I push all the doubts, the what-ifs, and the second guessing out of my head. This is what I wanted to use this vacation for, and dammit, I'm going to take charge.

I shove Pierce onto his back before kneeling in between his legs.

"Oh shit," he groans out, and I can't help the smirk from spreading on my face. This is what I need right now, to remember that I *can be* this woman. I can take charge of my life and turn this impressive man into a puddle underneath me.

"I think I like having you at my mercy." Wrapping my hand around his already hard erection, I tease him like he likes to tease me: soft and slow and not enough to actually get him off.

"I think I like being at your mercy. You are insanely sexy when you're in charge," he pants out, arching his hips to try and get more friction.

Hearing the way I'm affecting him makes my brain shut off and forces me into action.

I grip him a little tighter and lick the tip of his dick, coating my tongue in the precum leaking from him.

God, he tastes good.

I dip my head, engulfing the bulbus head before sucking gently. His hips buck off the bed and his moans reach my ears making me wet with the power to reduce him to this.

Without overthinking, I sit up and kneel over him, putting his dick right up against my clit.

His hands reach for my hips. "That's it, love, take what you need. Use me." He lets out a low groan.

Rotating my hips, I get the friction I'm craving and tilt my head back as my hips continue to move.

His grip on my hips never change, he doesn't try to control my movements, he just lets me use him, and it's the hottest thing I've ever felt.

I need more.

I sit up on my knees a little, reaching for his cock and lining him up with my opening before sinking down the slightest bit.

"Holy shit, wait!" He pulls my hips up and sees the disappointment on my face. "You feel so fucking good, Jane, too good, but I need to get a condom." He scrambles, still holding me to him, reaching for the bedside drawer and grabbing a condom.

I cannot believe I forgot something as important as a condom, and it has my head a little fuzzy. Heck, he has my head a complete mess, but I'm determined to stick to my plan and separate my emotions from the mind blowing sex.

"Put it on me." He holds out the condom.

"What?" I jolt back. I've never, in my life put a condom on a man.

"Take the condom, and roll it down my cock, love."

I hesitantly grab it and rip it open.

"I need the breather because your bare cunt on my cock has me too close to the edge." His crass words send a shiver down my spine. The power I feel from it makes me feel drunk and determined to make him lose control.

I carefully roll the condom down his length before he grips my hand in his.

"Nope, I think that made it worse." He's gritting his teeth, and his eyes are closed in concentration.

I did this. I'm making him lose control, and I fucking love it!

I don't waste any more time lining myself back up with him and sinking down on one smooth stroke.

"Jesus fuck, love, you're going to unman me," Pierce grits out.

"Better figure it out because I want at least two orgasms," I say with all the confidence in the world.

I love this version of me. I wish I could be this version all the time. *So do it. Nothing is holding you back. Tell Pierce what you want from him, quit your job, and figure it out.*

His eyes pop open and pride is evident in his stare. He takes one hand off my hip, moving his thumb to my clit and circling it in the way he knows will make me come in minutes.

"Ride my cock love. Ride me until you're breathless, dripping, and satiated."

His words spring me into action, and I don't think I could stop for anything. All my focus is on the pressure building low in my stomach, the clench of my inner muscles against his rigid cock.

"Oh God!" I scream as the force of my orgasm hits me like a tsunami.

"That's one. Keep going."

I bounce harder as my orgasm continues to roll through me. He angles my hips back a little, and he instantly hits the spot inside of me that makes me see stars. I swear my next orgasm starts as soon as the last one ends. I come so hard, I think I black out because the next thing I know I'm lying on Pierce's chest panting as I try to catch my breath.

Before I know what's happening, Pierce rolls me to my back and pulls out of my before ripping off the condom and stroking himself in between my legs.

The sight alone is one of the sexiest things I've ever witnessed. But when he pushes two fingers into my already abused pussy, finding the spot I love so much inside of me? I lose it. I come on his fingers, feeling rung out and exhausted.

"Look at me, love. Look at my cock as I paint you with my cum."

I sit up as best as I can right as spurts of cum jet out of his tip and land on my lower stomach and pelvis. He moans my name as he comes and my heart pounds in my chest. *Lust not love, I have to remember that.*

He's barely finished when he dips down and licks a line from my opening, up past my clit and through his orgasm that's coating my skin.

Holy erotic perfection.

He braces himself around my head before he dips down and kisses me in a slow languid kiss. I can taste both of us on his tongue making this the single most sensual experience in my life. When he pulls back my head is in shambles.

"Did I die?" I ask, completely serious. I've had some incredible orgasms with this man, but I've never felt anything like what I just felt.

He laughs as he rolls over to the side.

"No love, but that's as close to nirvana as I've ever been."

We look at each other for a long moment. I feel so much right now, but I can't say any of it. The fear of rejection is too much for me right now.

This is a vacation hookup.

I just wish my stupid heart would get the memo.

Chapter 21
Pierce

*F*riday

How has this week gone by so fast? I'm not ready to let Jane go, even if it's only temporary until I can make my way to Austin.

Jane leaves tomorrow and with our last full day here, I wanted to show her a piece of me that no one gets to see.

We're currently driving to the other side of the island to the Oceanview Academy.

"It's gorgeous over here." Her voice breaks the silence in the car.

"This side of the island is why I bought the property for The Vanstone."

"So why isn't The Vanstone over here?"

"Because I had different plans, you'll see."

We pull up to the entrance, and I start to get nervous. The only people who know about this are the people working here, Sydney, and the board members of my foundation.

I look over and see Jane's eyes lit up in wonderment.

"This is Oceanview Academy. A little backstory before we go in." I take a deep breath. I'm about to share a whole lot of my fucked up history with Jane. I don't want it to deter her away from me. I just want her to understand where I came from.

"My parents were only together a short time. Met because my mother was doing a late gap year. She travelled around, mostly England for a few months, before she jumped into the work force. They never got married, and when they got pregnant with me there was a pretty shitty custody battle. As I've told you previously, I spent most of the time with my mother, and summers were spent with my father. He comes from old money so when he wanted to be out of my mother's life he just stayed in England when she went back to the States.

"The courts in America deemed the need for him to pay child support. He protested for most of my life, honestly. He would send my mother the bare minimum, sometimes not even that, but she didn't have the financials to really fight him on anything.

"She would talk about what she would do with the money if my father ever gave her what he was actually obligated to, and she always said she wanted to start a school somewhere that didn't have access to education. She had these grand plans to build a foundation to help under privileged kids all over the country, and some outside as well.

"She never got to live out her dreams, so I made sure to live them out for her."

We're both silent in the car for a long time, and I start to wonder if this is a good idea.

"That's incredible, Pierce. She would be very proud of the man you became," she says quietly.

My chest fills with pride and love, both for my mother and for Jane. Her understanding, her heart makes it impossible to have ever resisted her.

"I'd like to show you around, if you're okay with it."

"Absolutely. I'd be honored."

We both get out of the car, and I'm feeling extremely vulnerable. I'm forty-two and I've never opened up to a woman like I have to Jane; it's scary to put yourself out there. She could decide to be done with me tomorrow, and I wouldn't fight it.

I would literally give her anything she wanted, even if it means it isn't me.

We walk in silence, hand in hand through the front doors and to the administration office.

"Good afternoon, ladies. I was just going to show Ms. Hatley around our facilities if that's okay with you."

"Of course, Mr. Vanstone. No need to ask, you know where everything is," Melba, the principal here, tells me.

"Pierce, please, Melba. We'll swing back by before we leave." I wink at her. Her calling me Mr. Vanstone has been a battle for years, so it's become a little inside joke between us.

We tour the grounds, I show her all the little things my mother thought were important to schooling like the art and music rooms, the outside area with places to play and do sports, and classes that are more useful in the real world like how to interview, how to manage your money.

We stop into one of the empty classrooms, and Jane's eyes light up.

"I love how this is set up! You have different areas around the room so everyone isn't just sitting at a desk. It helps different types of learners actually learn the information." She turns to me with a bright smile on her face.

"That would mostly be Melba's doing. She believes every kid learns in their own way, and we both wanted to make sure everyone has the opportunity to thrive, not just collect a grade."

"God that's so amazing. I wish we prioritized the kids like this."

I gesture for her to head down the hallway.

"It's funny she wanted a focus to be on more real world functionality because that's exactly what I teach at Phoenix House when I'm there. I hold classes about how to interviews for jobs, how to find resources for food and shelter if needed—basics that aren't really taught in schools," Jane adds as we make out way around the grounds.

"Great women think alike then." I smile at her. God my mother would have loved her, there's no doubt in my mind.

"And around the side of the building is the community garden. It helps supply for not only school, but the island as well. The resort actually pays the school for their season vegetables every week. So, a lot of what you eat there, comes from here."

"Oh Pierce, that's just amazing."

I shrug. "It may seem like I only care about what bigger and better properties I can add to my portfolio, but I do try and offset a lot with places just like this. The Eloise Ford Foundation is responsible for infusing the places we put resorts with schools for the locals, for whatever their specific needs are, but we always make sure a community garden is started and maintained for their benefit."

"The Eloise Ford Foundation?"

"My mother's name, well her middle name. I didn't want to have the Vanstone name connected to this," I admit.

"God, I love it. I've always wanted to use food to help people. Whether that be with food science to make sure nutritious options are available everywhere, or community gardens just like this that bring access to otherwise baron areas." Her excitement is palatable.

"So why don't you?" I ask, genuinely confused why she stays on teaching if this is truly what she wants to do with her life.

"It's complicated." She sighs. "I chose the safe option back in college, and I've stuck with it. And it's not like teaching gives me a ton of funds to make any of it a reality anyways. Plus, if I just quit, I think my mom would lose it. I've kept teaching partially out of obligation to her." She brushes it off like it's something that could never happen, but my brain is already running a mile a minute trying to come up with a way to make this happen for her.

"Do you want to stay and play with the kids?" I offer, knowing she won't want to talk about me throwing money at anything she wants.

"Yes!" She jumps up and starts walking back to the playground area.

If there is anything I've learned about Jane in the past two weeks, it's that my money doesn't mean shit to her. So now, on top of moving my entire company to Austin, I need to find a way to make her dreams a reality without just throwing money at them. But it'll be a challenge to figure out a different day because I'm soaking up as much Jane time as I can before she heads back home.

Chapter 22
Jane

S^{aturday}

I laid in bed last night with silent tears running down my face.

How did I ever think I could be the woman who spends time with an amazing man like Pierce and not fall for him?

I was doomed from the start; I know that now.

And after learning about his foundation and the reason he does it! How was I supposed to keep my heart safe?

It's now Saturday morning, and I officially leave paradise in six hours. I'm not ready. I don't want to go back to my boring, unfulfilled life. But that's what I have to do because Pierce and I haven't actually talked about anything past this week. I take it to mean this is all we get. All the confidence I've cultivated the last two weeks can't help me force me to start the difficult conversation.

Two weeks of finding myself.

Two weeks of feeling more like myself than I ever have before.

Two weeks of reevaluating everything I thought I knew I wanted in life.

Two weeks of not playing it safe.

And two weeks of falling for a man so unattainable my heart is already cracking in two.

It's not like I can just drop my life and travel around with Pierce. And there's no way Pierce can drop what he has going on to what? Visit me periodically? There's no way.

So I'm going to relish in the feel of his strong forearm draped around my torso and his hot breath against my neck as he sleeps behind me one last time.

This extended trip has made me realize a lot about myself. I like who I've been here, and I want to bring it home with me. I want to take more chances, really take the next month or so to evaluate if I want to continue teaching and figure out my options if I choose to leave. It's a lot of potential change really fast, but I don't want to lose this new me.

I also think I need to take a break from dating. I don't even know how I could date anyone outside of Pierce any time soon. He's probably ruined me for all men, honestly.

"Stop thinking so loudly." He presses a kiss to my shoulder.

"Sorry, just making a mental list so I don't forget anything," I say, discreetly wiping the tears from my face.

His arm around my middle tightens as I speak the truth neither of us have wanted to face.

But there's no more ignoring it.

I'm leaving.

"Can I make you breakfast?" he murmurs in my ear.

"Since when do you cook?" I ask on a laugh.

"I can manage the basics. Just because I choose to utilize the five-star restaurants here instead of cooking for myself doesn't mean I can't." He presses another kiss to my shoulder.

"I could go for some breakfast."

"Wonderful, I'll cook yours after I eat mine."

"What—" He burrows himself in the blankets, pushing me to lie flat on my back before sliding his hands up my thighs.

He wastes no time, licking my clit as he pushes a finger into me. I'm already wet for him, which is no shocker, but dang it if I'm not close already.

I reach down and run my fingers through his hair before gripping it and drawing him closer to me.

"That's right. Use me, love."

"Shut up and get me off." I shove his head back down.

He chuckles. "God I fucking love it when you're sassy."

"Pierce," I whine.

"Have I ever let you down?"

Not yet, but I'm about to have my heart crushed in a few hours.

It takes him less than five minutes to get me off, and I'm glad for the distraction, however short it is.

I finish putting my toiletries in my bag and zip up my suitcase sitting on the bed. Looking around, I'm grateful for the two weeks I've spent here. Not only because of Pierce, but because this was a once in a lifetime trip. It's brought more clarity to me, and I truly feel like I've learned more about myself here.

I've done more here in the past two weeks than I have in the last five years at least.

And I should be ecstatic about that. But Pierce is heavy on my mind right now.

Biting the bullet, I decide it's time to stop hiding from him and go eat breakfast. He is cooking for me after all.

The sight the greets me when I walk out of the bedroom is something I wish I could burn into my retinas and hold onto long after I leave here.

Pierce in nothing but his boxer briefs and an apron flipping pancakes.

I realize quickly he has his earbuds in when he lifts the spatula to his mouth and starts singing off key to the music only he can hear.

Laughter bubbles up my throat causing me to clamp my hand over my mouth to muffle it. He spins around, spatula still poised at his mouth with a smirk.

"You like the show?" He pulls an ear bud out.

"Love it." I giggle.

"Breakfast is almost ready, have a seat and I'll bring it to you." He winks. "Coffee?"

"Please."

He turns back around and fills up a coffee cup, doctoring it up just the way I like it.

We fit together so damn well ... why can't we live closer? Why can't this last beyond these past two weeks?

Placing the mug softly in front of me, he places a kiss on my cheek before heading back to the stove and plating our breakfast.

I rub my chest where my heart aches.

I just need to get through breakfast and goodbyes then I can cry the entire flight home. I'll give myself that before I need to return to real life and be an adult.

"Okay," Pierce says, pulling me from my thoughts. "We have scrambled eggs that started as fried eggs, but I fucked them up. Toast and some bacon. Very gourmet." A flush takes over his cheeks as he sets down his simple breakfast and it's so endearing.

"Looks delicious," I say as I pick up my fork and dig in.

"Should have just ordered room service," he grumbles as he sits next to me and digs in.

"Nope. I like this better." And I do, his eggs are seasoned well, and the bacon is cooked perfectly. It may be simple, but I like this peeled back version of Pierce. It makes him feel attainable.

No! He's not attainable so don't even think about it. Start locking up that heart, girl.

We eat in comfortable silence, both lost in our thoughts. I wish I was feeling the bravery I've had this week because I want to know what he's thinking. I want to ask if we can make this work, but I'm too scared to hear the answer. I think I'd rather take this experience and keep it a happy one. Not ruin it with forcing him to crush my very fragile heart.

No, it's better this way.

Pierce's fork clatters to the table and I turn my attention to him.

"I'm going to get dressed really quickly. I want to take you somewhere." He gets up without waiting for my response and my heart pounds in my chest. I'm not sure if I can handle whatever he wants to show me.

If it's something good, I'll just fall harder. If he's taking me somewhere to tell me we're officially nothing more than a fling, I swear I'll break down in ugly tears right then and there.

But I want these last few hours with Pierce. I want to keep this feeling I have when I'm with him for just a little bit longer.

He returns in loose, cream linen pants and a white linen short sleeve shirt. He looks more relaxed than I've ever seen him outside of the bedroom and I hope I had as much of an impact on him as he's had on me.

"Ready?"

"Yeah, I think so." *God, I hope I'm ready.*

He places his hand on my lower back, leading me out the front door and to his fancy car. I don't even ask how things magically appear anymore. He can make anything happen with a simple text.

We're quiet yet again as he drives us to wherever he's taking us. The longer we're in the car, the more familiar the landscape looks.

When he pulls up to the beach we went to all those days ago, I don't know how to feel. I want to be the cool unaffected woman, but my heart is pounding out of my chest. The anxiety of what could happen is almost debilitating right now.

Pierce gets out of the car after parking and walks over to my door. Taking a deep breath, I paste a smile on my face as he opens my door and holds his hand out to me.

"Back where it all began." I smile up at him as we walk to the deserted beach.

"Felt fitting," he says as he sits in the sand, motioning for me to do the same beside him.

"I wasn't expecting you," he murmurs. "I've never wanted to keep someone here past their stay, and yet I couldn't let you go. Hell, I still don't want to, but I know it's not possible for you to stay."

"If only." I smile over at him.

"I'd like to stay in touch if you are amenable to it. I know the distance would prevent a lot of things, but I don't think I can give you up completely."

"I'd like that," I say cautiously. It's not a declaration of more, but it is a promise to stay in touch. I don't think I realized how much I wanted to keep contact until he said it. Giving him up cold turkey may have completely broken me.

"I'll try not to bombard you with texts." He smiles sadly.

Even if we don't stay in touch for long, even if I never see him again, this was worth it. Not just because of Pierce, but because of me. I think the separation from everything in my life has allowed me to really let loose and be who I want to be, not who I'm expected to be. And I *fucking* love who I've been this week.

A small smile graces my face as I think about something as simple as cursing, but it's the freedom more than anything. The freedom to be whoever I want to be without judgment. The freedom to not stay where I'm at simply because it's what's expected.

The waves comfort us in our silence, and I wish I was a woman who could just drop all my responsibilities and stay. But I'd never let my friends down like that.

And who knows what will happen between me and Pierce. Miracles happen, we could end up together in some crazy world where everything works out.

"These past two weeks have been ... nothing short of eye opening. I hope you know how much of an impact you've had on me in such a short amount of time." Pierce speaks his words to the ocean, but his words hit my heart directly.

"Same," I barely get out. My throat feels tight, and the back of my eyes burn with unshed tears.

The sound of ocean waves engulfs us. Their soothing nature barely calming my racing heart. I want to say so much, but what is there to really say?

I want to stay here.

I don't want to fly halfway around the world and never see you again.

I want more.

No. Everything left unsaid needs to stay there because there is no easy answer. No way Pierce and I being a couple happens anytime in the near future, if ever.

God, this sucks.

I look down at my phone and see it's almost time to head to the airport.

"I've got to head back soon."

"I know." He pulls me to him, setting me in his lap. His hand cups my jaw as he stares into my eyes.

"This isn't goodbye, okay? This is a *we'll talk later*." His tone leaves no room for argument, and I am desperate to believe him, but I also need to protect myself.

"Okay," I whisper. Leaning into the hand holding my jaw, I close my eyes and soak in his touch. If this is the last time I feel it, I'm going to sear the feeling into my brain.

His lips brush against my cheek, forehead, and finally my lips.

He says this isn't goodbye, but it sure as hell feels like it is.

"Let's go get your bags, and I'll drive you to the airport," he says quietly as he pressed his forehead to mine. I wordlessly nod and start to climb out of his lap.

The drive back to the resort is uneventful, so is the drive to the airport. I'm too lost in my own head to make small talk and either Pierce feels the same or is allowing me this small reprieve.

He parks and turns to face me.

"This isn't goodbye," he reminds me.

"Just a *we'll talk later*." I smile at him. "I know. I've got it from here but thank you for the phenomenal time. You'll never know how much this has meant to me." Leaning forward, I press a kiss to his lips and pull back before he drags me in for more. I jump out of the car and pull my bag from the back seat. I give him one last wave before walking into the terminal.

It's fairly empty in here right now, so I get to the check in counter in record time, giving them my name and ID.

"Alright Miss Hatley, I have you on flight 1142 leaving at 2:30 p.m. You're in seat 2A, and when you make it through security, take a left and you'll walk right into the first class lounge.

"What?" I'm dumbfounded. First class? There's no way.

Pierce.

Still surprising me even as I'm leaving.

"Thank you very much." I grab my boarding pass and head throughs security.

I should really be more excited about sitting in the first-class lounge. This is undoubtedly the only time I'll get this level of luxury but I can't get my thoughts away from Pierce. Instead, I drink two glasses of wine and try to keep a lid on my emotions until I board.

They finally call for my flight, and I sag with relief. Boarding is seamless, and before I know it we're taking off. I get settled with another glass of wine, and that's when the waterworks start. I turn my head to the window and cry for everything that could have been. Cry for finally finding a good man and having to let him go.

Guess I'm the only one who doesn't get to be lucky in love.

Chapter 23
Pierce

I 've done some hard shit in my life but sending Jane home on that airplane last week is hitting dangerously close to number one on my list.

I know she felt like it was a goodbye, but nothing could be further from the truth. I just didn't want to get either of our hopes up when none of my plans are set in stone yet. My need for control made the decision not to talk to her about anything in the future, and I know now it was probably the wrong move.

And the biggest thing I have to do before things get finalized is talk to my father. I don't need his approval, but he does hold some shares in my company. A stupid decision on my part many years ago, but here we are. *Maybe I should just buy him out if he gives me a hard time.*

Shaking my head, knowing he would never sell me his shares if he can help it, I refocus my attention the listings in Austin Sydney sent over this morning. We've got some great options, I just need to pick which one will work the best.

A knock at the door pulls my attention. "Come in." I bolster my voice, knowing it's my father. I can't show any weakness around him or he'll just exploit it.

Alfred Bronstein looks exactly as one would expect by his name. He's tall, but his portly belly is a clear sign of his gluttony. His rosy cheeks grow ruddier when he drinks, and his hard green eyes, the same as mine, miss nothing. He's a hard man, and one I've given up on trying to impress.

"I thought you were at the Mariana Islands property for another week," he says without preamble and takes a seat in front of my desk.

"I decided to cut the trip a little short because I had some other things to work on."

He snorts. "Buying yet another property, son?" He says *son* like it's a curse, and I have to force myself to stay calm. I rarely make it longer than ten minutes in the room with him, but this conversation needs to happen before I pull the trigger on this big move to Austin.

"In a way. I'm going to be looking at moving our headquarters to the States."

"And why would you want to do that?" He looks bored.

"Because London has become stagnant, and the company needs the change." It's true enough, I'm stagnant here so forcing the company, my company to change with me makes the most sense.

"London is never stagnant. That's a preposterous statement." He brushes me off.

"Well, this was more of a courtesy anyways. I'm moving the company's headquarters to the States, it wasn't a question."

He blusters, his cheeks turning rosier by the second.

"You can't do this if I say no. I own shares and that means what I say goes. I forbade you from thinking of this asinine idea." It really is exhausting talking to him. It amazes me he got so far in his life when he says shit like this. If he really knew what he was talking about, he would realize he's making an empty threat.

"You hold ten percent of the shares to *my* company. That means, I get to do whatever the fuck I want with *my* company. I gave you those shares as a courtesy and some misplaced loyalty to a man I called my father.

You've since dispelled that relationship, and you're lucky I don't buy you out."

I've had enough. I've beaten around the bush too much with this man, and I'm sick of it. He's my father by name only, and he's lucky he gets a pretty sizable income from my company so he can sit on his ass and bitch about his miserable life to whoever listens.

"How dare you speak to me like that? The only reason you are what you are today is because of me, boy, and you best remember that," he says with a scoff.

"Sure, we'll go with that." I roll my eyes. It's not worth the fight because he won't hear me anyways.

He sputters, trying to find an argument, but I'm bored of this all. It solidifies my decision to move even more. Leaving this city, getting as far away from my father as possible is the right decision for me. Jane just happens to be the cherry on top of the very delicious sundae.

"You ungrateful little shit." His face turns an alarming shade of red. God I hope he doesn't have a heart attack in my office. I don't want to have him spend any more time in here if I can help it.

"You owe me for all the times I put up with you. For helping you start this god forsaken company and for taking you under my wing so you could be this successful. You will not leave London."

I ignore him, although the hurt is still there. I worked so hard to garner his respect, and this is how he still sees me. Instead of engaging in conversation, I send a text to the head of my security asking him to come and escort my father out of the building. I'm also revoking his access to the building for the time being until I solidify plans and figure out how to lessen his involvement entirely.

"Are you listening to me?!" His voice is getting louder and louder by the minute.

My door opens and security comes in.

"Mr. Bronstein, if you could come with us, please."

"What is the meaning of this? You can't be serious. I'll sue you, Pierce, for assaulting one of your shareholders. Is that the reputation you want?"

"Mr. Bronstein, please," security continues.

I make eye contact with him to show him I'm serious. He can put up as big of a fight as he wants, but I'm done with this shit. He stares a moment longer before standing up in a huff and walking to the door.

"I'll see myself out. I don't need you fucking goons to walk me out like I'm a child." And with that, he leaves.

"Follow him, please. Make sure he doesn't cause any trouble on his way out." I sigh.

Tapping my fingers on my desk, I watch as everyone leaves my office. Alone with my thoughts, my head goes to Jane and my future.

Do I really want to keep dealing with this shit? Is buying him out the best option? Should I just rethink my company as a whole?

Fuck.

A gentle knock at the door followed by Sydney's head poking in pushes my thoughts to the side.

"Hey, you okay?" she asks. I may give her impossible tasks to complete on a daily basis, but she really is a great assistant.

"Yes. No. I don't know, you know how he is. I just think I've hit my breaking point with him."

She walks in and sits in the chair my father just vacated.

"Have you thought about buying him out?"

"It's been on my mind for the last few months, it just feels like a fight I'm not ready to engage in right now."

"I'll look into it." She nods, determined. "Have you looked at the listings I sent over earlier?"

"I was looking before he came in here. There are a couple with potential. I want to take out all of the ones that aren't within twenty miles of Austin, and hopefully narrow down our options to two or three and choose from there. Do you have a favorite?" I ask. She has wonderful taste in properties, and if I'm undecided I like to get her opinion on things.

"I'm preferential to the property on the north side. It's away from the hustle of downtown and other major companies, but you'll have room for growth."

"And what if I want to downsize?" I ask. The idea popped into my head as my father was berating me.

Do I really need to keep growing my company? I've got more money than I could spend in ten lifetimes and I'm not getting any younger. And if things with Jane work out the way I want them to, I don't want to prioritize my work over her. I want to prioritize our life together.

"You want to downsize?" She sounds shocked, and I can understand why. I've never, in the twenty plus years I've grown this company, wanted to scale down anything. I've always wanted bigger and better.

"I'm thinking about it. I mean, really, what else is there to do? Buy more properties? Build more resorts? It's the same shit I've been doing for two decades. What else do I have to show for my life?"

"Is this about Jane Hatley?" she asks tentatively. We don't get personal with each other. If we talk, it's always been about work, but right this second, I think I could use a friend.

"If I want to create a life for us so we can really be together, I can't travel fifty weeks out of the year. I can't keep up with schedule I've set for myself, and I don't think I even want to. Am I crazy for even thinking about downsizing?"

"I don't think it's crazy, I just think the logistics need to be figured out to see if it's even manageable. What does a downsize look like to you?"

I look out the window contemplating. "No more buying properties. Possible selling some off. Keeping the ones that are special to me and possibly creating a more exclusive brand with limited number of hotels and resorts." I muse out loud.

Her chuckle reaches my ears and I turn my gaze from the window to her. I raise my eyebrow in question.

"I don't know how you could get much more exclusive, but I understand your meaning. I think it's doable, but it'll be a process to accomplish."

We both sit silently, thinking about the logistics behind such a big project. But my gut reaction is downsizing feels right. If I truly want to be the man suitable for Jane, I need to change my lifestyle. She deserves that much. And besides, I doubt I could go longer than a weekend without her if we're together. These past couple of days have been hard enough.

We're four thousand nine hundred and twelve miles apart and I know I won't be able to stand the distance for much longer. I know that much at least.

"Okay, let's make a tentative plan to downsize. Can you get me a general plan in the next couple days and then hopefully we can start implementing in the next week or so."

"What are you going to do about your father?" she asks.

"Talk to our lawyers about forcefully buying him out. It's past time to be rid of him."

She gets a small smirk on her face and nods.

"I'll get started on it now, sir." Getting up. She leaves me to think about the massive amount of change I've decided in the last twenty minutes.

The main thing on my mind now that I've made the decision to buy out my father is Jane. I texted her when her plane landed to make sure she got there okay, and I got clipped response in return.

I wanted to give her a day or two to settle back into her normal routine before attempting to start up conversation again. Or maybe my heart was a little too fragile to get rejected and waiting a couple days meant putting off the inevitable.

No, I know she feels the same way I do. I just need her to see I'm not giving up so easily.

I pull out my phone and pull up our text thread, debating on what words would make her see I'm serious about keeping in touch.

Me: How's life in Austin?

Fuck. I sound fucking stupid. Erasing it, I try a different direction.

Me: I've been missing you. Life isn't the same without our beach trips and cooking escapades.

There, straight to the point. No pussy footing around. And as much as I miss the sex, I know if I say anything about it right now, she'll think that's all I'm missing.

The ellipsis pops up on my screen.

Jane: I miss it, too ...

My heart clenches painfully in my chest. I need to figure out a way to buy out my father and move my entire operations to Austin like yesterday. The less time it takes, the sooner I can be with my woman. And I fucking need to be with her.

I just need to make sure my life is where it needs to be before I tell her all of this and fully commit to a relationship with her. That is, if she even wants one.

No, she'll want one. I'll just have to make sure she doesn't forget about me and knows she's constantly on my mind.

Me: What interesting things are there to do in Austin?

Jane: I'd have to ask Bea, she's the one who gets out all the time. I'm more of a homebody.

Me: Works for me. Would you rather watch a movie or read?

Jane: Today? I'd rather mindlessly watch a movie, I think.

I swear I can hear the melancholy through her words and I need to find a way, even from almost five thousand miles away to cheer her up.

Me: Maybe when I get home tonight we could watch a movie together.

Jane: Considering it would be one in the afternoon here, I'll be teaching at Phoenix House.

Fucking time difference. I may not be able to make it happen today, but I'll adjust my whole fucking schedule to be able to watch movies together.

Me: I forgot about the time difference. Maybe later this week, I can make it happen. Would that be okay with you?

The uncertainty in my words makes me cringe. I've never been this hesitant in my life, let alone with a woman. But Jane is different. Everything about her makes me want to be a better person and show her I'm worth the time and effort.

Jane: I think I'd like that.

Fuck yes! Long distance date night, here we come.

Chapter 24
Jane

Returning from my extended vacation has been … difficult. It's been a week, and I'm still feeling off. I'm not quite sure of anything in my life right now, and I don't really know how to cope with it. I've been holed up in my apartment, avoiding all my usual responsibilities because I just don't know how to deal with it all. Hell, I don't think I want to deal with it all. I left the island with all this confidence, and somehow it's all just disappeared.

The one constant is Pierce. We've texted a little bit and tonight is supposed to be our "date night."

And all I want to do is cancel.

As much as I want to say screw it and go along with whatever is happening with Pierce, I just don't think my heart can take it. I know, especially with the distance between us, nothing will happen with us in the long run, so why get my hopes up? Why act like a real relationship can bloom over the phone?

My phone pings on the coffee table, and my anxiety kicks up thinking it's Pierce again.

Bea: Hey! Are you still good to come in and teach the job readiness class at Phoenix House tonight?

I instantly feel like crap because she should never doubt my willingness to come and teach at the center. But I've been distance myself from our group so what exactly did I expect? And it's not like I'm actually taking care of myself so it's a very valid question even if she doesn't know how bad it is.

Plopping down on the couch, I rest my head against the back of it. My head is a jumbles mess of too many thoughts, and my brain won't slow down enough to really think about what I want in my life. It's been this way all week and I can't break the cycle.

Picking my phone back up, I reply to Bea.

Me: Of course! I'll be there. Let me know if you want to add any other classes this summer. I'd love to maybe add a class or two for when they actually get the jobs ... like how to handle the stress of it while also being productive.

Bea: I love it! Let me talk to Pen and Riggs about the schedule and we'll set it up.

Me: Perfect. See you tonight.

An impulsive decision starts forming in my head. I genuinely have no idea what the right move it here, but I think I just need to step back from it all. I need to step back because I have no idea how to make it all work right now, and I don't need the added complication of Pierce in the mix. All that does is cloud my head with hopes that are logically impossible. I need to focus on my actual future right now.

Me: I'm going to have to cancel our movie date tonight. I'm sorry.

I think on it and decide to at least give him the curtesy of being honest.

Me: I don't think it's a good idea for me to get so attached to you with this much distance in play. I'm sorry, Pierce.

Sighing, I toss my phone on the table and close my eyes. I hope I'm making the right decision. I may help out at the Phoenix House on a regular basis, but damn if I'm unable to use the tools I preach in class in my own life right now.

I'm thirty years old. I should have everything figured out right now, and I just feel ... like a child again. Back in school where I'm two years younger than everyone and just trying to fit in. I'm not happy. I don't have the life I thought I would by this age. I sure as heck don't have a man.

You could have one, but you just pushed him away like you have everyone else.

And dang it if my inner voice isn't spot on.

My phone rings this time, and I hesitantly pick it up.

"Hello."

"What did I do? What *can* I do?" Pierce's voice is on the edge of frantic and determined at the same time.

"You didn't do anything. This is all me. You are the perfect man in the wrong place and the wrong time," I whisper.

I wasn't prepared to bare my soul right this second, but I know the kind of man Pierce is, and I know being honest with him is the only way he forgets about all of his attempts to stay in touch, date, whatever it is he wants.

He's silent for a long time before I hear his intake of breath.

"And there's nothing I can do to change your mind?" He sounds ... controlled, and my heart flutters in my chest at the thought of him not giving up easily.

No heart, no fluttering. We're trying to disconnect from him not fall harder.

"I don't think so. I'm a mess right now, and I'm not sure I can really be what you want at the moment. I need to figure out things in my life, like if I want to continue teaching, and where I go from there if I quit, before I commit to anything more." I definitely skirt around the fact I'm already extremely attached to this man, but it doesn't change the fact a long-distance relationship would be absolute torture for me right now.

"I'll admit, I'm not one to back down from a challenge. But I respect you and how you're feeling. But Jane?"

"Yeah?" I whisper, scared of what he's about to say.

"This isn't over. I can't just let you go, Jane. I'll respect the fact you don't want to be anything more than friends, right this minute. But I'm not giving up. I'll do whatever it takes to prove to you I'm in this for the long haul."

My heart stutters in my chest.

Isn't this what every girl dreams of? Isn't this exactly why I read so many romance novels?

So why do I feel both excitement and dread at the thought of this man who's incredibly out of my league making an effort for me? It feels too good to be true, and that's exactly why I can't get my hopes up no matter what he tells me.

"Jane?" His question makes me realize I've been stuck in my head for too long.

"I ... I don't know Pierce." It's all I can say. Because I genuinely have no idea what a man of his means could make happen if he really is serious. I also can't think about the alternative which results in a broken heart for me.

"That's okay, I know enough for the both of us right now. Just ... Don't completely shut me out, okay? I promise to respect your space."

A laugh bursts out of me. "We have nothing but space between us and that's the problem."

"You know what I mean," he says, not letting me lighten up the mood.

I don't respond because I have no idea what to say. I'm so torn and confused, I'm not even sure which was is up anymore.

What I do know is I need to focus on my career and what I want from it first and foremost. Then I can worry about everything else. If I don't know what direction my career is going, how am I supposed to deal with anything else?

Focusing on multiple things right now seems like too much for me to handle.

"I have to go get ready to teach at Phoenix House. I'm sorry Pierce." Whether I'm apologizing for ending our conversation, or because I know I'm pulling away from everything he's saying, who knows. I just know I need to get off the phone with him sooner rather than later.

"Just remember I'm not giving up, love. I'll talk to you later." He hangs up without another word, leaving me more confused than before our phone call.

I don't have time to analyze it though, because I do have to start getting ready to go to Phoenix House. I don't have everything set up like I usually do since I've been neglecting my life this week. Heck, I haven't even fully unpacked yet.

Yeah, probably a sign you need to focus and figure things out.

Loading up my bag with all my paperwork, making sure to grab my computer too, in case I need it, I decide to head over to Phoenix House early. I don't want to think about my conversation with Pierce and overanalyze everything more than I already have.

Walking into Phoenix House gives me a sense of normalcy I wasn't expecting. I've been spiraling and just being here is enough to calm me down.

I drop my stuff off in Pen's empty office—she just got back from the honeymoon today—and head to Bea's. The door's shut when I get there, and I knock and wait. We've all learned if the door is shut to not barge in. Her and Riggs are notorious for office shenanigans, and I'd rather not see any of it.

"Come in!" Bea calls from behind the door.

I open the door gingerly and peek around it before committing.

"I'm alone, geez. Honestly, I wish you guys would stop. It was one time and it was Pen who got an eye full. Y'all need to be worried about catching Pen and Andy in a compromising position not Riggs and me." She rolls her eyes.

I laugh at her response because she's not wrong.

"You know it's fun to mess with you. So how have things been here?" I ask.

"Busy, really busy, but good. Riggs and I are already looking at what needs to be done in the next few months before I need to go on maternity leave."

My heart gives a little clench. I'm so dang happy for her, but dang it makes me feel like I'm behind the curve yet again.

"Good, so you aren't rushing when it gets closer and stressing out more," I muse.

"Exactly. But that's basically it. Tell me how you've been doing." She doesn't outright ask how my week with Pierce was, but I know she's hinting at it.

I let out a sigh. "I've been okay. Just adjusting to real life after vacation," I deflect. It's not a lie, but it's definitely skirting the truth.

"And was the extended vacation everything you hoped for?"

A sly smile takes over my face. Remembering my goals when I first got to the island, I can't help but feel proud that I accomplished them tenfold. I just didn't expect to fall for the hook up.

"It was very enjoyable." I smirk.

Bea laughs. "Good for you! You've certainly earned it."

"So anyways," I pivot. "How are you feeling? Morning sickness?"

"Ugh, yes. I think I'm finally out of the woods but holy shit it was rough for a few weeks. I was literally locking myself in here and throwing up in my trash can half the day." She gives an exaggerated shiver and I have to laugh.

"Sounds rough, I'm sorry. It's funny that every woman talks about how amazing being pregnant is and how it's the best thing ever. You don't really hear the negatives."

"Fucking facts. I swear, it's so miserable. I mean, I'm glad we're having a baby but this is already not a good time." She laughs. "I think they lie so that you'll join the kid club otherwise no one would willingly go through this shit." We both burst out laughing.

"You're really selling it to me."

"I think of it as adequately preparing you." She gives me a look.

"Yeah, I don't think that's in my cards anytime soon." I brush it off with a laugh. The girls know I've always wanted to be a mother. I may not be super close to my parents or have a functional relationship with my mom, but it's the one thing I've aspired to be better at. My relationship with my mom has never been strong, and I've always wanted to change that. But talking to her about this is an entirely different story. She's not very receptive to hearing about how I feel so I made a promise to myself a long time ago that things would be different when I had kids.

"You never know."

"Well, I'm going to go get my room ready, if you need anything I'll be in there." I ignore her comment.

She stares at me, a knowing look on her face. She knows exactly what I'm doing, but I don't think she'll call me on it.

I head back to the front desk and look at the schedule to double check what room I'm on today when the bell on the door chimes.

"Welcome to Phoenix House, how can I help you?" I ask without looking up yet.

"Hi, I have a delivery for Jane Hatley," a male voice says.

My head jolts up and I find myself staring at the most beautiful bouquet of all white magnolias and calla lilies.

Pierce.

"That's me," I tell him robotically. My head and heart are having a hard time catching up. I fully believed Pierce when he said he wasn't giving up, but dang the man moves fast. Too fast for my fragile little heart.

The delivery man drops off the flowers on the desk and throws up a wave as he leaves. I'm still standing there in shock.

It's just flowers, but it feels like so much more than flowers. And they are freaking beautiful. I've never seen such a gorgeous bouquet in my life. It's not ostentatious, it's just utterly classic, exactly like Pierce.

"Boyfriend or stalker? Or maybe a certain someone who owns a few resorts?" Riggs's voice startles me.

"Umm, Pierce. They're from Pierce."

"Interesting. Well, he could turn into a stalker but in a good way, you know? Like in those romance books where the guys are so obsessed with the woman he has to keep eyes on her every minute of the day," he muses.

I whip around. "Andy got to you too? Dang he's just converting everyone around here. I've read these dang books for years and no one wanted to read one. Andy steps into the picture and suddenly smut is all the rage." I roll my eyes.

"He's persuasive." He shrugs.

I laugh. "That he is. He got Pen after all."

"So, what are you going to do about your man?"

"He's not my man. And I'll thank him for the gorgeous flowers and move on." Even I don't believe it, but I'm not discussing this with Riggs if I can't even talk to my best friends about it.

He watches me for a moment.

"Let me know how that goes." He winks and leaves me to stare at the flowers from Pierce.

When he said he wasn't giving up, I believed him, but I didn't consider what it exactly looked like.

If these flowers are anything to go by, I might be hard-pressed to resist him no matter the distance and reluctance on my part. I thought coming here would help clear my thoughts up, instead, I'm more conflicted than ever.

Chapter 25
Jane

A week later, the first letter comes.

Jane-

I had a crazy idea. You told me you were the romantic of the group, so I thought what better way to work through the distance we find ourselves with than a letter.

My thought is to use this as a get to know you, well for you to get to know me, I guess.

Forgive my rambling, I honestly couldn't tell you the last time I've written a letter, so bear with me as I fumble through this.

I laugh at his honesty, and it makes me miss him so damn much.

Growing up, I never realized how much living in two very different households would shape me. I didn't have many friends because everyone hung out during the summer, and I was always shipped off to my father's. His house was more rigid than my mother's so playing with friends was a foreign concept there.

It wasn't until I spent time with you, specifically at Penelope's wedding, that I realized how disconnected I am from real connection. Friendship was never a priority to me, and I envy the people you've surrounded yourself with.

My heart clenches painfully in my chest as I read his words. For the little boy who struggled to make friends, to the fact that he's right about my friend group. I've felt a little more centered over this last week but I still haven't let the girls in on any of what I'm struggling with.

You've made me rethink a lot of things recently. Never doubt how much of an impact you have on people, even if it's not how you expected to be doing it.

Until next time,

Pierce

I sit on my couch and reread it five times. I'm still so unsure about all of this, about attempting to make things work with this man, but he just made a very compelling case. Who even writes letters anymore? He's right, the romantic in me in swooning like hell right now, but I still want to be cautious.

It's been two weeks since the first letter, and he's stuck to a pattern of one letter a week. This week's letter just arrived so I make myself comfortable in bed and gingerly open the envelope before pulling out the letter inside.

Jane-

I had plans to tell you all about my job and how it's come to be, but my thoughts brought me to my mother.

I told you a little about her and her death and how I've modeled my foundation after what she wanted, but I find myself stuck a little in my grief instead.

Grief is a strange thing. The initial punch I felt when learning of her death was so strong it felt like I wouldn't survive it. You hear a lot of apologies, and it just feels so empty. That makes me sounds like a dickhead, but the words are just something for people to say when they don't know how to comfort you. And let me tell you, no one knew how to comfort me because I wasn't close to anyone.

I felt numb planning everything but luckily my mother had everything planned out already because she knew her time was being cut short. It helped me not to have to think about what was really going on. I still don't remember a lot of her memorial service; I think it's just a black spot in my memory at this point.

And the old adage that time heals all wounds is true to an extent. The grief becomes less debilitating, but it never goes away. Take this letter for example. The wave of sadness I felt when thinking about my mother was so strong that I felt like writing down all my feelings might actually help me. And let you see a little more of me I suppose as well.

All this to say, life is short, and I don't want to waste time. I'm not letting you go, Jane. I hope you see that now. You've made me take a really hard look at my life, and I'm determined to figure out how to make all of this work. It might not be tomorrow, it might not be in the next month, but it's going to happen.

Yours,

Pierce

I wipe the tears trailing down my cheeks and stare at the flowers he sent me this week. This man is nothing like I expected when I met him on the island. He's so thoughtful. He's still sending me things even though I haven't been very receptive to it all. I've done nothing to show him we're on the same page.

Yet he's stuck around like glue, and if I can get my head and my heart on the same page for once, maybe, just maybe, we can make this work.

Chapter 26

Pierce

*T*hree months later

It's finally happening. I'm officially moving to Austin today, and it's taken way too fucking long to get to this point.

Three months and a week too long if you ask me, but everything that could go wrong with this move has. And I've been a less than patient man because of it.

Throughout it all, I've stayed in contact with Jane, sending her gifts periodically and writing her letters talking about how I grew up. I've been doing it all without knowing how she feels about them. She's been keeping things close to the chest, and I understand why, I just wish she'd have a little more faith in me.

But she doesn't really know your intentions because you've kept this damn move to yourself instead of letting her in on the process.

I rest my head back against the seat in my private jet, reflecting on why I didn't tell her. It probably would have made things easier for me. Hell, I might have even gotten to know what was in her head when I sent her the amethyst necklace, or the letters giving her an insight into my past but not my future. Instead, I took a coward's route, thinking everything would come together perfectly if I just showed up one day.

Yes, taking an extra month to find a building and yet another to find me a place to live really fucked up my plans.

Now, I can only hope it isn't too late.

After she cancelled our movie date, I let her pull back. Resorting mostly to texting so she would feel like it was less of a commitment, but I did continue my weekly letters. I'm not sure if she read them because she didn't respond to them specifically, but it was almost therapeutic to let it all out.

The last time I was able to physically talk to her was about two weeks ago and she sounded fucking miserable. She said she still didn't have a clear direction of what she wanted to do about teaching.

And all I wanted to do was tell her not to worry. She could do absolutely anything her heart desires because I would be there to support her and cheer her on. But I couldn't because I thought it would be a fan-fucking-tastic idea to not tell her about the drastic moves within my own company.

Regret weighs heavy on my chest, but I can't change the path I chose. I can only show up and then keep showing up until she sees I'm in the for the long haul.

The flight attendant stops next to me. "Another gin and tonic, Sir?"

"Yes please. Thank you, Adam." I hand him my empty glass and return to my tumultuous thoughts.

Sydney told me time and time again that keeping this all a secret from her would have the opposite effect I was going for, but I stood by it because I couldn't imagine it taking this fucking long.

And yet, here we are.

It feels like I've moved farther away from her instead of closer. At least emotionally.

My phone buzzes on the table on front of me and I see Sydney's name.

"Yes," I clip out. Although we've gotten more friendly over the past months, I'm not in the mood to talk to anyone right now.

"Hope your flight is going well. I just received a phone call from an irate Mr. Bronstein." She pauses.

"I'm sure you did. I had the lawyers send over the buyout contract this morning."

"He definitely isn't going to play ball and when I told him you were unavailable, he made some ... interesting threats."

"Threats against you?"

"Among other things like the company and yourself."

"What exactly did he say to threaten you?" I don't give a shit if he threatens me or my company but I'll be damned if he decides to take it out on my hard working assistant.

"Umm, he said he was going to come down to the office and show me what a real boss does." Her voice is a little shaky.

"Are you currently at the office?" I ask, getting angrier and angrier the more I hear. How dare he threaten anyone, let alone someone who has no say in what's happening. If he needs to threaten anybody it needs to be me.

"I'm at the office wrapping up the last little bit we had to close the office completely."

"And when are you flying out?" I could have had her come with me, but she insisted she wanted to handle the last few things to close the London chapter of my company completely then she would fly out to Austin after. Everyone else who is transferring is already in Austin helping set things up.

"I should actually be heading to the airport in less than an hour."

"Lock the doors and I'll send some security your way to stay while you finish up and to escort you to the airport. I apologize for the vile threats to you. It shouldn't have happened."

"Pierce, it's really not that serious. I'll be fine."

It wasn't fine and I absolutely didn't trust the man I barely called my father.

"It's happening. Call me when you're on the plane." I hang up without further conversation and dial a security company I have on retainer.

After getting them set up and confirming someone is with Sydney, I turn my thoughts to my father.

I certainly didn't expect him to lie down quietly, but threatening an innocent woman is beyond the pale. His drastic actions mean he's relying on the shares of my company to support his income. Oh, how the mighty have fallen. A measly ten percent in my company is the only thing holding him afloat. I wonder what he's gotten into. Gambling? Whores! The list could be endless. I honestly don't care, but if I figure it out, I can use it as leverage to make him take the buyout without all of this drama.

I pick up my phone as Adam delivers my drink and send an email to a PI I've used before, asking him to dig until he finds what I need.

What a cluster fuck. All I wanted to do was downsize and move to be with Jane. It wasn't supposed to be this complicated. Leave it to my father to be an epic asshole.

I take a deep breath and think about Jane again. If my father is pulling this shit with Sydney, I can only imagine the lengths he would go to if he knew about Jane.

No, I won't let that happen. I need to finalize his buyout and make sure he is taken care of before I bring Jane into this mess. I won't risk her safety even if it is a long shot.

Fuck, what a disaster.

My phone pings with a return email from my PI telling me he'll have the information to me as soon as he finds something and I breathe a sigh of relief.

At least this won't drag on. It pays to have endless amounts of money to throw at people to get shit done.

Lifting my fresh drink to my lips, I take a sip and start to plan.

When my PI gets back to me, I'll send dear ol' dad a nice message telling him to stand down or I'll blast what I found to the media. He can't stand the hit to his image so this should work.

Less than an hour later I receive a call from Sydney.

"The London office is officially shut down," she says with a lightness in her voice.

"Wonderful. There was no trouble?" Security didn't say anything, but I want to double check anyways.

"No trouble. Pierce, I wanted to tell you what he said about you."

"Sydney, it's fine. Things will be taken care of shortly, and he'll be long forgotten." I brush her off.

"He said he would send a blast to the media about how you lure guests at your resorts to your place and get them to have sex with you by any means."

"Let him. He doesn't have proof because I've never done such a thing."

"He sent pictures to my email. Of you and Jane," she whispers.

"And you're just now telling me this? What the fuck, Sydney?"

"You hung up on me before I could relay it," she reminds me. Fuck, sometimes I'm an asshole.

"Forward me everything. Please," I add, trying not to take my anger out on her. She's an innocent party in this.

"Done. I'm sorry, Pierce."

"Don't apologize for his vile actions. He threatened you and when that didn't work, he took things to the next level. How did he even get those pictures?" I switch my phone to speaker and pull up the email Sydney forwarded me.

There in perfect clarity is Jane and I on the beach. Right before I took her back to the cabana and had my wicked way with her.

Seeing this somehow taints our experience, making me angrier by the minute.

The next set of pictures are little unclear, but you can tell they were taken from outside of my villa. Catching us both in very compromising positions. My blood boils.

How dare he use such a special time in my life for his own fucked up gain. How desperate must he be to stoop to this level. I scroll through all the pictures, the memories now clouded by the fact they weren't private and are now being used to blackmail me.

"Pierce?" Sydney's voice sounds from the speaker.

"Sorry, what was that?" I was so angry I missed what she said.

"I said we'll figure this out. I can call the lawyers and have them send—"

"This is my battle. Thank you for immediately jumping into *fixing* mode, but your job now is to get Austin up and running. I'll handle my father like I should have done years ago." I hang up on her again, realizing I never say goodbye to her. I'll change it in the future.

Next, I call the lawyers and explain the situation. They advise doing nothing because it's most likely a bluff, but I tell them point blank that's not going to happen. Not with Jane in the crosshairs. I will not take the risk.

I hang up on them too, not liking what they're telling me.

All I can do now is wait for the PI to get back to me and hope it's enough to fight fire with fire.

I also need to go to Jane. I can't wait until this all blows over. Making sure she's safe and unaffected from my father's bullshit is paramount and the only way I accomplish it is by being close to her.

Downing the rest of my drink, I feel jittery and unsettled. Everything is out of my hands at the moment and I fucking hate it. I need the control. I need to know Jane is safe and won't be pulled into the harsh and unforgiving world my father wants to drag her into.

Do I tell her about the pictures? Would it make things better or worse? For once in my life, I don't know the correct answer. I don't know if telling her makes her push me away. All I know is I physically can't have her push me away any more than she already is. I need to get closer to her. I need her to see we're it. We are meant to be together, and I'm willing to walk through fire to protect her and prove to her I am worthy.

I land in two hours. So, I have two hours to plan, two hours to hope my PI gets back to me, and two hours to figure out what I'm going to say when I knock on Jane's door this afternoon.

Chapter 27

Jane

I t feels weird to not be getting ready for the first day of school, but it also feels right.

I took a long time to come to the decision not to go back to teaching. But after many tears and a lot of soul searching, it felt like it was time to let it go.

Teaching will always have a part of my heart, but it's time to do something for me. Something that makes me completely happy and fulfilled.

I haven't told the girls yet, but we're doing our usually brunch today so I guess now's as good a time as any.

I walk into Scrambled, a brunch place on our normal rotation, and head to the corner table they usually put us in.

I instantly feel the anxiety welling up inside of me. My palms are sweaty, my heart rate is up, and all I can think about is every possible scenario where things could go wrong. They could hate me after I've majorly pushed them away. They could say quitting my teaching job is stupid. God, there are so many options. I've been ducking out of brunch almost every week lately because I just needed to figure things out and now I hope they'll forgive my distance.

Instead, the girls cheer when they see me and jump up for hugs as relief hits me square in the chest.

I missed this.

The time for reflection was good, but I missed getting all the updates. Heck, Bea's like five months pregnant, and I've barely talked to her about it. I can feel her little baby bump as she pulls me in for a hug.

I'm the worst friend.

I can feel my face getting red from trying to hold in the tears, but I won't let them fall. It's not the time to have a breakdown. I can do that at home later, not in front of the entire restaurant.

Bea pulls back and looks me up and down before narrowing her gaze in on my face. I know she can tell I'm getting emotional.

"Okay, sit. We've ordered you a mimosa, and I'm going to need you to start talking." Bea points to the empty chair.

"I'm not going back to teaching." Ripping off the band aid feels scary, and I clench my eyes closed to avoid their judgement.

"About damn time," Pen mutters.

My eyes pop open as I stare at her incredulously.

"What?" I ask in disbelief.

"You're a fucking great teacher, don't get me wrong, but your passion lies elsewhere. You've always wanted to do bigger and better things. I never understood why you went the teaching route," Pen explains.

I look around to see Larkin and Bea nodding.

"How in the world would you know that? I don't even know it! It took me all dang summer to decide to not go back, and I still feel like it might be a mistake." I'm flabbergasted. They so easily saw I wasn't really happy, but they never pushed me to do anything. I doubt I would have listened, and they probably know it too.

"When we all met in college and started getting closer, do you remember what you were majoring in?" Larkin asks.

"Sustainability, emphasizing on food sustainability," I say robotically.

"And then you ended up adding teaching as your double major," she continues.

I nod, unsure where she's going.

"When you made the switch, you could just see it didn't excite you the way food sustainability did, even though you still managed to get an extra degree out of it. It wasn't our place to say anything, and you were dead set on teaching because your mom wanted you to teach."

I sit back stunned.

"You are a damn good teacher," Pen says. "Don't doubt that. Any kid that had you as a teacher is damn lucky because you put your whole heart into it, and they could only benefit from that. But putting your heart into something and being truly happy in your career aren't one in the same."

"Well, I feel stupid," I murmur.

I've been battling this internally for almost a year and here my best friends just explained it all perfectly in ten minutes.

"You aren't stupid. It's easier to see things objectively when it's not happening to you," Bea chastises.

I sit back and down my mimosa in one go. I've been pushing them away since we got back from the island when I could have just talked to them and figured things out so much faster. *No, you needed to figure this out for yourself. They're right, sometimes it takes you figuring it out to really make the change.*

"I know that look. No, talking to us earlier wouldn't have solved anything for you. This is one of those things you need to figure out all on your own otherwise you'll never know if you made the choice, or you just took some advice from your friends and ran with it," Larkin says and I smile at how well we know each other.

"I still have no idea where to go from here," I say knowing only one of my many issues is solved.

Pen shrugs. "That's okay. You've got time. If you need help you know we've got your back. Hell, Bea's place is huge if you need a place to stay."

"True, although in like four months you'll be sharing the house with a screaming infant," Bea adds.

I smile brightly over at her, suddenly so emotional. "I'm so fucking happy for you, you have no idea," I whisper.

Three sets of eyes widen in shock.

"Who is this Jane, and what did you do with the old one?" Larkin asks.

I sigh. I might as well dive into the whole situation with Pierce. I've been keeping too much to myself it seems. Pushing my best friends away hasn't done me any favors even if it felt like what I needed to do at the time. And the pressure of keeping it all in is finally boiling over.

"So, you know I met Pierce at Pen's wedding..." They all nod. "And then I stayed an extra week."

"Did he set Andy and I up on that insane honeymoon just so he could keep you on the island for an extra week?" Pen asks, finally putting things together.

My cheeks heat with embarrassment.

"He sure did. We got into quite the argument from that too." I also think about what happened after the argument and I beg the horniness I'm feeling to chill out.

"Continue," Bea says giving Pen a look that says not to interrupt.

"We've kind of been staying in touch since then."

Silence greets me and I wait them out. I know they'll have a lot to say.

"What does *kind of* mean?" Larkin asks.

"Well, much like I distanced myself from you guys, over the past few months"—I give them an apologetic look which Bea waves away immediately—"I did the same to him. Except he kept pushing to stay in touch. He regularly texts me, and when I'm feeling weak, we talk on the phone ... and he's been sending me things."

"Things. What things?" Pen asks.

This is where I need to decide how much to let them in. For the most part, the gifts aren't out of the norm, at least I assume they aren't for a billionaire, but the letters he sent are something else entirely.

"Flowers, food, little things here and there," I deflect. Although I'm not sure why. It feels amazing to finally talk about Pierce.

"And that?" Pen's eyes zero in on the necklace I'm wearing.

"And this," I concede.

"Damn," Larkin whispers.

"It's entirely too much, but dang it if this isn't the prettiest necklace I've ever seen. It would be a shame not to wear it, right?" I ask.

"Oh, totally."

"Absolutely."

"It's gorgeous."

They all talk over each other.

"But he lives in London, and I live here." I deflate.

"Is the distance the only obstacle?" Bea asks.

"It's probably the biggest one. He's also way older than me, and you know I've always wanted the nuclear family. I can't imagine him wanting kids at his age."

"Did you ask him if he wanted kids?" Larkin asks.

"No. We weren't really focused on the future when we were together."

"And how about since then? He's obviously putting in quite the effort," Larkin says pointedly.

"He is, but you guys, he's a freaking billionaire. We don't even live in the same world." I throw my hands up, exasperated.

"Money doesn't mean shit, you should know that since you're friends with us," Pen says pointing to her and Bea.

"Millions is a lot different from billions," I counter. "And you guys threw that into the foundation and Phoenix House. He's still jet setting and growing his empire."

Pen rolls her eyes.

"How do you know he's jet setting and working a lot?" Larkin asks, genuinely curious.

"Ugh, I hate it when you guys are logical! I don't know technically. I just assume because it's been three months and sending things is one thing, but making an effort to actually see each other is another. I've been on summer break, he knows this. I could have flown out to meet him somewhere." Even as I say it, I know I've been sending him the wrong message if I actually wanted that to happen.

"And I'm a jerk for wanting that when I've been pushing him away," I muse out loud.

I flag down the waiter for another mimosa and I drop my head to the table.

"Many a brunch have been the time for realizations. You aren't alone." Bea rubs her hand on my back as I laugh at her statement.

I lift my head up as the girls join my laughter.

"Brunch solves the world's problems." Pen holds up her glass just as my new drink gets delivered.

We cheers to the power of the almighty brunch and dissolve in a fit of laughter.

Once we've settled down and had our food delivered, I think about everything I've learned today.

"So, do you think I should throw caution to the wind and go for it with Pierce?" I ask. They know I have terrible taste in men, and they are honest to a fault if they dislike the man in my life.

"I think this is something you need to do some soul searching about. The money concern is ridiculous, and you know it. You're just using it as an excuse," Pen says. "But the age difference has the potential to hinder your overall life goals. But it's something you need to talk to him about, not guess at how he feels about the subject," she says pointedly.

I sigh. "I know, you're right. I just feel like I'm more vulnerable with him than I ever have been with a man. I don't want to put myself out there just to be crushed when he thinks I'm some silly little girl for wanting this dream life."

"I just want you to think back to the brunches we had after we all met our men," Bea says. "You happened to give a lot of great advice during those times, do you remember?" I nod. "Every single one of us took a scary as hell leap of faith, but it led us to our happily ever after's. And you helped us get there. I don't want to push you one way or another if truly feel like he isn't the guy for you. But if you feel like he is, Jane you've got to take the leap. We'll be here for whatever happens. But you'll never know unless you try."

I *know* she's right, but it's so hard to put yourself out there. I've dated a ton in the past, sure, but I've never had this bone deep need to see where it goes. This feeling it could really be something magical.

And it is absolutely fucking scary. Quitting my job feels like child's play compared to this, and that took me almost three months to commit to.

"Don't make an impulsive decision now," Larkin adds. I'm sure she's seeing the panic on my face. "Think about it, call us whenever you need to and eventually the answer will come to you."

Nodding, I shove some of my eggs benedict in my mouth to avoid having to talk about this more.

"So, how's baby?" Larkin asks Bea.

"So good! We saw them wiggling all over the place during the last ultrasound so that was fun. It put a real image to the feeling of them rotating and kicking me all night long, so that's super weird." She laughs.

"You aren't finding out the gender?" I ask, feeling left out of my friend group for not knowing the answer. But it's by my own doing.

"Team green all the way. We won't know until I push this thing out of me." She smiles.

"Sounds like an alien movie if I'm honest." Pen laughs. "And this is why I'll stick to being the cool aunt."

"No lie." Bea chuckles.

The rest of brunch is spent talking about babies, and all the other things I missed out on while I isolated myself from my best friends.

They weren't wrong, I needed to figure things out on my own, but it doesn't necessarily mean I need to completely isolate myself from them if I feel like this again.

I get a rideshare back to my apartment, lost in my head about how to approach things with Pierce.

The girls were right, I'm assuming a lot in order to protect myself. But how will I ever get the life I've always wanted if I don't at least ask Pierce how he feels about things?

Finally, home, I plop down onto my couch.

This has been the longest summer ever, and I still have a ton to figure out, but at least I have a little more clarity now. Things are starting to feel right, and it makes the weight on my shoulders lift a little.

A knock at my door annoys me. I swear, if it's one of the girls, they're getting yelled at. They have a dang key and we literally just left each other.

It sounds again and I peel myself off the couch. "I'm coming, geez!" I yell.

I make my way to my front door and open it without thinking to look. What greets me surprises the ever-loving shit out of me.

"Pierce?" I'm confused and shocked and my gut reaction is to slam the door in his face. Throwing caution to the wind? Yes, that's the plan. But I've only just decided this. I'm not freaking prepared. The impulse to avoid an interaction that I'm not mentally prepared for is so strong. So that's exactly what I do.

Chapter 28

Pierce

Well getting a door slammed in my face certainly wasn't the reaction I was hoping for.

"Jane?" I ask tentatively. I'm honestly not sure what to do in this situation.

"What are you doing here?" Her question is muffled by the door.

"I thought surprising you would be good idea. I was clearly wrong, and I apologize for that."

I got off the plane and immediately came here, but I can see maybe I should have thought this through a little more. Given her time to get used to the idea of seeing me in person. But I was so hung up on *needing* to see her. Selfishly, I was only thinking of myself.

I hear her head thump against the door.

"Fine." The door opens suddenly but Jane's smile is all wrong.

She's putting on a face, and I can't stand the fact she feels the need to do so with me.

"What brings you to the great city of Austin?" she asks with a little too much enthusiasm.

"I—" My mouth snaps shut. This isn't how I want to tell her everything. I need her happiness, her bright heart, and she's bleeding the opposite at the moment.

She lets out a sigh and opens the door wider.

"Come in, there's no use in talking in the hallway." The tension in her body is still there, but she slumps a little in defeat.

I fucking hate everything about this, but I also can't say no to more time with her. Getting to see the apartment she calls home is a bonus at this point.

"I apologize for surprising you," I say as I sit down on her sofa. All her furnishing is muted shades of grey. She also doesn't have much in the way of photographs which shocks me. If you would have asked me what the apartment of the woman I met on the island was like I would say it was full of bright colors and pictures of her loved ones. This is the complete opposite.

"It's not your fault. It's just been a weird day, and I wasn't expecting any more excitement." She finds a seat on the chair across from me. If there was a bigger way to send the message that I was unwelcome, I didn't know what it was.

"Care to talk about it?"

She looks at me with an appraising eye. "Not really."

I tip my head to her in concession and wait her out. If she really doesn't want me here, I'll leave and figure out another way to get her to hear me out.

She sinks into the chair more and tips her head back.

"I'm sorry," she whispers. "I wasn't expecting you to just show up here. I'm not ... prepared."

I see my mistake immediately. Sure, we've continued to talk, and I've sent her things I thought she would like and spilled my heart into letters, but it also wasn't an invitation to just show up at her door.

"I understand completely. I apologize for putting you in this position, it wasn't my intention. I'll be in Austin for a little while," I tell her while standing up. "I would love it if we could get together at some point. Let me know time and place and I'll be there."

No need to tell her I've moved here permanently just yet, not with the reception I received today. I can work up to it.

She holds my eye, searching for something, but I'm just hoping she can see how much I genuinely missed her. She must find what she's looking for because she gently nods before standing up.

Guess this is my cue to leave, as much as it physically pains me to do.

She walks me to the door, and I pause before walking through the threshold.

"It was wonderful to see you again, love." I lean down a press a chaste kiss to her cheek before pulling back and walking away. She wraps her arms around my neck before I pull back, and I respond in kind. The feel of her in my arms is a soothing balm.

"It's good to see your too Pierce," she whispers before pulling back. She finally has a real smile on her face, and I'll count that as a win today.

I've got time to get her on the same page. But for now, I'll head to my new place and attempt to get settled in while thinking of ways I can get her to at least talk to me.

My new place is nice. It sits on Lake Travis and is mostly secluded from my neighbors. Sydney showed me a few places, but I felt like this place was more Jane, so I didn't even question it. If, in the future, she wants a different place we'll get one, but for now this works. Now, sitting here on the sprawling deck, I'm wondering if I've done the right thing. Not moving here, I know without a shadow of a doubt moving here was what

I had to do, but not talking to Jane about. Not including her in my plans might have just bit me in the ass.

What a fucking asshole I am. All the time I spent with Jane on the island should have given me a clear sign she likes to be in control and in the know. And from what she's told me, people haven't always believed in her decision-making skills. And I just took the decision right out of her hands.

I'm used to being in charge, being absolutely sure my decisions are the correct ones that will grow my business, my wealth and whatever else I needed in life. And somehow, in a matter of months, Jane's flipped me on my head.

Now I need to figure out a way to give her back control. To let her have options as much as I fucking hate it. I want to be her only option, the one she wants irrevocably.

I take a sip from the glass of whiskey I have sitting on the arm of the chair and watch the carefree people on the lake.

My brain feels like it's underwater. Nothing I come up with is right. I can't just force my way into Jane's life, I need her to come to me. And in order for her to do so, I need to have patience. I'm not a particularly patient man, I'm sure if you ask Sydney she'll tell you I actually have no patience so this will be a learning experience for me. At forty-two fucking years old I'm learning to have patience. What a novelty.

I chuckle to myself thinking about Jane's fictious response. She'd probably tell me the patience would be worth it as she teased the ever-loving shit out of me. Owning my body as much as she owns my heart.

My phone pings next to me, and I'm reluctant to look at it. It's probably Sydney letting me know she made it and is getting settled into her place. Nothing should need my immediate attention at work right now anyway.

The sun setting is making me aware of how different this day ended up. My phone pings again, interrupting my self-loathing thoughts and spiking my irritation.

I'm no closer to figuring out a solution and the last thing I want is to deal with a work crisis.

Pinking up my phone, I prepare to call Sydney without looking at the texts and dealing with this as fast as I can. But when I see Jane's name on my phone instead, I nearly jump out of the chair almost knocking my whiskey onto the deck before calming my shit down and opening up the messages.

Jane: I'm sorry for how I reacted earlier. I'm not the best with surprises on a good day, and I certainly wasn't expecting you to just show up at my door.

Jane: I think I'd like to see if you, if you're still open to that. I have a pretty wide-open schedule so let me know what works best for you. If you want to that is.

Her hesitation and uncertainty are written in every word, and I don't think, I just type. I never want her to be unsure with me and it honestly makes me a little physically ill she feels this way.

I send her a simple message, just my address and the word *anytime.* I want to leave the ball completely in her court. If she chooses not to come, I'll except that for the time being. But if she comes to me, it's game on.

———◆◆◆———

An hour later, the buzz of my front gates gets my attention. My heart immediately pounds in my chest, and I feel flushed all over. I almost trip over myself to pull up the video at the gate and when I see the most gorgeous face staring back at me, I feel a calm like I've only felt in her presence.

I buzz her in immediately and race to the front door to meet her. I could play this cool, sure, but why hide the fact I'm fucking thrilled she's here, at the house I picked for us to be together in.

Her practical sedan pulls up to the front and she stares out the windshield at me. I give her a smile I hope reassures her and I see her shoulder deflate a little as she takes a deep breath and gets out of the car.

"Some house you've got here. Rental?" She digs.

I can't contain the grin on my face, knowing she wants to know if this is temporary.

"It's mine."

"Oh." She flushes, bobbing her head.

"Would you like to come in, or do you want to stay in my driveway?" I chuckle when she rolls her eyes and slowly makes her way to me.

"How did you even manage to get a house on Lake Travis? I thought it was impossible because no one ever moves from here." I raise my eyebrows at her. "Duh, you're like beyond rich. How could I forget," she mumbles.

"I didn't force anyone out. It was just good timing when this one became available," I say as I lead her through the foyer.

"Well, it is truly beautiful." She stops in front of the floor to ceiling windows in the living area which take up the entire back wall of the house.

"Yes, it is." My eyes stay hooked on her.

I can't believe she's really here. I want to ask her so many questions. I want to say fuck talking and show her how much I physically missed her these last couple months. My head is stuck in a whirlwind of what to do when her voice pulls me from my own indecision.

"Why are you here, Pierce?"

"Would you like to sit outside or inside for this?" I ask, knowing this is going to take some time.

"That sounds ominous, but outside would be lovely." She moves over to the open patio doors on her right.

"Can I get you something to drink?" I ask, attempting to be a good host at the very least.

"A water would be great." Her tone is a little clipped and I know I only have this one chance to lay it all out there. Be honest and upfront and pray it's enough to break through.

I grab two water bottles from the refrigerator and head out to join her on the patio.

We both sit in the silence for a few minutes. I'm trying to get my words right, and I'm sure she's just waiting me out. I do have a lot to explain after all.

"I didn't plan for you," I say quietly. "When I saw you on the island, I had no idea the impact you would have on me. Did I want to sleep with you immediately? Yes, I won't deny that, but somewhere in the first night together everything changed.

"The next week we spent together felt like something I would never have in my life. I've been devoted to my business far longer than anything else in my life, and I was fine with that, until I met you. I manipulated things a little to get you to stay, but I don't apologize for doing it. I would do it again in a heartbeat." I look over at her, but she's staring out into the water, tapping her fingers on the water bottle.

"When you had to leave I felt like my heart was being ripped out of my chest. It still does honestly, even though you're right here. I knew I needed to figure things out on my end before I could be the man you could rely on.

"Traveling as much as I was, wasn't going to work anymore. Adding to my portfolio was only going to hinder my new goal."

"What's your new goal?" Her question barely audible above the sound of the water.

"You," I tell her simply. And it really is this simple. I want her, whatever I have to do to get her I'll make happen. Because I don't know that I want to live this life without her anymore.

"Why me? I mean it's not like I've been open and receptive the last few months. Hell, I've basically ignored you more than I've talked to you. How in the world could you want that?"

"Because I know if you take away the circumstances, and you put us together without the obstacles we've had, we're made for each other."

I let her take in my words. I know they're going to be a lot for her to take in right now, but I know being completely honest is going to be the only way I get to keep her.

"I set this plan into motion our second week on the island. Effective today, my new headquarters are in Austin, and I'm starting the process of downsizing my company." I pull the band aid off, except it sure as hell feels like super glue as I wait for her response.

Her head whips around to meet my stare.

"Are you crazy?"

Chapter 29

Jane

I can hear how shrill my voice is, but I'm so shocked right now I don't really know how to respond.

"Crazy about you." He smirks, and I roll my eyes.

"Yeah, that was bad," he concedes. "I apologize. I don't feel this is crazy at all. I think I found something I want and need more than my company. I've been in this world a long time, and I've never really knew what my purpose is in all of this. I know I'm good at my job, hell I'm the best at my job, but is it really my purpose? And if it is, how fucking sad is that? My purpose is to build fancy ass resorts for rich assholes who treat people like shit on a regular basis?"

He looks over at me impassioned by his words. I see his point, but this is all insane. Who moves across the damn country for someone they spent two weeks with?

You've always wanted your own book worthy romance. Now it's staring you in the face, and you're running scared.

Because this doesn't happen in real life! I internally scream at myself.

"I should have told you my plans from the get-go. I know that now, but I just wanted to make sure everything was perfect before I told you everything. I needed you to see everything I had done."

"Nothing's ever perfect, Pierce," I mummer.

"I know. But you deserve as close to perfect as I can get." Her earnest tone is going to be my undoing.

When I texted him, I didn't expect him to send me an address. I definitely didn't expect him to tell me he had freaking moved here, but it's his bone deep honesty making me feel like this could be real life.

"How have you made all this possible in what, three months?"

His laugh pulls my attention.

"Oh love, I wanted to be here a couple weeks after we left the island, but nothing seemed to be on my side with this transition. There were … multiple issues that arose stopping me from being here sooner."

"Why didn't you just tell me all of this? I would have flown to London to spend some time with you. I've been on break this whole time with nothing but time on my hands." I realize the hurt is bleeding through my voice when he turns to face me completely and grabs both my hands.

"I fucked up, badly. I will spend every single day making it up to you. All I can say is I thought having everything in order was the right way to do this, and instead, it caused us to miss out on months together."

"That's why you sent me all those things?" I wonder out loud.

"Among other reasons."

I raise my eyebrow at him, wordlessly asking for an explanation.

"I sent you the gifts because I couldn't stop thinking about you. And every time I saw something that reminded me of you, I sent it to you." He shrugs. "The letters were…" He sighs. "The letters were my way of showing you who I am—how I came to be Pierce Vanstone. I wanted you to know my past because I see you as my present and future."

Stunned.

I am fucking stunned by this man.

I stop thinking, stop overthinking, stop the second guessing, and just *feel.*

Dropping the water bottle carelessly onto the deck, I stand up and walk to Pierce's chair only a couple steps from mine. He looks up at me with nothing but hope and want in his eyes. Gripping his shoulders, I climb on his lap, straddling his legs. He's gripping the armrests of the chair so hard I can feel the tension rolling off of him.

Wordlessly, I lower down on his lap as I lean in to kiss him. It's all it takes for him to grip my hips and pull me closer to him as he devours my mouth. Our tongue battle for dominance as I rock on his lap, feeling how hard he is.

Moaning into his kiss at how much I've missed this, he pulls back abruptly.

"If you don't want me to debauch your right here on the patio say so now because I'm to the point of no return. We go inside now, or I'm fucking you right here." He breathes into my neck, sending a shiver down my spine.

"Here. I want you right here," I whimper.

He stands up, holding me up by my butt, and walks over to a lounger on the other side of the deck. He lays me down so gently, with so much care; I almost believe he's going be sweet and slow. Until he rips my shirt over my head and has my bra off in less than a second. He does the same to my leggings, leaving me in my silky navy boy shorts.

"I have fucking missed you, love," he whispers reverently. His gaze hitting every single exposed inch of me until I'm squirming on the lounger. Desperate for his touch, for the pleasure only he can give me.

I have no words; I'm just a mewling, whining mess of need, and Pierce must see it because he finally puts me out of my misery.

His fingertips trail a line from my neck to my collar bone, down to circle each nipple before descending down my belly. He pauses, looking up at me with a feral look in his eyes.

"Tell me no one has touched you. Tell me it's been only me since we met."

"Only you," I pant. "I couldn't even get off with a vibrator," I admit.

His eyes darken as he tears my panties off.

"You need an orgasm, you come to me from now on. When I'm not so pent up I'll teach you how to use that vibrator with me." He winks mischievously.

"Shut up and get naked already!" I throw my head back already so worked up it feels like I could come from just one touch.

"God, I fucking love you when you're bossy," he says as he unbuttons his shirt with practiced efficiency. I watch as more of his body comes to light and a thought pops into my head.

"What about you? You haven't been with ... anyone have you?" I ask shakily.

He stops suddenly.

"Love, since I met you, it's been either you or my hand, and I've only used my hand when I'm truly desperate for you. No one else. There will be no one else for me, even if you decide you don't want me anymore," he murmurs the last part as if it physically pains him and a little piece of my heart floats away to him.

"Then show me how desperate you are for me."

In the matter of a minute, he's completely stripped down and crawling on top of me.

"You want to see how desperate I am for you? How much I fucking missed you and this pussy? I'll leave your tight little cunt used and dripping from my cock, then I'll lick both our orgasms up and do it all again until you're so boneless you can't walk away from me again." His chest rises and falls as he gets more and more worked up.

His words simultaneously hurt me and turn me on. I didn't want to walk away from him the first time, but maybe this is how it was all supposed to play out. Who knows, all I know is if he doesn't sink his dick into me in the next five seconds I'm going to scream.

"Pierce, fuck me, please. Now. I can't take it." My head trashes from side to side.

"I'll give you what you need, love. Trust me," he whispers in my ear as his fingers circle my aching clit.

My back arches in pleasure from just the barest of touches, and I know this is going to be fast.

His thumb takes over as he plunges to fingers inside of me and I come instantly. He covers my screams with a kiss that consumes as much as my orgasm does.

"Fuuuckkk, you feel phenomenal wrapped around my fingers love," he says as he pulls back from the heart stopping kiss.

I feel like I'm in a daze. I don't know which directions is up and I couldn't care less.

He pulls up completely, taking his dick in his hand and rubbing it up and down my orgasm.

"Shit, I need to get a condom, love. Hold on a second." He goes to leave, and I stop him with a hand on this thigh.

"I'm covered," I say as he stills. "I have an IUD and I'm tested every year because I'm paranoid."

"Think very carefully about this, Jane. If I take you bare, I'm never going back. You're mine to keep."

God, I don't think I've ever been surer of anything in my life.

"No condoms," I whisper just before he surges forward, gripping my ass hard in one hand as the other guides himself to my opening. He kisses me like I'm precious, a gift, and I feel pressure behind my eyes. I will not cry during sex, but I'm so overwhelmed I don't know how to feel right this moment.

The stretch as he slides inside of me again makes my head fuzzy. I've never done drugs, but I imagine this is how it feels.

"Breathe, love," Pierce whispers in my ear as he holds steady inside of me.

"Holy shit, I forgot how big you are." I slowly release the breath I was holding.

"This is going to be real fucking fast if you keep talking like that." He grunts.

I chuckle. "Sorry."

"Fuck, laughing doesn't help." He pumps his hips and every muscle in my body goes lax.

"I'll stop, I promise," I say on a moan as he starts a punishing rhythm.

"Never. Fucking. Stop. Jane. Ever." He punctuates every word with a hard thrust. "I don't care if I have to fuck you all night to make sure you can't walk, I'll do it no matter how fast you make me come each and every time."

"That would be a hardship." I smirk.

"I'll take care of that smart mouth too." He winks and the pleasure mixed with how playful this all is sends me flying. My orgasm hits me out of nowhere, and I completely lose it. My body trembles and my mouth pops open in a silent scream. My breath catches in my throat and my entire body clenches up tight and releases as waves upon waves hit me.

"Oh shit," I vaguely hear Pierce as he thrusts as deep as he can while he comes.

The feeling of him coming inside of me is something I didn't know I needed. I've never been with a partner bare before and I never really thought of it as a thing before. But holy hell do I need to feel it every single time we have sex now. It's powerful to feel the effect you have on a man. And this man in particular? I feel like a goddess, all powerful and sexy.

We're both trying to catch our breath as I run my hand up and down Pierce's back. I thought I would never see him again and now suddenly he's not only within my reach but wants me too. It feels like a dream, like a fairytale and I don't know what to do with it.

"Let's get you cleaned up in the shower so I can get your dirty again." He smiles as he looks down at me. He's the happiest I've ever seen him, and my heart pounds painfully in my chest.

"You did promise to make sure I couldn't walk, and I'm not sure I'm there yet." I smile back at him.

"Minx." He growls as he lifts me up from the lounge, still inside of me, with ease.

"Lead the way, caveman." I let out a quick giggle and sigh happily.

"I'm *your* caveman." He nips at the skin on my neck.

"That you are."

After many, many rounds throughout the night, we finally crashed sometime before sunrise.

I'm deliciously sore and wide awake a few hours later.

My mind is racing with everything that's happened in the last twenty-four hours.

I pushed a lot of people away this summer and somehow, I've landed right side up.

Things like this don't happen to me. I picked the safe career. I've picked safe, albeit terrible men for me. And now suddenly I have no job but am a million times happier and a man who surpasses every single dream man I thought I had.

How is this my life?

I've been watching Pierce sleep as my mind goes a mile a minute and the only thing I keep thinking is: Why can't I have this?

Why can't I create the life I've always wanted? I mean hell, the man I thought I'd never see again moved his entire freaking headquarters to the city I live in. If that doesn't say *I'm not leaving you* I don't know what does. And that's not mentioning all the little things he's sent me or the letters which told me all about Pierce Vanstone and what a phenomenal man he is.

Can I have everything I've ever dreamed of?

"What's got you thinking so hard over there?" Pierce's gravelly morning voice makes me smile.

"Just life." I sigh dreamily.

His eyes pop open and connect with mine. No words are needed, we both know what last night meant. We're giving this thing between us a real shot.

"Are you hungry?" I ask, sitting up and getting ready to head to the kitchen to make breakfast.

Instead of answering me, he runs his hand along my stomach before pulling me back down to the bed.

"Good morning, love," he says as he leans in for a kiss.

Butterflies take up residence in my belly at something so simple, yet so meaningful.

"Morning. Sorry I woke you up."

"You didn't. My body clock usually has me up early no matter what time I go to bed. This is actually late for me." He chuckles.

"Seriously though, can I make you breakfast?" I ask again. I want to cook for him. I want to be the person who takes care of him.

"If you want to make me breakfast, I would absolutely love that. I can also order us food, or we can go out to eat."

"I want to cook for you."

"Perfect." He presses a kiss to my nose before getting out of bed and heading to the bathroom.

I walk into his closet and stare at the sheer size of it. I swear my apartment could fit into just his closet. I finally find a regular T-shirt and toss it on before heading out to the kitchen.

I find my phone in my discarded purse on the table in the foyer and open up my cooking playlist before I start gathering ingredients.

I'm in the middle of chopping some onions when the music stops and my phone rings. I walk over to it and see it's my dad.

"Hey dad, what's going on?"

"You need to get here fast, Jane. Your mother's in the hospital; she had a heart attack a few hours ago, and the doctors are telling me it doesn't look good," he chokes out.

I stand frozen with my phone to my ear unable to talk, unable to move.

"Jane. You need to get here," my dad says again, harsher this time.

"I—I'll be there," I whisper as he hangs up the phone without another word.

"Jane?"

I look up in a daze. I can barely see Pierce in the haze taking over my vision.

"Jane!" I hear him rush over to me, taking the knife from my hand and putting it on the counter.

"What happened? What's going on?" he asks frantically,

I gulp several times, trying to get the words out and by the fourth time I'm able to tell him the bare minimum.

"I have to go," I whispers. "I need to get to Kansas. My mom had a heart attack." I feel the first tear fall as I collapse against Pierce.

"Okay. I've got it love. I'll get you there. Let me handle it." He's rambling, but I can't talk above my own tight throat. A steady stream of tears fall from my eyes, but I'm not uncontrollably sobbing.

Am I in shock? Probably, but at this moment I'm more worried about get there in time to focus on anything else.

"Pierce," I croak out.

"I've already got the flight started, love. Who can I call to let them know what's going on? Where are we flying to?"

"The girls. I need to tell the girls. Overland Park," I tell him disjointedly.

"Okay. Let's get you some clothes and then I'll have some more delivered when we get there."

He leads me to the bedroom where he finds a pair of basketball shorts and helps me get them on. Next, he throws on a T-shirt and sweats and pulls me up and leads me to the garage, grabbing my purse on the way.

"I'll get us there, okay, Jane?"

I nod, but I can barely hear anything over the whooshing in my ears.

Chapter 30

Pierce

I t takes me five minutes to text the pilot for my private plane, call in a favor from a doctor friend in New York, and tell Sydney what's going on so she can help me get set up with a rental house, or a hotel to stay in. I also send a text in Jane's group chat filling in the girls briefly, but I'll be checking in with them as soon as we're on the plane to get an actual plan together.

We jump in the car and twenty minutes later we're pulling up to the executive airport. Jane was quiet the entire drive, barely making a sound as silent tears streamed down her face. My heart cracked in two every time I looked over at her because it feels like I'm not doing enough.

Now, I'm leading her up the stairs of my jet while simultaneously thinking about all the things I can still do to help.

My minds going a mile a minute, but one thing is clear: I'm utterly useless. The only thing I can do is make sure to support Jane in whatever she needs right now.

I make sure she gets settled before talking with the pilot.

"Sydney sent you the details, correct?"

"Yes, sir."

"We need to get there as fast as possible," I say bluntly. I know logically he can only get us there so fast, but I don't care at this point. I need to get her there before something else happens.

"We'll be flying into the Kansas City Airport, and from there I believe it's only twenty minutes to Overland Park. Sydney is already getting you set up with transportation. The flight should be about an hour and forty five minutes." His no nonsense tone sooths my feeling out of control a little, and I take a deep breath.

"Thank you. I'll let you get us up in there air then." I turn to walk down the aisle and stop dead in my tracks when I see Jane curled into herself on one of the plush chairs toward the back.

I grab a blanket from one of the overhead bins and make my way to her.

"Hey love," I whisper, draping the blanket over her shaking body. The shock is starting to wear off, and her body is racked with sobs. Taking the seat next to her, I pull up the arm rests in between us and pull her to me.

I let her get the worst of it out while running my hand soothingly up and down her back. Or at least I hope it's soothingly. I'm lost here. I'm not the man who comforts people or knows how to deal with people when they're upset. I'll do anything for this woman, but I'm wholly out of my element here. I only have my experience with my mother to go by and I won't say I handled it the most effective way.

"I—" She clears her throat. "I don't know how to feel." Her voice barely audible over the sounds of the airplane.

"There isn't a right or wrong way to feel."

"I don't have the best relationship with either of my parents. I started pulling away from them the last few years even though we still do our usual phone calls. But it's all so hollow."

Her voice is getting stronger the more she talks, and I refuse to interrupt her, so I let her get it all out.

"You know I skipped a couple grades and was always the youngest in my class by a long shot, and I think my mom felt like she needed to over protect me from a lot of things. When I was in high school, mostly my senior year, it was suffocating. I was about to head off to college far away from home and she became overbearing and wouldn't let me do anything outside of school.

"I thought going off to college would help gain me some freedom, and it did for the most part, but I had to distance myself from my mom to make that happen."

"Where was your father in all of this?" I ask.

"On his recliner, watching TV, most likely." She scoffs.

"He's never been into confrontation and pretty much anything my mother says goes. If my mom and I aren't close, my dad and I have almost no relationship. He went along with anything my mom wanted, still does."

We're both quiet for a minute both lost in our thoughts of less than stellar parents.

"We got into a huge fight a year or so ago. I was talking about not wanting to teach anymore and she ... heavily disagreed with my thinking. She's always been the one to push for a safe career, a career fit for a woman, and I always chose the same because I thought it's what I was supposed to do."

"Not what you wanted to do," I surmise.

"No. But she said she didn't know how I could want to give up teaching when I was teaching the generation of the future and whenever I met the right man, I would just stay at home with the kids. So, in her mind I was only even going to teach for a few years before I became a baby making machine." Her voice falters.

"I'm sorry. I didn't mean to unload all of this shit on you."

"Never apologize Jane. I want to hear it all, the good, the bad, the shit you hide from everyone else. I want it all. And it's not a bad thing to work through your feelings now before we land and head to the hospital," I add.

I know when my mother died, I was young yes, but I also didn't have time to process any of it. It was just a thing that happened, and I had to figure out how to cope without support.

"What if she doesn't make it?" Her whispered fear makes my heart clench painfully in my chest.

"Then we figure out how to cope with it. Together. I won't sugar coat it and say she'll pull through, I know well enough it isn't always the case, but I will be here every step of the way."

"Thank you." She curls into my chest more and cries more.

———◆———

An hour and a half later, I'm gently waking Jane up.

"Hey love, we're here."

She looks up at me with bleary eyes, red-rimmed from crying.

"Already?"

"It was a quick flight. I believe Sydney got us a driver so we can head straight to the hospital, if you'd like."

"Yeah, that's probably what we should do."

She sounds despondent and hollow, and I know there's nothing in the world I can do to fix it no matter how much I *need* to.

We wordlessly deplane and head to the nondescript SUV waiting for us on the tarmac.

I'll have to give Sydney a bonus because everything's been smooth, and we haven't had to give any direction.

We finally make it to the hospital and Jane grabs my hand in a punishing grip.

"I don't know if I can do this."

"You are stronger than you give yourself credit for, Jane. But if you need a little time we can run to the hotel for a while," I won't be the one to tell her what she needs to do. Do I think she should go see her mom before it's too late? Yes, but when you have a less than ideal relationship with a parent it's hard to take that first step.

"No, I need to go in there." She nods to herself, resolute in her decision.

"I'll be here every step of the way unless you tell me to get lost, okay?" I pull her back to me, cupping her cheek and brushing the errand tears away.

"Please don't leave me," she whispers as more tears fall.

I press a kiss to her forehead. "Never, love."

Pressing her forehead to my chest and taking a few deep breaths to sooth her tears away, before straightening and nodding.

"Let's go."

I follow her determined steps to the front desk where she asks for Alice Hatley's room. We're directed to the ICU waiting room and my heart starts to pound.

Fuck, I thought I would be okay.

I haven't spent a lot of time in hospitals since my mother died, but I thought I would have a handle on it by now. But the rushing of memories flood my system, and I pinch my eyes shut as I pray I can get through this.

I didn't go to the hospital after my mom passed because she was already transferred to the funeral home. But being here right now makes me imagine what her last days were like, without me or any support. My breathing picks up a little, and I clench my fists. I need to get through this for Jane though.

And it's that thought that calms me down enough to walk into the waiting room with Jane.

"Dad." She nods to a portly older man with a full head of graying hair.

He grunts in return. No hello, no hug, no words of comfort.

My fists clench at my side in an attempt to hold my temper at bay, but it's Jane pulling me to sit down that pulls me out of my head.

"It's fine," she murmurs.

It's not fine, but it's not my place to say anything right this second.

"What's the latest news?" she asks her father calmer than I would have expected.

"Nothing, that's why I'm still sitting in this god forsaken room," he grumbles.

"Is she in surgery?" Jane asks, not letting his shitty attitude deter her.

"Yes. They're supposed to come talk to me when she's out, but it's been hours." It's then I see a crack in his armor. His wife is in surgery, and he's scared, but he doesn't know how to cope with it all.

"Can I get you both anything? Coffee? Food?" I offer because I'm sure he hasn't eaten since getting here and I know Jane hasn't had anything since last night.

"Who are you?" Jane's dad gives me a hard look.

"Dad—"

"I'm Pierce Vanstone, Jane's boyfriend." I hear her let out a squeak of surprise beside me. "Now, can I get you anything?" I repeat.

"Your boyfriend?" He whips his head around to Jane. "You think it's appropriate to bring a man you've never talked about, your so called boyfriend, to the place your mother is dying?" His face is turning red.

"I'll thank you to watch your tone with Jane. I'm here as support and I'm not going anywhere. Now, would you like coffee or something to eat?"

He stares at me like I'll cave, but he doesn't know me and doesn't know my feelings for his daughter. I'll be making her a priority while we're here and he'll just have to deal with it. Taking out his pain on his daughter will not fly while I'm around.

"I'm fine," he grumbles.

"What about you, love?" I ask turning my attention to Jane.

"I ... I'm okay." She sighs.

We sit in silence for a while. I pull out my phone and check in with Sydney who says everything is fine and to not worry about things there. I also pull up the group text I created with the girls' numbers.

Me: I'm sending the plane back shortly. You should have about two to three hours before it's ready to fly back here.

Bea: Okay, we'll be ready. I packed a bag for Jane, too. I know she'll want some of her own things.

Pen: What hotel are you guys at? I'll book our rooms.

Me: Already taken care of. Just give them your names at the front desk.

Pen: Thank you. Seriously, thank you for taking care of her and keeping us updated.

Larkin: How's she doing?

Me: Not great honestly, but that's to be expected. Her father's a peach, but we're still waiting for her mother to get out of surgery.

Me: I'll keep you updated if anything happens, ladies.

Bea: We'll head straight there when we land. Thanks for getting us all there so quickly.

I put my phone back in my pocket and press a kiss to Jane's hairline.

"Sydney? Do you need to get some work done?" she asks.

God, even with her mom in emergency surgery she's still worried about me.

"Work is taken care of, don't worry about that, just—"

"Hatley family?" An older woman in scrubs and a weary look on her face calls from the doorway.

Jane pops up and rushes to her as her father follows. I trail behind, not wanting to be in the way, but needed to be close to Jane.

"Well, we had to do a little damage control when we got in there so we ended up giving her a double bypass. Everything is looking good so far, but the next twenty-four to forty-eight hours are huge. Once we hit the forty-eight-hour mark we should be able to move her out of the ICU barring any complications."

Jane nods as she sags in relief while her father stays stoic as ever.

"I have a heart specialist flying in shortly as well to check in on her," I tell the doctor. "Dr. Marchmant from New York Presbyterian."

The doctor nods. "Dr. Marchmant and I went to med school together he's a wonderful resource to have. I'll be waiting for his call." She turns to Jane and her father. "Do you have any questions for me?"

"When can we see her?" Jane asks.

"She's still coming out of anesthesia, and when she's more stable it'll only be one at a time, but we should be able to let you see her within the hour."

"Great, thank you so much doctor."

Jane's father doesn't say a word during the entire conversation.

As the doctor leaves, Jane's shoulder slump forward.

"Well, that's good she made it out of surgery right?" she asks me and her father.

"She's not out of the woods yet," he gripes.

"What's your name? We haven't formally met yet." I hold my hand out to him. He grips my hand in what I suppose is meant to be a strong grip, but I pull him toward me a little.

"Names Daniel and we don't need you here."

"Well, Daniel." I pull him closer to me so only he can hear me. "I will do whatever it takes to make that woman happy. You will not take anything out on her, and I will be by her side throughout all of this so get used to it. I'm not going anywhere."

I squeeze his hand a little tighter before letting it go and stepping back. Jane's head ping pongs between the two of us—probably wondering what just happened.

"Care to go grab some coffee while we wait, love?"

She nods and grabs my hand as I lead us to the cafeteria.

Chapter 31

Jane

I 'm in a daze, just going through the motions, because I don't even know how I'm supposed to be feeling right now.

Between my dad barely saying two words and Pierce being overly attentive, I feel like I could scream or cry—or better yet, go hide in a corner while I scream and cry.

My mom is officially awake from the anesthesia, so my dad is in there right now talking to her while I bite my nails down to nothing because I'm so anxious.

Talking on the plane ride over here with Pierce about my relationship with my mom was a little eye opening. How are you supposed to act when a parent you aren't close to has a huge health scare? How are you *supposed* to feel?

I'm not any closer to answering those questions, but I know I don't want any more regrets in my life, so as soon as I'm able to talk to my mom I'm going to be honest and open with her.

Tilting my head back against the chair, I let out a heavy sigh.

"You doing okay, love?" Pierce's voice is like a soothing balm over all my uncertainty.

"Yes. No. I don't know. I'm not sure how to feel honestly. I'm glad she made it out of surgery, though."

"It's a crucial step, and you don't need to know how to feel right now. A lot has happened in a few hours, and it'll take some time to process everything." His thumb works circles on the back of the hand he's holding.

My dad finally comes back after almost an hour.

"She'd like to see you before visiting hours are over," he says with no inflection.

"Okay." I get up shakily as Pierce pops up and helps me.

"Are you going to be okay by yourself?"

"You going to break all the hospital rule is I say no?" I attempt a smirk but fail when his face turns serious.

"I would do anything for you."

I know in my heart of hearts he means it; I just don't have time to focus on it. I need to see my mom and really talk to her before I can focus on things with Pierce.

I nod and pull my hands from his as I turn to go to mom's room.

I stop in front of her door and struggle to take a full breath.

Pull your big girl pants on and go talk to your mom.

I pull open the door and my breath catches in my chest. She looks so pale and fragile it feels like my heart stops in my chest. She has so many wires attached to her, and I don't know where to put my focus.

"There's my Janey." Her voice sounds brittle, and I can feel the pressure behind my eyes already.

"Hey, mom." I sit in the chair I assume my dad pulled over next to her bed and grab the hand closest to me.

"How are you feeling?"

"Oh, I've been better." She chuckles and then grimaces.

"Your father tells me you've brought a man with you."

She's lying in a hospital bed after having her chest cracked open and she cares more about a man I brought with me. Why am I even shocked?

"Yeah, Pierce. I met him while I was at Penelope's wedding." I sigh.

"Your father doesn't like him." Her serious tone puts me on edge.

"Well, I'm dating him so he's going to have to deal with it. He also got me here faster than I could have on my own so I think we should be a little more grateful for that."

"Watch your tone with me Janey," she says with as much sternness as she can mutter.

"I have some things I want to tell you." I brush aside her warning. I need to get this out because I truly don't know if I'll have another chance regardless of how well she's doing at the moment.

"I quit teaching. I don't want to be stuck anymore. I want to use my food science degree and try and make a difference in the world with food." It all spews out like word vomit.

I'm looking down at my clenched hands but when there's no response I look up and meet my very angry mom's eyes.

"Why in the world would you quit a stable job? And to do something so ... so ... unpredictable? Is it because of that man?"

"It's because I've played it safe my whole life. I chose teaching because you said it was a safe, smart option. People always need teachers, and I don't disagree, but I'm not passionate about it."

"Where is this coming from?" she asks, uncertain.

"It's been building a long time. I always wanted to do more with my life, but I felt stuck. And it's scary to uproot your life without having a true back up plan. But I have some money saved so I'll be fine until I figure things out."

"But ..."

"All my life, I was the outcast because of my age. I know you did your best to protect me, but I think we both took it to the other extreme. My friends are doing such incredible things with their lives and honestly, I'm jealous."

"Teaching is nothing to snub, dear."

"I know that, I do. But what if I could create a program to help all those kids who don't have access to food on a regular basis? What if I can help underprivileged areas get the food they need and deserve?"

She sits quietly looking at me as if seeing me as a completely new person.

Honestly, I feel like one.

"I never wanted to hinder you," she whispers.

"I know. I don't fault you for the way you approached things. Hell, being two years younger than everyone was hard, and I don't think anyone knows how to navigate it." I laugh.

A small smile lifts the side of her mouth.

"What made you finally decide to jump into this?" she asks, more accepting than I've ever seen her before.

"Pierce," I say quietly. "Well, the time I spent on the island with him is more accurate."

"And Pierce is the man in the waiting room?"

"He is." I can't help the smile on my face.

"Your father isn't very fond of him." She huffs out a small laugh so she doesn't hurt herself.

"Yeah. Pierce is very ... commanding and I'm sure dad didn't love being told how things were going to go. But he's a good man." *The best man.*

"I think I'd like to meet him," she muses.

"I can make that happen. Are you really okay with all of this? I know it's a huge risk, and it's so different from what I've been doing. But I just feel like I need to do it."

"Honey, I'm proud of you no matter what you do. I think maybe I tried to hold the reigns too tight with you, but you're my only child, and I just wanted to do things the right way."

"I know, mom. But I think this is what I need to be doing with my life."

"Then do it and have no regrets." Her eyes shine with tears, and I lean forward to hug her as best as I can.

"I will. I love you, mom. I'm glad you're feeling better."

"Me too, dear." She pats my arm. "Now send in that boy."

I laugh out loud at my mom calling Pierce a *boy*, but I give her cheek a kiss and agree.

"Jane?"

"Yeah, mom?"

"I love you, never forget that okay?"

"I won't." I smile at her. "I love you, too."

Feeling lighter than I ever have before, I head out to the waiting room with a huge smile on my face. Pierce quickly gets up to meet me.

"How'd it go?" He looks concerned.

"Really good actually. She'd like to talk to you if you're willing."

"I'd love to." He looks shocked but proceeds to give me a kiss before heading to the ICU doors.

I plop down into one of the hard plastic and barely padded chairs with a happy sigh.

"He shouldn't be going to see her." My dad's hard voice interrupts my happiness.

"She asked to talk to him. I'm not telling her no."

As glad as I am I was able to clear the air with my mom, I don't think there's hope with my father. He just doesn't ... care. I don't think I'll ever change his ways, and I just need to be okay with that.

About ten awkward and silent minutes later Pierce comes back to the waiting room.

"Well, visiting hours are over for the night. I made sure to ask the nurse to call me if anything happens and they can't reach you. Mr. Hatley, do you need a ride back home? Or would you like to stay closer? We have a room available for you at the Hilton down the street."

"I don't need your room." My dad stands and turns to the elevator.

"It's yours if you change your mind. Just tell the front desk your name." Pierce continues like my dad isn't being a passive prick to him.

I understand he's shaken from what happened to mom, but he definitely doesn't need to take it out on us.

"We'll see you back here in the morning," I tell him before we all enter the elevator and ride it down silently.

Finally getting out into fresh air even though it's late makes me feel alive. Things with my mom went surprisingly well and she's doing good all things considered. I have Pierce by my side, and I feel like I can finally take a breath.

"Let's go to the hotel, love." Pierce steers me to the SUV and helps me in. I realize I'm still in his button-down shirt and basketball shorts and start laughing hysterically.

"What's so funny?" He raises an eyebrow at me.

"No wonder my dad was pissed at you. Look what I'm wearing!" I can't stop the laughter and soon tears follow. I can't tell if I'm laughing so hard I'm crying or all the emotions of the day have finally caught up to me, and I've officially lost it.

"Alright let's get you to bed." He chuckles, wiping the tears from my cheeks. He shuts my door and makes his way around to the driver side before swiftly starting it and pulling out.

We drive less than five minutes before pulling up to the fanciest hotel in my hometown. He parks and helps me out as we head inside.

Before we reach the check in counter three women stand up from the chairs in the lobby and when I figure out who they are I promptly burst into tears.

"I'm going to grab our key then we can all head up to our room," Pierce says, leaving me with the girls.

"Oh my god, how are you guys here?" I barely get out through my sobs.

"Pierce," Bea says as she pulls me in for a hug. Larkin and Pen wrap themselves around me and we stay huddled together until Pierce clears his throat, back as fast as he left.

"Shall we head up, so you all aren't in the middle of the lobby?"

"Yup," Pen says as she disengages first. I try to wipe my tears away, but they won't stop falling. We make our way to the elevator, and I pull him down for a hug.

"Thank you," I whisper in his ear before releasing him with a smile.

"Nothing to thank me for."

"So, how's your mom?" Larkin draws me away from Pierce's heady stare.

"Actually, pretty good considering. Let's get up to the room so I can take a quick shower then I'll fill you guys in." They all nod in agreement as the elevator dings our floor.

We all enter our large suite, and everyone sits down on the plush couches.

"Okay, give me like ten minutes and I'll be out," I tell them as I head to the bathroom.

"There are clothes on the bed for you, love," Pierce adds before chastely kissing me and tapping my ass.

I waste no time rinsing off the day and the stress, and by the time I'm done I feel much more human. I head to the bedroom and find half the bed covered in shopping bags. I peak in and see everything from lingerie to T-shirts and jeans. I find a bag with a pair of leggings and tank top and toss them on while throwing my hair up in a messy bun.

I come out and see the coffee table covered in food and my stomach growls so loud Pierce looks up at the sound.

"It's been a while since you ate." He holds his hand out for me. I join him in an oversized chair and look at the girls who are all giving me shit eating grins.

Everyone patiently waits while I shove half a burger in my mouth along with some fruit when I come up for air.

"Oh my god, I feel so much better." I groan as I push my plate away.

"So fill us in," Pen says scooting the edge of the couch.

"How much do you know? About what happened with my mom?" I ask.

"We know she had a heart attack and was in surgery for a long time, but she made it out okay. She's in the ICU, right? You'll know more in the next day or two." Bea sums everything up quite perfectly.

I look at Pierce. "You've been busy. Thank you," I tell him. He bows his head but doesn't say anything as the girls and I talk about everything that's happened in the last day.

I tell them about my conversation with my mom and how well it went. How I finally feel like the pressure is off and maybe I can really have a good relationship with my mom now.

Pierces phone rings so I scoot off of him as he pulls it from his pants. His face hardens when he sees the number and hits decline.

"You okay?" I ask quietly.

"Perfect," he says pulling me back on his lap just as his phone rings again. He yanks it out of his pants and stops short when he sees who it is. He answers the call quickly.

"Yes? This is he." His eyes shift to mine before he hands the phone to me. I hesitantly put it to my ear.

"Hello?"

"Ms. Hatley, hello I'm the nurse at the ICU unit tonight. We're going to need you to come to the hospital as soon as possible."

"Is everything okay?"

"We really you need you to come in so we can discuss it."

"Umm, okay. I'll be right there," I hang up numbly.

I look up at my best friends and they all have grim looks on their faces.

"She's okay, right?" I ask. "She's going to be okay?"

Their eyes fill with tears and Pierce squeezes my hand.

"Let's get over there and hear what they have to say. It could be nothing, maybe a change in level of care." His words are logical, but his tone tells me he doesn't believe it's that easy.

I take a shuddering breath and stand up, robotically following Pierce as we head back to the car.

We get to the hospital quickly, thank god, and when we reach the ICU waiting room the nurse pulls us into a small meeting room where my father is already waiting.

"What's going on?" he demands.

"The doctor will be in momentarily," she says just as there is a knock on the door.

It's an older man followed by the doctor we met earlier.

"My name's Dr. Marchmant. Pierce called me earlier to check in on your mother, and you met Dr. Keely earlier. I'm sorry to tell you Alice passed away. She had a hemorrhagic stroke, and there was no way to save her. It happened fast, and she wasn't in pain," he says as the whooshing sounds takes over my ears again. I feel like I'm underwater, and I can't find a way to come up for air.

I vaguely hear my dad yelling, but I can't make out the words. I sit staring at the floor, unable to connect what I was just told to something that makes sense.

I hear Pierce's voice next, and then I see him in my line of sight.

"Do you want to say goodbye?" he asks, pain so prevalent in his voice.

"N—" I clear my throat. "No. I think I'd like to leave."

Pierce wastes no time pulling me out of the chair and leading me to the elevator. He doesn't say anything as he drives us back to the hotel, and neither do I.

When we get back to the room, I notice the girls are gone. I don't think I can handle them right now anyways. I automatically head to the bathroom and turn on the shower as hot as I can get it before climbing in fully clothed.

Sinking down against the wall, I finally let myself feel every ounce of pain.

Chapter 32

Pierce

Watching Jane despairingly walk into the bathroom rips my heart in two. Not only am I devastated for her, I'm dangerously close to letting my own personal dealings with the death of my mother pull me under.

And I can't let that happen.

I have to take care of Jane, even if it kills me in the process.

Walking toward the bedroom, I hear the shower turn on and immediately head to the bathroom.

When I see Jane sitting on the shower floor, hugging her knees to her chest, I don't hesitate. I climb into the shower fully clothed and sit on the floor, pulling her into my lap.

Her shoulders shake as the reality of tonight hits her, and her gut wrenching sobs steal my breath. She buries herself into my chest as she breaks down and the pressure I feel behind my eyes is telling me I'm very close to joining her.

I never had closure with my mother, and although she made the choice for me, I don't know that I would change the way things were. When Jane said she didn't want to say goodbye I understood where she was coming from. Some might see it as callus or cold, but I know it for what it really was. She wanted her last memory of her mother to be a mostly happy one. One she was able to control the narrative and not one that would probably traumatize her long after the worst of the grief settles.

I don't know how long we stay in the shower, but I know it's long past the time for soggy fingers and lukewarm water. When I feel her start to shiver, I know I need to take charge and at least get her in bed.

"I'm going to pick you up, okay? You're freezing and I need to get you warmed up," I whisper in her ear. A barely there nod moves against my chest, and I tuck my arm under her legs and slowly stand with her in my arms. I shut off the water and gently place her on the vanity as a I grab a couple towels.

"Can you lift your arms up for me love?" I ask.

She looks up at me with a trembling bottom lip, hollow eyes, and a red splotchy face, and I feel utterly useless. All I want is to make this better, but I can't. I want to take all this pain away from her and put it on my shoulders. But I can't.

She holds her arms up for a few seconds and I waste no time ripping her drenched tank top off. I know I have limited time as she's likely to crash any second from exhaustion.

Unhooking her bra, I slide it down her arms and toss it on top of her shirt I threw on the ground. This next part is tricky, I wrap her arms around my neck and use one hand to lift her slightly off the counter to pull her leggings and underwear down before setting her back down and taking them the rest of the way off.

I grab a towel and dry her off as fast as I can, wrapping her with it as I strip out of my sodden clothes as well. Not caring how cold I am, I pick her up and walk her to the bed before digging through our bags and grabbing some underwear for us both and a T-shirt for Jane.

"Okay, last time and then you can sleep love." My voice is scratchy, and I'm quickly losing control of my emotions.

I pull the towel off of her, swiftly putting the T-shirt over her head as she shoves her arms into it. Sliding her feet into the underwear I move them up her legs, helping her lift up so I can cover her fully.

"Can I get you anything? Water?" I know when I learned my mother had passed away, I didn't eat for a few days because I just couldn't be bothered to do much of anything, so I can't imagine food sounds good to her right now. But water would be smart to attempt to keep her hydrated.

"I'm going to grab you some water," I tell her without waiting for her answer.

"Pierce," she croaks out.

"Yeah, love." I sit down next to her on the bed trying to hold back the tears that are precariously close to falling.

"Thank you," she rasps.

I can't respond, too caught up in feeling helpless and at the same time like I'm not doing enough. Throw in remembering how I felt when my mother passed away, I'm a fucking mess.

Pulling her to my chest, I hold her to steady myself before pressing a kiss to the crown of her head.

"Let me get you some water, then you can sleep," I murmur against her hair, holding her to me a little longer before I release her and get up.

In the kitchen area, I grip the counter until my knuckles hurt. The tears fall without permission.

I may be the last person equipped to handle any of this, but I'll be damned if I let my own hang ups get in the way of taking care of Jane. Taking a deep breath, I refocus and push myself off the counter. Grabbing two water bottles from the fridge, I open them both and take a long swig from one as I walk back to the bedroom.

Jane is fast asleep when I come back to the room so I set her water on the nightstand and watch her for a couple minutes.

Tomorrow.

Tomorrow I'll help get things set up. Start planning the funeral for her and everything else that needs to be done.

Tonight, I'm going to grieve with her.

———◦———

I'm woken up by my phone buzzing on the nightstand. I blearily reach for it and try to focus on the name lighting it up.

Sydney.

"What?" I ask in a harsh whisper.

"Have you checked your email at all?" Her tone has me sitting up and moving to the living room area as quietly as I can.

"No. Shit went downhill here fast so I haven't even thought about work," I admit.

"Is everything okay?"

I let out a sigh. "Not really. Jane's mother passed away last night."

"Shit."

"Yeah. So, what email do I need to look at?"

"Umm, this is like the worst possible time for this, I'm sorry. Tyler in finance sent you an email and it's ... it's' not good."

"What the hell," I mutter as I pull my phone away and open up my email. "Give me a second."

I scroll through the endless bullshit I couldn't care less about right now and find an email from Tyler marked URGENT.

"God dammit," I grit out.

"Yeah."

"So, my father tried to get an insurance policy essentially. He had Tyler doctor the numbers so he could whistle blow the company, and me, for tax fraud, so he could get the reward for turning me in. And all of this because I didn't jump when he threatened blackmail."

"It appears so. He just didn't bank on Tyler having a conscious and emailing you directly to tell you the plan."

I tip my head back, trying to think logically. This is usually what I'm good at but this is the worst possible time for this shit to come. I don't have the brain power to allocate to this problem right now, and I don't know if I will in the near future.

"I need a huge favor," I tell Sydney.

"Of course," she readily agrees.

"I need you to look into the finance department and make sure no one else is involved. See if there could be any connection to my father with any of them. I'd also like you to call the PI and fill him in and have him look into my father's finances to see why he's resorting to such drastic actions for some petty cash. He's already digging, but hopefully this new information will help him get it faster. And can you check in with the lawyers on how fast we can buy him out?"

What a cluster fuck.

"Already looking into it. I have the PI looking through your father's finances and such as we speak, and I'll be combing through the finance department. I'll let you know as soon as we have anything. And I talked to them about a week ago, and they we're just finishing up the actual contract. They said it took some time to dig into the buy-sell agreement and make sure it was ironclad so your father couldn't come back and claim something bogus to cancel it out. They sent an email saying it was sent, but I haven't heard anything since."

"Thanks Sydney. I'll be out of commission for the foreseeable future for all other work situations. But if something comes from your digging, please don't hesitate to let me know." I also make a mental note to give her a raise and an even bigger bonus for having to deal with all this ridiculous bullshit my father's doing.

"Don't worry about a thing at work, I've got it handled. Can I do anything to help with Jane? Is she okay?"

"She's definitely struggling, but that's to be expected. I don't think there's much to do at the moment, but as soon as we figure out a timeline, I may need help getting the funeral plans underway and making sure everything is set up."

She may not want my help, but I'll be damned if she has to do this all on her own. And I doubt her father will be any help when it comes down, not that I can really blame him, but he doesn't seem like the type to go above and beyond to help out his daughter in any context.

"Not a problem. I'll start looking up places in the area and different options so you'll have access to it whenever you need it." Sydney doesn't even hesitate and I'm eternally grateful for the help.

"Thank you, Sydney. I appreciate it more than you know."

"That's what I'm here for," she says distractedly, and I can already hear her fingers going a mile a minute on her computer even though it's three in the morning.

"Keep me in the loop, and don't work all night," I say before hanging up the phone.

What is happening in my company right now? Is this a sign to just sell it completely? Hell, I don't even know anymore. And I'm not in the head space to be making these decisions right now anyways.

I hear a strangled cry from the bedroom and rush back in time to see Jane's tiny body curled into a ball shaking with sobs. Climbing into bed,

I pull her to me and run my hand up and down her body to try and sooth her.

No matter what happens with my father, as long as I have this woman in my life, I'll be the happiest man in the world—even if it means abandoning my company completely.

Chapter 33
Jane

Everything feels surreal when I wake up. Like everything that happened was part of a television show or something. But then it hits me.

My mom died last night.

I barely remember Pierce bringing me back to the hotel.

I peel my crusted eyes open and rub them with the heels of my hands. Everything hurts right now. I have a pounding headache that causes me to wince when I turn my head and see the curtains open.

"Hey, love." Pierce's quiet voice sounds beside me.

"Hi," I croak out, not turning to face him.

"How are you doing?"

"Everything hurts," I say clearing my throat.

"I'm not surprised. Can I get you anything? Some tea? Food?" His voice is gentle, and I feel his palm rub up and down my back.

"Tea and maybe some Tylenol? My head hurts so bad."

"Done." His hand moves from me as I feel the mattress dip as he gets out of bed. I instantly feel colder without him next to me, but I know I need to get a handle on this headache so I can attempt to function.

While he rummages around in the kitchen of the suite, a million thoughts run through my head.

How do you just accept your mom dying?

Do I just get up and carry on with my life like nothing happened?

I know there are plans that need to get figured out, and I doubt my dad will be much, if not any help so that'll probably land on my shoulders.

What *are* the next steps? Is someone supposed to call you and tell you? Are you supposed to know this stuff already?

I guess I need to figure all this out once I'm feeling a little better.

Pierce returns and kneels by my side of the bed.

"Here's the Tylenol and some water." He hands it to me as he helps me sit up. I wince again as the pain intensifies.

"Your tea." He places a mug on the nightstand.

He doesn't ask how I'm doing or if I'm okay, and I'm grateful. Is anyone ever okay after something like this happens? And Pierce of all people would know since he lost his mom.

Oh God, his mom.

He never got to say goodbye properly and now he just had to sit through all of this with me. This is like a double whammy, right? Bringing up all his memories and feelings of missing out on closure. Now I feel terrible for him.

"Are *you* okay?" I hear myself ask him. It's like I'm having an out of body experience. My mind is racing but I'm not in full control over what's coming out of my mouth right now.

He tilts his head at my question, brows furrowed trying to understand my question.

"I'm ... I'm just worried about you and trying to make sure you're okay," he finally says.

"I just want this headache to go away and then I can start figuring things out."

"Jane ..."

"I'm fine, really Pierce. I'm just going to stay in bed a little longer. Just until the Tylenol kicks in."

His stare meets mine, and I see the pain in his gaze. I can't determine if it's my pain or his, and it just makes me more determined to put my grief aside and deal with my mom's funeral.

I can't be a bigger burden to him than I already am even though I know he would turn my ass red if he heard me say that.

I pick up the mug of tea and take small sips, letting the warmth fill my stomach.

"Do you want me to call the girls up here?" Pierce asks, no doubt trying to figure out where my head is at.

"That would be great. Can we have them wait like an hour though?"

"Absolutely." He picks up his phone, and I assume he's sending a message to the girls.

I sip my tea until the mug is empty, final feeling some version of normal as Pierce gets up and sits next to my on the bed.

I finally turn my full attention to him and try to come up with the right words.

"If this is too hard for you, I understand. You don't have to stick around. I'm sure you have a lot happening with your properties."

His angry eyes meet mine.

Apparently, my words weren't right at all.

"You think I would just leave you? Do you really think my job is a priority over you?"

I feel my eyes start to well up with tears again and I start angrily whipping them away.

"I don't know what I'm saying. I'm just trying to make sure I'm doing the right thing."

"Jane, there is no right thing right now. You are allowed to feel every emotion under the sun and be irrational and cry all fucking day. It doesn't matter. I just want to be here for you, for whatever you need and I'm not leaving your side."

I wipe my face off again and heave in a deep breath, trying to calm myself down.

"I'm sorry. I'm a fucking mess." I huff out a distraught laugh.

"Never apologize for anything you feel—especially right now." He holds his arm out as an open invitation to lay on him and I take it eagerly.

It takes me a while, but I finally calm down enough to start feeling a little better, physically anyways, and I sit up from Pierce's chest.

"I think I'm going to take a shower before the girls get here."

"Okay. Do you need anything from me?" he asks.

Shaking my head, I start to climb out of bed. "I'll be good. I just need to wash everything clean, you know?" I don't know if I'm making sense to him, but I know I want to wash off all of last night and come out a new woman. Well, a more put together one who can figure out what all needs to be done for a funeral.

The concern on his face lets me know I'm not really fooling him, but I don't have the energy to worry about it right now. I need to focus on what needs to get done today.

I climb into the shower set as hot as I can possibly stand it and let it beat down on my body.

I feel like I'm in a daze. My mind shuts down and my body finally loosens up from being so tense over the last twenty-four hours. Everything feels ... blissfully blank.

I don't know how long I stay in there, but the hot water is cooling slightly so I take it as a sign to get out.

I dry off and quickly realize I didn't bring anything to change into. I head to the bedroom to grab some clothes. Pierce is nowhere to be seen, but the bedroom door is closed.

I walk closer and hear Pierce's voice.

"But what did the PI say? ... And that's the only connection you've found so far? ... There's more to this. He has to have someone on the inside. Keep digging and let me know if you find anything else. Thanks, Sydney."

Stepping away from the door, I move to the bags on the floor with all the clothes Pierce had delivered.

I know he said I was a priority over his job, but I can't help but feel like he's needed there. I know no matter what I say, he won't budge but the guilt of taking up his time won't dissipate.

I throw on a pair of jeans that somehow fit me perfectly and a super soft purple sweater. The sweater feels like a constant warm hug, and it's just what I need to feel a little more stability at the moment.

I hear the main door open and know the girls just showed up.

I take a centering breath, pushing every overwhelming feeling away and turn on the planner part of my brain.

I slowly open the door and see everyone I love sitting in the living room.

Do I love Pierce?

This is probably not the time to attempt to analyze my feelings for him.

Everyone's attention turns to me as I join them, plopping down into the oversized chair that's empty.

Sympathy. It's all I see written on every single one of their faces, and I absolutely hate it.

"So I think I need to go back to the hospital and figure out where they need to send the body." I can feel the disconnect happening. My brain is thinking logically, like it's not my mom we're talking about, but just some task that needs to be accomplished.

"I had called them last night and gave them instructions," Pierce says.

"Oh. Umm, okay. Does my dad know?" I'm more than grateful Pierce stepped in when I normally would be mad at him for doing so because I don't think I could walk back into that hospital right now and not lose my shit.

"He does. There's an appointment set up at the funeral home tomorrow where all the decisions can be made."

"Thank you." I bow my head to him.

"What else needs to be done today?" I look around at everyone questioningly.

"Jane ..." Larkin says.

"I'm fine. Really. I just want to make sure we get everything done in a timely manner. I should probably go check on my dad as well," I muse.

The girls and Pierce give each other concerned looks. I know this doesn't seem healthy, but I'll have time to really grieve later. When I'm back home and alone.

"So today, I think heading to my parent's house—" I trip over myself because it's technically just my dad's house now, right? "And check on him. Make sure he's doing okay and then try to see if he has a general plan for a funeral. Like cremation, burial, I'm not sure what she would have preferred but I'm sure he'll know."

Jane, Larkin and Bea jolt back in their seats and Pierce runs his hand over his face.

"Do you want us to go with you?" Bea asks.

"Umm, I don't think so." I look over at Pierce and he nods back. "I'll have Pierce take me over there so I should be fine. You guys can hang out here until I get back, or go explore or whatever, and then when we get back if you want to help me plan or brainstorm that would be helpful."

"Of course. Anything you need," Larkin says.

"So let's plan to meet back here for dinner then?" I ask, getting up and grabbing my shoes.

"Sounds like a plan," Pierce says with a bit of sternness in his voice, leaving no room for the girls' rebuttal.

I know this isn't what they expected, but it's what I need right now. I don't want to think about what happened. I don't want to think about the reality of my life right now. I just want to get things done so I can go home.

Chapter 34

Pierce

I t's been almost three weeks, and I'm officially losing my mind.

I know grief is a fickle bitch, but I'm struggling with how to help Jane right now when she doesn't want anyone near her.

The girls and I have been checking in on her every day. Well, the girls check in, I've been basically living on Jane's couch and then running to the office to get a little bit of necessary work done any time the girls show up.

Every time Jane comes out of her room, she walks past all of us like we aren't even there, and my heart can't take it anymore.

At least things with my father seem to be dying out. Sydney and I received confirmation right after the funeral that the buyout agreement was officially sent, and so far, we haven't heard anything from him. I can only assume it means he's going to go away quietly.

I've also been working on a special project while Jane's been ignoring me and buried in her grief.

Not only am I scaling back the company as a whole, but I've also been creating a non-profit branch specifically to help feed those in need. *Exactly what Jane is passionate about.*

It's called The Hatley Foundation. And I've been talking with Bea and Pen about possibly connecting it to their foundation but that's still in its early stages.

Sydney's also been extremely busy. I found an old farmhouse with acreage on the outskirts of the city, and I've put her in charge of re-vamping the entire thing so it's ready for Jane, and hopefully myself, when she's past the worst of her grief. It's amazing what money can make happen in such a short amount of time. I'll keep the lake house because it's a great location, but I think this farmhouse is exactly what Jane wants long term.

Jane's best friends have been a wonderful help with it as well. I let them in on my plan, as everyone was feeling helpless. They've been helping pick finishes and decorate so it's everything Jane had envisioned in a dream home.

I have to say, I've never been one who cared much about friendships, but these women, and their husbands, are what I imagine true friendship is supposed to be. They've brought me into their circle like I was always meant to be here. It's been ... eye-opening to have the support they've shown me.

And today, they've planned a girls' day in an attempt to get Jane to talk. Hell, I don't think anyone cares what she actually talks about, we just want her to engage in life again.

I'm currently running through the logistics of putting in a vegetable garden at the farmhouse and how fast I can get it done while Jane sits on the couch next to me eating crisps and mindlessly flipping through channels.

And my heart fucking hurts for her. I just don't know what else to do to make it better, hence why I'm attempting to help make all her dreams come true with the house and foundation.

My phone buzzes with a text.

Bea: We're so late, sorry! But we're on our way now.

Pen: What she means is we bought half the grocery store's junk food supplies and then spent an hour picking out wine.

I barely hold my chuckle in at their antics.

Me: No worries. I don't have anything pressing at the office so take your time.

Larkin: How's she doing today?

Me: The same. She's been flipping through channels for the last hour and not actually watching anything. Completely ignoring me as usual.

Larkin: Fuck, okay. Maybe our good old fashioned girl's day will help us get through to her.

I put my phone down and wrap up the email I was writing. When the girls get here, I need to check in at the office and then I want to head out to the farmhouse and look in on the progress. I'm hoping everything will be done in the next couple of weeks. Sydney says I'm crazy, but what good is having all this money if I can't make shit happen fast for the woman I'm in love with?

I've given up trying to play it cool. I'm in love with Jane, and I'm doing everything in my power to make this grief a little more bearable.

It's strange, though. I thought I would feel the grief of losing my mother all over again. But in some bizarre twist of fate, it feels like Jane's mother gave me a sense of closure with my own mother's passing.

My thoughts are disrupted by the sound of keys in the front door. Jane doesn't even look away from the television.

The girls file in, shooting me a look that says *has she moved at all today?* I shake my head as I close my laptop and pocket my phone as I stand up.

"What are we watching today?" Larkin asks as she plops down on the couch next to Jane. Pen and Bea head to the kitchen to drop off all the food and wine.

I follow them, speaking in a hushed tone so Jane doesn't overhear.

"I'm going to the office for a little bit then heading over to the house to check things out. If you need anything, I can be over here within half an hour, so just call me." They nod.

"I'm really worried about her," I confess.

"We all are. We'll see what we can manage today, and I'll keep you updated if anything changes," Bea tells me.

"I know, I just wish I were able to do more."

Pen laughs out loud. "If you do any more, we're all going to move in with you. Pierce, you're already doing so much, even if she doesn't know it yet. We knew this was going to be a long process. We just have to stay patient."

I *know* she's right, but it doesn't ease the ball in the pit of my stomach.

"Okay. Just ... keep me updated."

"You know we will. Go rule the world, we'll be here with her," Bea says.

"I'm leaving," I say with a smile, holding my hands up and moving toward the front door.

I stop abruptly before walking back to Jane on the couch. Pressing a kiss to the top of her head, I whisper against her, "I'll be back."

I feel her sink down into the couch a little, and I take solstice I'm able to relax her even if she still won't talk to me.

Walking to my car, my head is on everything except work. I just feel like I should be doing *more*. But then my phone rings and I try to switch gears.

"Yes, Sydney?" I sigh.

"You need to get to the office, like now."

"I'm on my way there. I should only be about fifteen minutes."

"Brace yourself."

"Shit."

"Yeah. I'll see you when you get here." The silence after she hangs up if deafening. She wouldn't tell me to get to the office if it wasn't an emergency, and I can only think of one thing it would be.

My father.

I race over to the office, not even saying hello to anyone as I walk into the building. When I get to my office, Sydney is sitting in a chair in front of my desk chewing on her nails.

"What happened?"

"Well, I found out a lot of information about your father, but it doesn't really matter anymore."

"And why's that?"

"Because he just CC'd us on an email he sent to some news outlets. He already sent the pictures."

"Fuck!"

Fuck! I can't even think. I should have known it was too quiet on his end.

I pull out my phone and scroll through my email looking for it.

When I find it and pull it up my heart sinks. He sent every single picture of Jane and I on the island to gossip rags and popular online magazines he could find. The more risqué ones are blurred out. How fucking nice of him.

"I'm already on damage control, but it'll take time and the pictures will likely already be out there," Sydney says.

"Okay. What did you find out about him?"

I need to get to Jane immediately, but I also need to know what I'm working with so I'm able to shut this shit down permanently.

"He invested in a pyramid scheme, well more like he helped *facilitate* a pyramid scheme. It looks like his partner ended up screwing him over. He's desperate for money, and he thinks this is the way to get it since you had the buyout papers drawn up."

"What a fucking prick. Okay, I need to go warn Jane, prepare her. God I don't even know. But are you able to get me some hard proof of this so there is potential to expose him and this partner?"

"Absolutely."

"Great. Work on that, I'll figure out what to do with the info in a little bit. I need to go to Jane. She's unwillingly involved in this, and I need to warn her and make sure she's okay."

"Don't worry about what to do with the information, I've already got a handle on that. Go take care of Jane, and I'll handle everything else. Lord knows that woman doesn't need more shit on her plate right now."

"We need to bury him. Whatever it takes. I don't wany him to ever pop into my life again."

I can feel the anger rising to the surface. How fucking dare he put Jane in the line of fire. I don't give a shit about me, but he fucked with the wrong woman, and he will pay for what he's done.

Any sense of familial love is gone. He crushed it like he crushes everything in his life.

"Send me any articles you find too ... please," I tack on. I refuse to be like my father in any way. Jane's made me aspire to be better, and that starts with how I treat people like Sydney, no matter how pissed I am at the situation.

"Done."

I'm already walking out the door, but I call out over my shoulder, "I owe you a very big raise!"

"Yes, you do!"

I don't even have the energy to chuckle at her response. I trust her to take care of this, but I need to be the one to tell Jane. I don't want her to see it online and then find even more reason to push me away. And I need her to know I'm taking care of it. That the man responsible won't be allowed to get away with his reprehensible actions.

As I'm walking back to my car my phone vibrates in my pocket. I pull it out and my heart races.

Jane: Thank you for taking care of things. I'm sorry I'm a mess.

I'm a mix of elated she's finally reached out, and so fucking mad that I have to ruin this fragile yet huge step she's taken. Everything I'm about to tell her will negate everything I've done these last few weeks.

Letting my father smear her name and body around the internet is a failure on my part. I never should have underestimated him. And no matter what I've done for Jane thus far, it doesn't matter now that the pictures are out there.

But I want to hold onto the elation a little bit longer.

Me: Don't ever apologize, love. I'm on my way back. We can talk more when I get there. I also have something I need to discuss with you.

Even if she doesn't engage in conversation with me, she needs to know what's going on. I just hope this doesn't push her away for good.

Chapter 35

Jane

We ended up having a celebration of life ceremony at a park my mom loved. It was perfect and I'm glad I had my best friends and Pierce there to help me because my dad was exactly zero help. If he barely talked to me before my mom's death, he now refuses to say two words to me. Pierce is the one who ended up getting him to talk, shockingly enough, but it got the job done so I'm happy.

We've been back in Austin for a few weeks, and I've been hibernating in my apartment for most of that time.

The entire first week I was back, I locked myself in my bedroom and cried. I don't really remember much else, but I know the girls and Pierce dropped by multiple times. They would sit in front of my door and talk to me through it as I cried my body weight in tears.

Now, I'm just angry at the world. Anytime I come out of my room and someone, usually Pierce, is sitting on my couch, I ignore them and move on with my day. I'm angry they won't leave me alone, angry that I barely got closure with my mom, angry that I can't seem to feel anything but anger. I want to talk about it, I want to move forward. It's just too hard to talk about, and I don't even know where to begin.

Larkin left a couple books on grief the last time she was here, and I've been looking through them. All the standard stuff about the five stages of grief makes a ton of sense, but I'm not ready to look deeper and analyze my feelings right now. I just don't want to feel so damn angry. I don't know how anyone could just accept that a loved one is never coming back. But I'm probably the last person to be thinking logically about any of this right now.

At the moment, I'm eating sour cream and onion chips while flipping through the television channels but not really watching anything while Pierce sits on the other end of the couch on his laptop.

What I'm stuck on is why the universe had to make the last conversation I had with my mom so fucking hopeful. I was so happy it looked like we could finally have a relationship where I could tell her about my life in weekly phone calls. Invite her out to Austin to see what my life looked like and see how well I'm doing.

It's like I finally decided to not play things safe and go after what I want, and the universe threw up a big middle finger at me.

I'm just glad I was able to get at least a little closure before everything went to shit.

The sound of keys in the door makes my shoulders tense up. Pierce closes his laptop and stands up to greet the girls who are walking in with their hands loaded up with all sorts of stuff.

Great. Here comes the pep talks and attempts to get me to talk.

"What are we watching today?" Larkin asks as she sits in the space Pierce just vacated.

I don't answer her, but I do inconspicuously look toward the kitchen and see Bea, Pen, and Pierce talking.

I'm sure they're discussing how I've completely lost it.

A few minutes later, Pierce is about to leave but he stops short. He walks over to me and presses a kiss to the crown of my head before whispering, "I'll be back."

I don't know what it is about those words, but the tension I'm holding lessens a little. As much as I've made it my job to ignore everyone, the fact he's still here, still showing up tells me he's in this for the long haul.

And thank God for that, because his strength and the girls showing up every single day feels like the only thing keeping me going.

He leaves without another word as Pen and Bea join us in the living room.

"Okay, we aren't going to force you to talk but do you want to just get drunk and see what happens?" Pen asks.

It's so out of left field a laugh bursts out of me. And I keep laughing until tears are streaming down my face. Then the tears of laughter turn to ugly sobs.

The girl circle around me, wrapping me up in their arms and it only makes me cry harder.

A few minutes later, I finally catch my breath and calm down. The tears letting up enough to attempt to get some words out.

"I'm sorry," I croak.

"Nope. No apologizing," Larkin says.

I collapse back into the couch and wipe my face off with the blanket I've had wrapped around me.

"This sucks." I don't even know what to say or how to approach the fact that I've pushed everyone close to me away for the last few weeks. I know they understand and don't hold it against me, but I suddenly feel like need to be done with the bullshit I've been pulling.

"It totally sucks," Pen agrees.

"I haven't been a very good friend lately," I whisper.

"Nope. None of that. We are not here to hear you say you're sorry or tell us you've been a bad friend. We're here because we want to help you in any way we can get through the worst of this grief. We don't want to negate it, Jane. We just want to support you through it," Bea says.

"I know."

We sit in silence while I think about how to put into words how I've been feeling. I don't want to stay stuck in this anger bubble I'm in and talking to my best friends is the best way to get out of it.

"The first week home was hard. I think it all kind of hit me. I was in work mode in Kansas trying to get everything set up since my dad didn't want any part of it, so I just pushed it all to the back of my mind. Then when I came home, I was just alone with my thoughts, and I couldn't escape the sadness."

Larkin reaches over to hold my hand. I squeeze it back in thanks.

"Then I just got angry, you know? Like how dare my mom be so accepting of the decisions I had just made to start living my life the way I wanted to and then just die? How dare she give me this hope that things would change. I know that's so irrational."

"You aren't supposed to be rational right now," Bea adds.

"I know, but it's just strange. Like how do you just move on? How do you just continue on with your life after something like this?"

"Very gradually. And you never really move on. It just becomes a part of your life. You make an effort every day to not let the grief pull you under, and eventually it lessens," Larkin says.

I take in her words.

It all sounds so easy.

"You take it one day at a time, Jane," Bea says from her spot on the loveseat.

Tears trail down my cheeks.

"You guys brought wine?" I ask through my tears.

"Yep! On it." Pen jumps up and heads to the kitchen.

At the same time, I pick up my phone.

Texting Pierce, who has been by my side this entire time, is long overdue. I don't know that I have a lot to give him right now but letting him know I see him and all he's done for me seems like a good start.

Me: Thank you for taking care of things. I'm sorry I'm a mess.

Pierce: Don't apologize ever love. I'm on my way back, so we can talk more when I get there. I also have something I need to discuss with you.

Awesome. I probably pushed him away one too many times and he's trying to let me down easy.

I suck in a shaky breath as Pen hands me a glass of wine. She also grabbed as many bags of chips and cookies as she could and unloads them onto the coffee table.

"Thank you, guys. I don't know what I would do without you," I whisper. My voice sounds scared, like I already know this is the end of the road with Pierce and I'm just trying to hold onto the only thing in my life that's been by my side: my friends.

Bea grabs the remote and flips through the channels before landing on an *Ocean's Eleven* marathon.

We barely get fifteen minutes in before I hear keys in my door, and something about the sound makes me break.

Pierce opens the door, and I turn around and let him have it.

"How did you get a key to my place? I didn't give you one so how do you think it's okay to just waltz in here like you own the place?" I'm bordering on yelling at this point but I'm so scared.

Scared he's about to break my heart because I'm too much to handle right now.

Scared he's given up on me.

Scared I found the man of my dreams only to lose him before we really even got started.

"Jane ..." Larkin says.

"No. Answer the question," I say still facing Pierce.

"I had the girls make me a copy so I could stay here and help you." He says it like he knows exactly what I'm doing right now, and it pisses me off more.

If he's about to break my heart, I want to have the upper hand.

"Jane, love this isn't what you're thinking it is. And we can talk about all of that later, but right now I really need to talk to you about what's been going on."

Okay, I'm confused.

"What?"

"We can leave ..." Pen offers.

"Stay, you all need to be informed of all of this too."

"What are you talking about?"

He sighs before grabbing a chair from the little dining room table I have and moving it into the living room. He takes a seat and runs his hand through his hair, clearly agitated.

"My father lost all his money in a pyramid scheme. At the same time, I've been downsizing my company and moving here. I also determined I was going to buy out his shares of the company, so he had zero say in anything I did in the future. He objected to the idea of moving the offices here, so I cut him off." He runs his hand through his hair again and now I'm worried.

"He had someone take pictures of us on the island. Pictures that show us in compromising positions." His face is so pained, and I want to comfort him, but I'm also trying to make sense of what he just told me.

"He then threatened me with them."

"What the fuck?" Pen's voice rings out.

"It gets worse." He looks over at Pen apologetically.

"When I ignored his threats, he turned to more questionable methods. He buddied up to an employee in our finance department and had him doctor some tax forms. He was going to turn me and the company in for tax fraud, but he didn't bank on the employee coming forward and telling us.

"I sent him the buyout contract a while ago and hadn't heard anything, so I thought I was finally home free."

My heart sinks in my gut.

"He sent the photos out almost half an hour ago to gossip rags and online magazines."

He drops his head into his hands completely miserable.

"How bad are these pictures?" Bea asks, jumping right into mama bear mode.

"Very bad. I'm not worried about the impact on me but I'm very worried about how this will affect you." He looks at me with so much pain in his eyes.

"What do you mean? Affect me how?" I'm so confused.

He tilts his head in question. "These pictures, if seen by your administrators or parents will create problems for you. I would be shocked, if these come to light, that you wouldn't be fired."

The girl's heads ping pong back to mine and it's then I realize he doesn't know. So much has happened over the last few weeks, but it all interrupted a very important detail.

"I'm not teaching any more Pierce."

"What?" He looks alarmed now and I'm seriously starting to worry about his health.

"I didn't go back. God, we have so much to talk about. I'm sorry for that," I offer. I am sorry, because we could have had this conversation ten times over, but I was too lost in my grief.

"Okay, well that alleviates the biggest issue I suppose. But the pictures will still be out there. Sydney is doing everything in her power to get them pulled, but once they're out there they'll always be on the internet."

"Can I see them?"

"Of course." He scrambles over to me pulling out his phone. He opens up an email and lets me read the entire thing along with the attached pictures.

I'll be honest, my mind might not be in a very healthy place right now but all I can think about is how good we look together. Sure, there are some that show a lot, but everything is blurred so it's not like you can see my boobs or anything.

And it's not like I have a career to ruin now anyways.

"May we?" Pen asks Pierce.

He nods but doesn't move his eyes from me. I hand the phone to the girls, and they all go through them. Pen's got a smirk on her face, Larkin is blushing a little and Bea's the only with a little concern on her face.

"How can this affect Jane in the future? If she creates a non-profit, or gets another job?" Bea asks.

All logical questions, so I'm thankful at least one of us is thinking clearly.

"I'll be putting out a statement condemning the photos and I'll do my best to protect Jane in the process. I'll pull the attention to me and off of Jane and hopefully that will be enough. I'm also in the process of forcing some well-earned consequences on my father. If things go to plan, it'll come to light what my father has done, and it will lessen the legitimacy of the photos."

He makes eye contact with me and I see pride in his gaze. He's proud of my decision to leave teaching. And Bea mentioning a non-profit lets him know the direction I'm looking to go.

If I can ever get out of this haze of grief.

"So … should I be worried?" I ask Pierce.

"I … I thought this would play out differently," he admits.

"So did I," I say offhanded.

"What did you think I was coming over to talk about?"

I'm suddenly very embarrassed that I assumed Pierce would leave me when all he's done is shown me he won't.

Sometimes just being present is enough to show a person you care about the most that you aren't leaving them. And I was choosing not to see that until now.

"I thought you were coming over to tell me you were done with me," I confess.

"Love—"

"We're going to head out. Call us if you need anything," Pen says in an exaggerated whisper before winking and dragging the girls behind her.

I push down the chuckle threatening to break free.

Now is the time to embrace Pierce, embrace our very new relationship and let him be here for me.

"Are you busy the rest of the day?" I ask.

"I'm all yours," he offers immediately.

"I want to tell you about how I've been feeling, but I think it's going to drain me. Care to move this to the bedroom?"

He doesn't answer, just gets up from his chair and sweeps me into his arms, blanket and all. I snuggle into his chest, comforted by his familiar scent and ready to stop hiding from the world and the man who means more to me than I ever thought he would.

Chapter 36

Pierce

S tripping out of my button-down and slacks takes me all of three minutes, and then I'm sliding into bed next to Jane. She rolls over, putting her head on my chest as I wrap my arm around her, pulling her close.

I wait for Jane to talk first because I know if I do, I'll end up telling her how in love with her I already am and I'm not sure she's ready to hear that.

"This is hard," she whispers.

"When my mother died the only thing I remember is not really eating for a week. The rest of it is kind of a blur. I remember how I felt, but I don't remember what I did for a good chunk of time after she passed."

"Do you feel like you forgot her? I mean silly question because you started an entire foundation for her, but—"

"I've never forgotten her. Details get fuzzy, but I remember very specific things, events, if you will. Things that were quintessentially my mother," I tell her.

She nods against my chest, and I give her the time to absorb what I've told her. Grief is different for everyone. And lord knows I didn't handle mine the best way, but I was also in college and didn't know you could ask for help for this type of thing. I know Jane has a lot more resources available to her as well as friends who will be there every step of the way.

And me. I'm not going anywhere.

"I'm sorry I pushed you away. I have a bad habit of that don't I?" She asks the question in a such a small voice it breaks my heart.

"I understand what you're feeling better than most, and I know sometimes it's just easier to lock yourself away rather than face it head on."

"I just thought if I didn't face it, it wouldn't be true. I could just pretend it never happened. Which is so irrational, of course it happened and hiding from this ... this pain is only going to make it worse."

"No one is faulting you for taking time to yourself. Were the girls and I worried? Yes, but that's just because we care so much about you and want to make this easier on you."

"You just have to live through this huh? Take in everything you're feeling and learn to cope with it."

"Basically. It's not easy and it never quite feels like you're done grieving, but the pain from it? The pain lessens. It gets easier to talk about, and soon you're remembering good times with them and focusing less on the fact their gone." I don't know if this actually helps her, but I'm not going to sugar coat how hard this time in her life will be.

"Can we talk about something else?"

"Anything."

"Why did you keep this stuff with your father from me?"

"Because it wasn't something I wanted you to worry about. I was trying to protect you from it all, and I failed miserably at that. I am truly sorry the photos released. Sydney and my lawyer's will get them taken down, but once they're out there they'll never truly go away."

"Okay," she says chewing on her lip in thought.

"So, tell me about the decision to stop teaching," I offer as a reprieve.

"The island made me do a lot of thinking, face a lot of things about myself I wasn't particularly happy with. I've always picked the easy option. My career was safe, I picked safe boyfriends, and I wasn't really happy with any of it. I was happier doing all sorts of crazy things with you on the island than I have been in the last five years of my life.

"When you showed me the Oceanview Academy it sparked something for me. Teaching is great, but what if I could do more? What if I could help more kids in a more immediate sense. Everything your mother wanted and everything you've done inspired me to take a closer look at what goals I had for my life."

"That's amazing," I say in awe. If there is anyone on this Earth who could make a substantial impact, it's Jane. It's why I started the Hatley Foundation for her. We have been on the same page this entire time; we just haven't had time to actually talk to each other about.

I also know now is not the right time to lay all of the things I've been doing behind the scenes on her. She's just now coming out of her fog of grief, but she still has a lot to work through.

"And then everything happened with my mom, and I just feel stuck. Maybe I should just go back to teaching because it's a stable option."

I run my hand along her back. "Are you financially able to not go back? Even if you don't have all the answers right now, are you able to just sit on it for a few weeks?" I don't want to give all my plans away, but I sure as hell can move her into the lake house if she isn't able to just take the time to work through everything that just happened.

"Oh yeah, I mean I don't have money like you do." She chuckles. "But I have enough to get me by for a couple of months."

"You know all you have to do is ask, and I'll help in any way I can. I seem to have an abundance of money floating around," I say trying to lighten to the mood.

She smacks my chest as her chest shakes with silent laughter.

"Can I ask you something personal?"

"You can ask me anything you want," I offer. I'll tell her anything she wants to know. Nothing is off-limits.

"How do you see your future?"

Shit, I have to be careful about this one. I can't specifically tell her I see us living in a farmhouse I'm renovating specifically for her with plans to have a huge community garden to run our foundation out of.

"I see you in my future," I say generically. I do see her in my future, but I see her as my whole future. I just don't want to put that pressure on her right now.

"Do you ..." She hesitates. "Do you want kids?"

"Are you worried I don't?" I'm not side stepping the question, I just didn't even realize this was a worry she had about us.

"A little. You're forty-two so I don't know if kids are even on your radar."

"Do you want kids?" I counter instead of answering.

"Pierce." She looks up at me from my chest. "Just answer the question."

I can see the anxiety swirling around in her eyes and I definitely don't want to see that.

"I want kids with you. If you would have asked me six months ago if that was where I saw my life going, I would have laughed. Mainly because I had no one in my life I wanted to take that step with. And then you blew into my life and changed everything." It's as close as I can come to telling her about everything I've planned for us. But I don't want to overwhelm her now that she's started talking to me again.

"You do?"

"I want everything with you, love. But we don't have to worry about any of it right now. Right now, is a time to heal and we'll worry about everything else later. I'm not going anywhere."

"Promise?"

"You couldn't get rid of me if you tried, Jane. I mean, I haven't been sleeping on your couch for my own health," I joke.

Her giggle frees my soul. And I just know, we'll be okay. No matter how long it takes, no matter what it takes to get there. We'll be okay because we have a bond that is indescribably.

"You can sleep in here from now on, so your old back doesn't hurt," she says through her giggle.

"Ouch!" I throw a hand up in mock horror.

"You are quite spry for such an age so I guess I shouldn't give you too much shit."

"I'll give you spry." I tickle her side as she falls into a fit of giggles. And the sound is so fucking priceless to hear.

"Thank you for everything, Pierce," she says after I stop tickling her. As much as I want to push the boundaries further, I'm not jumping into sex until she tells me she's one hundred percent ready.

"Never thank me for being here, love. I couldn't have stayed away for anything."

She falls asleep shortly after. It's been quite the day, so I'm not shocked, but I stay up and think about what she asked me.

I do want everything with this woman.

And as soon as she's ready I'll have a ring on her finger, a foundation and job she loves, and possibly even a baby in her belly.

I never knew I could be this happy, but with Jane all things are possible.

Waking up with Jane in my arms feels like coming home. I knew how much I missed her, and I knew it would take time, but damn do I feel like a whole new man after a night with her in my arms.

She fell asleep early yesterday, but I just held her and thought about our future until it was closer to my usual bedtime. I knew she needed the sleep so shirking any responsibilities to ensure she got the rest was a no brainer.

I know I need to deal with some things today, but I don't want to leave the comfort of this bed.

Sadly, my phone makes the decision for me.

If Sydney is calling me right now, it's for a good reason. I let her know I wasn't working at all yesterday and as long as I could manage today. So, if she's calling me, I can no longer ignore my responsibilities.

I answer the phone on a whisper, hoping to let Jane sleep a little longer before I have to get up.

"Sydney."

"I know, I'm sorry. I wouldn't have called you if it wasn't necessary. I have a major update about your father."

I take a peek at Jane and see she's still sleeping. "Go on."

"He's been under investigation, along with his business partner, if you want to call him that. The SEC has enough on them both to arrest them and with this added blackmail he should be going away for a long time. The SEC have been in discussion with our lawyers and think it would be beneficial to get him into the office. Apparently, he's in Austin if his travel patterns are anything to go by."

"Well that's a turn of events. He's probably in Austin to see if there is any last chance to wring some cash from me. Can you set up an appointment with him? And let the authorities know. I'd like to have a little time to talk to him before they take him away."

I'm not even sad about this turn of events. He made his bed, now he has to lie in it.

I remember Jane and I talking on the island about how a forty-two-year-old still wants approval from his father, and now I can't fathom why I ever wanted it from him. He was never going to give it to me, and he was just using me and my company for my hard earned money. I was his gravy boat and now everything is falling apart for him.

He deserves it all after the way he treated my mother. And now I get to put the final nail in his bullshit.

"Done. I'll text you the time when I have one."

"Thanks, Sydney." I hang up and think about how much has changed in the last six months and how much happier I am because of it.

"Who was that?" Jane's sleep roughen voice hits me straight in the dick, but I have other things to focus on today.

"My assistant. Today's the day I finally get one over on dear old dad."

"What?" She looks alarmed, so I spend the next fifteen minutes breaking down everything that's happened with him.

"Can I come with you?"

"Why would you want to come with me?" I ask.

"Because you've been here to support be every step of the way even when I pushed you away, and I want to do the same for you."

Fuck, she has my heart and soul and doesn't even realize it.

"You can come if you want to, but I doubt it's going to be anyone's definition of a good time."

"I don't care. He's caused you a lot of trouble and you shouldn't have to go at that alone." She sits up and jumps out of bed like she hasn't just spent the last three weeks in misery because of her grief.

"Okay." I agree. I won't tell her no, especially if it's getting her out of her apartment and feeling some semblance of normalcy. It also feels fucking phenomenal to have someone on my side unconditionally. I've never had this before, and now I can't imagine my life without it.

"You should text the girls and let them know you won't be here, otherwise they'll show up!" I yell through the bathroom door as I walk to the living room and grab the spare suit I left here.

"Good call!" she yells back.

Twenty minutes later, we're in my car and headed to the office.

"I'm excited to see your new office," Jane says practically vibrating from excitement.

She's like a whole new woman today and I know she still has a lot to work through, but this is a huge step in the right direction.

She's also not helping my focus with the skintight pencil skirt she decided to put on. She said she wanted to represent me well and all I could think about was shoving it up her thighs and showing her how much appreciation I have for her.

But, it's not meant to be today because I have shit to take care of.

Sydney texted me a time and told me I have about thirty minutes before authorities show up and for the first time in my life, I feel no nerves, no hesitation about meeting my father head on. And it's all because of the incredible woman next to me.

We pull up to the modest office building and Jane immediately gasps.

"Holy hell, Pierce. You said you were downsizing!"

"This is downsizing." I laugh. The building is nice, all gorgeous stonework and five stories tall but it's not even half the size of our last headquarters.

"Can I ask you something random?" Jane asks.

"Always."

"What happened to all the people who no longer have a job because you downsized?" My Jane has a heart of gold.

"Many were offered a job at properties, if applicable. Some I gave excellent references for to comparable jobs they were eager to get. And some have moved onto other projects within the company." I don't tell her that a good number have moved to my foundation sector, both with The Hatley Foundation and The Eloise Ford Foundation. I'm hoping, with Jane's help, to grow this aspect of my life tenfold.

"That's good," she mumbles.

"I promise no one was left stranded, I made sure of it. Well, Sydney made sure of it," I concede.

"You owe that woman a raise." She huffs out a laugh.

"Several, actually. It's on my to-do list." I chuckle. "Come on, we don't have too much time before my father shows up."

I get out of the car and help Jane out before entering the building. It's like I'm seeing it with fresh eyes, Jane's eyes, and I'm finally proud of what we're accomplishing here.

Ten minutes later, Sydney is walking my father into my office.

"This place is ghastly," he says the minute he steps through the door. Sydney rolls her eyes before she exits, and I have to hold back my laugh.

"Thank you, now do you want to talk about why you're in Austin?"

"I don't have to answer to you. If I want to take a trip out here, I'll do so."

"It wouldn't be to watch the aftermath of the pictures you released, was it?" No more beating around the bush.

He looks around, slightly uncomfortable and finally spots Jane sitting on the sofa at the other end of my office.

"What's she doing here?" He sneers.

"She was in the pictures so it's only right she's here to make sure things are taken care of appropriately," I tell him smoothly.

"Your whore is not welcome here. And it doesn't matter because the pictures were already released."

"Were they?" I tilt my head.

Here's the best part. Sydney is a fucking rock star, and with the help of our lawyers and a hefty sum of money, no one actually posted the pictures. It seems my father is fairly inept at making sure scandalous pictures are going to the appropriate people. He sent the pictures to people who didn't have control over what makes publication, so there was a process to getting them approved. Giving us much needed time to clean up my father's mess. So, after negotiating and getting all copies back, and paying exorbitant fees, all well worth it, the pictures are no longer a threat.

Sydney really outdid herself with that one and has earned an extended vacation when all this shit with my father is over, all on my dime.

My father's face turns redder than I've ever seen before.

"You called this meeting. Was it just to tell me you beat me?" He blusters.

"Oh, no. I couldn't care less about beating you. I wanted to finally tell you how I really feel about you.

"See, when I was younger, after mother died, I wanted to make you proud of me. Get you to see me as a successful man. As the years went on, it became increasingly obvious that you really didn't care about me or my accomplishments. But I never gave up that need to prove my worth to you. Until I met Jane."

"You daft, piece of—"

"I'm talking now, thank you. Jane showed me I had plenty to be proud of, but more than that, she showed me that doing more just to try and garner your approval wasn't what I actually wanted to do anymore.

"So, I'm not. As you've already learned. I'm downsizing, working on some other things and—" A knock at the door interrupts me.

"Ah, perfect timing," I say as Sydney opens the door and lets the authorities file in.

"What is the meaning of this!" My father turns even redder—if that's even possible.

"And not buying you out. Because you no longer have steaks in any company." I smile.

The police read him his rights, he fights and cusses the entire time. Jane and I look on as it takes them several minutes to actually get him out of my office. When he's finally gone, I turn to the love of my life.

"Well, that was fun."

"How the hell is he your father? You two are nothing alike," she says in confusion.

Her statement is something I didn't know I needed to hear. I needed to know I was nothing like him, that I was better even if just little bit.

"Thank you," I tell her quietly, emotion clogging up my voice. I'm not emotional because of my father, I'm emotional because my woman was here to support me in this very crucial step in my life.

"I need to talk to Sydney for a minute and then we can head out," I tell Jane as Sydney walks back into my office.

Jane nods her head in agreement as I turn to face Sydney.

"You've been busy recently." I smirk.

"Oh, you know, all in a week's work." She's brushing it off, and for once I'm not going to let her.

"You saved a whole lot more than a buyout contract this week, and I thank you for that." She blushes at the praise.

The next few minutes are spent telling Sydney to plan an all-expenses paid vacation to anywhere she wants for a few weeks. When the disbelief wears off, she heads out to start making her plans.

"You ready to head back, love?" I turn to Jane.

"Absolutely. I think I want to cook for you tonight," she muses as she meets me by the door.

We're going to be just fine; I know that with every beat of my heart.

Chapter 37

Jane

Three weeks later

It's been one hell of a few weeks. After my heart-to-heart with Pierce and our subsequent trip to his office to straighten things out with his father, things for me have been going better.

I found a grief counselor that has helped tremendously, as well as an individual therapist to help me not only with the grief but coming to terms with losing my family. It's been a hard journey, and I'm nowhere near done, but I'm doing better.

Today, I'm doing something I haven't done in almost two months and its way past time.

Today, is brunch with the girls. And God, how I've missed it.

I'm the first to show up and I make sure to order everyone's favorite drinks, and just a regular juice for Bea. It's amazing how fast her pregnancy has gone, and I feel a little sad I've missed out on a good chunk of it. But in the words of my therapist, *We can't change the past; we can only be aware of our present and future. How we want those to transpire are entirely up to me.*

I've been slowly adding more classes to my Phoenix House course load, so I've been seeing Pen and Bea more than I had been. But I've still missed out on a lot. So today marks the day where I take my present and future by the horns and stop missing out on the things I love.

The girls show up one by one, all giving me a bug hug welcoming me back to brunch. I know for a fact they didn't do brunch without me, but I'm glad we're back to our normal and I'm not holding anyone back anymore.

"I've missed this!" I say as soon as we're all seated.

"Us too, girl, but we know a lot has happened and we're not upset we had to miss a couple brunches," Bea says.

"Well, I'm officially back and feeling mostly normal," I tell them as I take a sip of my mimosa.

"How's that grief counselor working out?" Larkin asks. She gave me the recommendation, and I jumped on it.

"She's so good. She's really making me think of things differently. I had a lot of guilt for not being closer to my parents, but she's made me see it's not so one sided like that. And the grief just amplified all these feelings I've had. Do you use her at the office?" Larkin's a social worker so I'm not shocked she's worked with all sorts of counselors.

"I've only recently started using her, but Theo's used her for years. She's helped a lot of kids we've had in the system so I figured it wouldn't hurt to throw her name your way."

"It's definitely helped. So, tell me what's new with you guys," I say. I don't want to focus on me today. I want to focus on having brunch with my best friends like I usually do.

Bea updates us on her pregnancy, and we start planning her baby shower. Larkin tells us all about a new card game her son, Gavin, is obsessed with, and I make a mental note to go over to their place and play some games with him. And Pen tells us all about this new romance book her and Andy are buddy reading. I take that to mean they are reading it together and then reenacting the sex scenes in their own bedroom, but I keep that to myself.

"So how are you and Pierce?" Pen asks with a raised eyebrow.

I let out a happy sigh. "So good. He's had some downsizing pains in his company, but everything seems to be doing better now."

"But how are you two together?" Larkin asks.

"We're actually really good. Taking things slow." Although at this point, I think he could breathe my way, and I'd want to jump him. I'm all for letting me heal and figure things out, but holy hell I'm horny as hell at right now.

"That's good. You've had a lot of change recently so I'm glad he's not pushing you too fast," Bea observes.

"Definitely." I hide my sexual frustration behind my mimosa as I take another sip.

"Any progress on the career change?" Pen asks.

I let out a huge sigh. "Kind of? Not really? I don't honestly know. I just started talking to my therapist about this and I'm not sure I'm any closer to a definitive direction."

"What are you leaning toward?" Bea asks.

"I want to do something with food. I have that food science degree just sitting there, and I've always loved the thought of using it more for feeding the hungry. Like more efficient ways to distribute food, or just working with a non-profit to help decrease the number of hungry kids in the area. Pierce had a community garden on the other side of the island that he showed me while we were there and that could be an option too," I ramble.

The three of them exchange looks.

"What?" I ask.

"Nothing, it sounds like a great idea! If we can help, you know we will," Larkin says with a little too much pep.

I know it's not that they think I can't do this, because we've never been the friend group who thinks anything is impossible, so it has to be that they know something I don't.

I stare at my friend a moment longer seeing if any of them will crack, but of course they don't.

"Alright keep your secrets," I mutter.

We spend the rest of brunch talking about everything and nothing. I think we're all just happy to be back at our usual brunch again.

I stopped at the store on my way home to pick up some ingredients for dinner. I've been cooking for Pierce and me more and more lately, and I think I want tonight to be extra special.

Because I'm hoping to finally lure him into getting me off in any way shape or form.

I seriously love him for not pushing me these last few weeks because I don't think I was in a very great head space for anything sexual. But now, I feel like if I don't get his hands on me I will little shrivel up on a ball and cry.

Walking into my apartment, I stop short when I see Pierce standing in my tiny dining room setting down a vase of tulips.

"Hi."

"Hi love. You're home early," he says as puts something in his pocket as he walks toward me and presses a kiss to my cheek.

"Those are beautiful. What's the occasion?" I ask wondering if I missed something. I wouldn't be shocked honestly; it's been hard to keep track of the days recently and I'm only now getting back on a normal schedule.

"Just wanted to get you some flowers."

Oh, my heart.

"Well, that's very sweet of you. I was going to make you dinner tonight."

"Sounds wonderful. I want to show you something today, do you think it'll last in the car for a little bit?"

My brows furrow and I tilt my head in confusion.

"You want to bring the ingredients with us to this place you want to show me?" Maybe he just wants to go to his lake house. I mean who could blame him. He's been practically living with me in my tiny apartment while his equally gorgeous and huge place sits empty.

He runs his hand through his hair tell me he's a little flustered.

Interesting.

"I want to take you somewhere, and there is a kitchen there. I was hoping we would spend the evening there." He looks so hopeful. There's no way I'm telling him no, not after all he's done for me and how patient he's been with me.

"Yeah, not a problem." I move to the kitchen and unpack the cold things before grabbing an old lunch bag and an ice pack from the freezer.

Pierce is acting weird, but maybe it has something to do with what he wants to show me. Honestly, it only makes me more curious, so I'll go along with just about everything right now.

I follow him out the to his car and we drive in silence for a couple minutes.

"So where are we headed to?" I ask.

"It's a surprise," he says quickly.

Okay, then.

"Sorry. I'm ... I'm nervous," he admits.

"Why would you of all people be nervous?"

"Because I want you to love this surprise, and I'm suddenly worried you'll hate it."

I reach over and grab his hand. This sweet generous man is worried I won't like something he's done?

"Impossible." I lean into his shoulder.

The rest of the drive is spent talking about our day and things that are coming up in the next couple of weeks.

We're on the road for just over a half an hour and I'm getting really antsy about this surprise. We're driving in open farmland now and I'm so confused what this surprise could be.

When he turns onto a fresh paved driveway that leads to a beautiful classic farmhouse.

I don't even have words the place is so gorgeous. When he pulls up the front, I turn to look at him.

"What is this place?"

"Come inside with me and I'll tell you." He gets out of the car and comes around to my side. I let him lead me to the front, but I'm genuinely confused why he brought me out here.

He pulls out a set of keys and unlocks the front door, stepping aside so I can enter first.

What I see when I step in has my breathing picking up and my heart thumping painfully in my chest.

If I were to have free reign on a house, this is exactly what I would want it to look like. It's modern but has a very lived in feel. There are bright colors everywhere in accents around the open living space. I feel Peirce's hand on my back, and I wipe around to face him.

"What is this place?" I ask again.

"This is yours … if you want it."

Mine?

"I … I don't understand."

"This has been a labor of love involving a lot of people. When your mother passed away, I needed to do something. I needed to help you in some way and the only way I knew how was to make your dreams a reality."

"How did you even know I'd like something like this?"

"As I said, a labor of love. The girls and Sydney are responsible for all for the decorating. It took longer than I wanted to get everything perfect, but I think it turned out well."

"Turned out well? Are you fucking kidding me?" My voice is reaching hysterical levels.

"You don't like it." His entire demeanor shrinks.

"I absolutely *love* it, Pierce. This is … I'm at a loss for words. And the girls knew about it this whole time?"

"They did, would you like to look around?"

"I would love to!" I'm bouncing on the balls of my feet now. I'm sure what he's done will hit me some time soon, but right now I want to go explore.

We walk around the first floor, checking out the pristine chef's kitchen, complete with dark emerald, green cabinets and a butcher block countertop. I already can't wait to make a meal in here. The dining room is big enough to fit about twenty people, but what stops me in my tracks are the giant doors leading out to the wrap around porch, and what's just beyond said porch.

"Is that?"

"It's the start of a community garden. When we were at Oceanview, you lit up talking about the community garden, and I knew if I found a place with enough space, I would make it happen. It's not very full right now because we just planted everything about a week ago, but it'll fill in."

I spin around to face him. "Where's the bedroom?"

"What?"

"Where's the bedroom, Pierce?"

"You don't want to go see the garden?"

"I want you to show me where the bedroom is so I can show you my appreciation."

"Jane, love, that's not why I did all of this."

"I know. But the thing is, I want it. So badly, and you just showed me this gorgeous house which I absolutely love but I need you to take me to bed. Now."

I don't think I've ever been so direct in my life, and it feels so *good*.

Something clicks in Pierce's mind because his entire disposition changes. He steps up to me and bends down, wrapping his hands around my thighs and picking me up in a matter of seconds.

I squeak and clutch his shoulders hard as he makes his way up the stairs.

I don't notice anything on the way to the bedroom, I'm too busy trailing kisses down his neck, across his jaw and the stubble he's let grow out before moving over to his sexy mouth.

"I like the scruff. I meant to tell you that earlier," I whisper against his lips.

"Then I'll keep the scruff."

He kicks open a door and unceremoniously drops me on a plush bed.

"Strip." His harsh tone leaves no room for negotiations, and I wouldn't argue if he begged me to. I'm freaking *ecstatic.*

I not so sexily yank my jeans and panties down over my butt and legs before finally being free of them, tossing them to the side. I move to my shirt, hastily ripping it over my head and doing the same with my bralette.

"You're so fucking perfect, Jane." The reverence in his voice sends shivers down my spine.

"Take your clothes off, Pierce," I whisper.

The corner of his lip lifts up in a sly smirk and I know I'm getting exactly what I want today.

The master in the bedroom is back.

"It's like you're begging for punishment," he says quietly.

"I can beg if you'd like," I offer with a smirk of my own.

"You miss this, love?"

"God yes!" My legs rub together to try and get some friction. I'm already so wet and turned on it's not going to take much.

He leisurely unbuttons his shirt, taking his sweet time taking off this shirt. Pulling the tails out of his slacks, he finally tosses it onto a chair in the corner.

When he kneels in front of the bed and drags me to the edge, I swear the thought of what he's about to do almost makes me come.

His hands slide up the inside of my thighs and I don't hesitate to fully open to him.

"Eager, are we?" He murmurs from his place in between my legs.

"Argh just hurry up and get me off! I can't take it anymore!" I snap.

Pierce's hands freeze on their descent, and I know I messed up. In the back of my mind, some distant hussy forgotten on the island is cheering about what's coming my way. But my immediate sense is that I'm about to pay for my impatience and I'm not sure if I'm really ready.

"Who does your pleasure belong to?" His deep voice reaches my ears.

"You."

"Do you trust me to know what you need and give it to you?"

"Yes." My voice trembles.

"Just remember that when you're wrung out and dripping and needy for my cock to stretch you."

"Oh my God."

"Pierce, not God. You come when I say you come, is that clear?""Yes." It physically hurts me to say yes because I need to come so bad. But I trust Pierce. He has yet to steer me wrong in the bedroom so I'm not questioning anything.

His hands continue their path up my splayed legs, and it sends a shockwave through my body.

"Oh, you are in trouble, love. Already so fucking wet for me and we haven't even started." His big hand spans across the bend in my hip as his thumb grazes my clit and I arch off the bed with how good it feels.

I reach down with one hand and fist his hair when his hand suddenly leaves me.

"No!" I cry out.

"Grip the sheets or put your hands above your head. If you touch my hair again, I will tie you up, is that clear?"

"Yes," I moan out as I throw my arms above my head and grips my hands together. This was not what I was expecting today. And outside of being extremely sexually frustrated, I'm so damn happy that the Pierce I met on the island is back.

I've missed this, missed him.

I don't miss the chuckle just before he returns his hand, making lazy circles around my clit knowing it's not enough to make me come.

He picks up the pace a little before I feel his lips drag across my other thigh. It takes everything in me not to plead with him to move where I really need him.

I don't realize my hips are moving until I feel him bite down on my thigh and give my pussy a little smack.

"Holy shit!" I cry out as my orgasm comes closer to the surface.

"I promise I will get you there, love. But you're going to have breathe through this, okay? If it really gets to be too much just tell me to stop." His tone changes to concern in the blink of an eye.

"I'm okay. I'm sorry. It's just been so long and I'm literally dying." My dramatics have him chuckling again, but he moves his thumb back to where I need him.

"I know, love. But I want you to understand why I'm doing this."

I frantically nod my head.

"Never push me away again." The vulnerability in his voice hits me straight in the chest.

"I won't be able to take it if you push me away again. I need you to let me in, come to me when you have a bad day. When the grief gets to be too much, let me take care of you, help you every single day. If you have a work problem, unload it on me. If I can't help, I'll find someone who will. But I can't manage if you push me away again," he whispers.

Tears trail down the sides of my face, and I know with every beat of my heart, this man was made for me.

"Never again." I sniffle.

He surges up and kisses me with everything he has.

"I'm going to punish you now, because I need you to know what happens if you ever withdraw from me again," he says in his strong, clear voice. He looks down at me, both with pain and lust in his eyes.

"Never again," I whisper once more.

He holds my gaze for a second before he starts kissing his way down my body. Wasting no time this round, he licks and sucks my clit with aggression until I'm bowing off the bed and a hairsbreadth away from coming.

Then his touch leaves me.

I feel empty and painfully close to the edge of oblivion that it's a struggle to not scream or yank him close to me again.

It takes a couple minutes for me to stop losing my mind; to stop thrashing and cursing Pierce's name before I settle back onto the bed.

During my struggle, Pierce doesn't utter a word.

It isn't until my wrung-out body is slack against the bed that he moves back between my legs and repeats his ministrations. This time, he traces his tongue over every inch of me except where I really need him.

He repeats this over and over again, bringing me to the edge just to back off and let it simmer away.

I'm losing my damn mind, and I'm a second away from screaming at him when he stands up and starts taking off the slacks, I didn't realize he still had on.

"How are you doing, love?" he asks with a grin on his face.

Chapter 38

Pierce

S he looks up at me like she's very close to the edge of murder, and if I wasn't so close to blowing, I'd probably do one more round of edging.

As it is, I don't think I could hold off for anything in the world.

I don't know what possessed me to punish her, especially in such a cruel way, but I needed her to know I'm with her no matter what. I needed her to know that the last few weeks have damn near killed me and I won't make it out alive if she does it again.

But now, if I don't get inside of her in the next five seconds I might combust.

My pants come off in a matter of moments and I immediately shove my hands under her arms and push her up the bed to make more room for me. My cock naturally nudges at her clit before notching at her opening as I do and it fucking hurts with how much I need her right now.

"Are we still good to go bare? I know we discussed it at the lake house, but I want to make sure we're still on the same page." She's thrashing around, arching her hips up to get me closer and her eyes pop open when she hears me.

"Yes! Same page, absolutely same page," she pants.

In my all my years, I have never taken a woman bare except that time with her at the lake house and I can't imagine taking her another way right now. But if she changed her mind, I would absolutely be okay with it.

Because this is Jane. The love of my life and the woman I'd marry tomorrow if she'd let me, and I'll do anything she asks of me. A need surges up in me, a need to not only fuck her senseless, but convince her to ditch the birth control sooner rather than later.

I want everything with this woman.

"Are you absolutely sure?" I check one more time.

"Oh, fuck," she whispers as I drag my tip up to her clit. "Yes please. Absolutely sure. Please Pierce!" She wraps her legs around my hips and digs her heels into my ass, urging me forward.

I listen to my love and thrust forward with one long stroke until I'm into the hilt.

I press my forehead into hers, shoving one hand under her ass to lift her up a little, and the other wraps around her shoulder, holding her to me.

I want to spill my soul to her. Tell her I love her, and I want to spend every second trying to make her the happiest woman in the world and promise her the life she's always dreamed of.

But I refuse to do so in the heat of the moment. I don't want her to think I'm only saying these because we're both horny as hell.

Nothing could be further from the truth.

Her eyes sparkle with moisture and I press a kiss to the corners of them before pulling my hips back.

Jesus fuck she feels like heaven and hell. Scorching heat and the wetness are about to pull me under along before I want it too.

"You feel so damn good," I grit out.

A happy sigh reaches my ears before her hips arch up off the bed causing me sink into her again.

"I missed this so much," she says.

I smile down at her as I set a pace sure to have us both reaching our orgasms in a matter of minutes.

My body is coiled so tight right now, I don't think I can talk anymore without coming at this point.

Tilting her hips a little more, I know I've hit her G-spot when she cries out and clutches my shoulders so hard her nails break through the skin.

But I love the pain, it adds to the pleasure skyrocketing through my body.

I trust into her three more times before she explodes with an orgasm that pulls me under. My body curls around hers, unloading weeks up of frustration and love into her body.

We don't move for a long moment, both of us trying to catch our breaths after the single best sexual experience in my life.

I finally release her from my hold, leaning back on my knees and watch as I pull out of her.

My cum leaks out of her so I use my thumb to push it back in. The primal feeling inside of me that I could get her pregnant overrides any sense of logic.

"You should get your birth control out," I say without thinking.

"Mmmm, okay," Jane mutters happily.

When I look up in shock, I see she's already dozing off.

She probably didn't hear me.

I quietly step off the bed and head to the bathroom for a warm washrag to clean her up.

After I clean her up, I move her gently under the covers. Standing over her for a few minutes, I take in the fact that she's really here, in the house I bought for her, and this sense of *rightness* washes over me.

This is the woman I was always meant to be with. I stare down at her sleeping form and am in awe of this woman. She's turned my life upside down in the best possible way.

And now I need to show her how much she means to me—show her she's it for me.

I walk to the closet, that's conveniently already stocked with clothes for both of us and throw on a pair of joggers and a T-shirt before heading downstairs to the office.

I may have remodeled this for Jane, but it still has everything I need to work from home.

I grab the stationary I used to write Jane the letters while we were separated after our time one the island and sit down to spill my heart and soul to her.

Jane, my love-
I'll never be able to find the right words to tell you how I feel about you, but
I'm going to try.
The first time I saw you, I knew I had to have you. When I took you to
lunch at the fancy restaurant and you were so uncomfortable in the setting,
I knew you were different.
When I persuaded you to stay an extra week on the island, I wanted to find
a way to keep you.
So, I did.
And it's quite possibly the best decision I've ever made in my life.
We've been through a lot in our short time together, but I think that just
means we can handle anything that comes our way.

I wanted this farmhouse to be yours even if you didn't want me, but I don't think I can stand by that anymore. I promise, every single day, to give you reasons to let me stay in your orbit. I promise to be the best version of myself, to help you reach your dreams and build a life together I know we'll both be proud of.

I love you. More than I ever thought I could love someone.

I want it all with you. Marriage, kids—however many you want—I don't care, I just want to do it with you.

You've made me realize I wasn't really living before you.

And now, I want to live all my days with you.

You make me a better man.

You make me want to do more in the world.

And you make me a fucking caveman in the bedroom.

I love you with every ounce of my being.

-Pierce

I don't second guess a thing, I just fold it up and put it in an envelope with her name on it. Then I head to the kitchen to put away the groceries we forgot about.

———— ◆ ————

Hours later, Jane slowly walks down the stairs.

She has a shy look on her face, and somehow it makes me love her all that much more.

"Morning, love, how did you sleep?" She's wearing nothing but the button-down shirt I had on earlier, and I'll be damned if my dick doesn't take notice.

"Really good. That mattress is the softest thing I've ever slept on, although I'm sorry I crashed."

"Don't apologize. You needed the sleep," I say.

She walks to me as I open my arms up for her. Wrapping her arounds around my back, she places her head on my chest and breaths me in.

"I have something I wanted to show you before we got a little ... sidetracked."

She giggles as she pulls back.

"Sidetracked is one word for it. Do I need to put on shoes?"

"You're perfect just as you are." I pull back and grab her hand, leading her to the patio doors.

We walk the path toward the gardens, and I can feel the excitement radiating off of Jane.

"This is just the start. I thought it might be nice to turn a lot of this farmland into a community garden and help feed people. Figure out the best way for distribution and try to reach more people than just the immediate area," I tell her as we make out way to the little seating area in the middle of the garden.

"How in the world did you do all of this so fast?" she asks in pure amazement as we sit down.

"I thought we got it done rather sluggishly, if I'm honest," I muse. I would have loved this done when we got back from Kansas but something things aren't within my power no matter how much money I have.

"You are insane sometimes, you know that?" She huffs out a laugh.

"I am starting to see that, yes." Laughter erupts out of both of us, and as it dies down, she rests her head on my shoulder.

"I made a new foundation branch in the company. Right now, it's just a blank slate but if you want it, it's yours."

"What?" She sits upright and stares at me.

"The Hatley Foundation. I set it up, well Sydney did a lot of it," I concede. "But it's all set up for meal distribution, funding school meal projects, anything you want it to do, we'll make it happen."

Tears trickle down her face, and I worry I overstepped, yet again.

"If you don't want to run it, that's fine. I'll still keep it in the company and appoint a director," I offer.

"I want to run it," she rushes out, and my heart feels about ten times lighter.

"Good, because I think you're the best person for the job." I tell her honestly. If she forced me to, I would find someone to run it, but it wouldn't be what was best for the foundation overall.

Her eyes search mine for a long second, and I'm not sure what she's looking for.

I've never been so content in my life, and I hope she sees that.

"I love you," she blurts out.

Her eyes widen in shock, but she doesn't take it back.

I can feel how wide my smile is because my cheeks start to hurt. I lean forward and cup her jaw in my hand.

"I love you. So fucking much." Pressing a kiss to her lips, I pull back and reach into my pocket.

"I've written you a few letters about my past, and now I wanted to write you one about my future," I say as I hand her the letter I wrote a few hours ago. I wasn't sure when I wanted to give it to her, but this just feels right.

Laying all my cards on the table feels *right*.

She stares at the envelope with a mix of trepidation and anticipation. Gingerly reaching out to grab it, she pulls out the letter and starts reading.

It's strange. I'm not even nervous for her to read it. I'm just ecstatic there don't seem to be anymore obstacles in the way of us being together.

The letter floats to the ground as Jane gets up and straddles my lap.

"You mean all of that?"

"Every single word. And I'll tell you every single day, show you every day if you don't believe me."

"Marry me." Her voice rings out strong and true.

"What?" I ask in disbelief.

"Marry me," she says simply. "Why should we wait if this is how we both feel? I mean what could possibly be harder to work through than the last few months of our lives? If my mother's death has taught me anything, it's to not waste time. To live my life the way I want to live it. And I want to live it with you. So, marry me."

Her wide smile matches mine as I grip her ass and stand with her still wrapped around my torso.

"How soon can we have the wedding?" I murmur as I nibble along her throat.

"I don't care. Is that a yes?"

"I should be mad you took my opportunity to propose away, but I'm just so fucking proud of you for going after what you want. It's a hell yes, and I'll go down to the courthouse tomorrow if that's what you want. Whatever you want, it's yours, love."

"I love you, Pierce." She sighs happily as I make my way back to our bedroom.

"Thank you for giving me a life I never thought I wanted. I love you."

An island vacation, a turbulent few months, and a woman who blew my world wide open shouldn't have resulted in the perfect love story. But here we are, walking up the stairs in our new home and creating the life we both always wanted.

Life couldn't possibly get any better.

Epilogue

*T*hree *months later*

The Northern Mariana Islands are just as beautiful as I remember them.

When I asked Pierce to marry me, I knew there was only one place for the ceremony. Did I expect a full-blown wedding to happen within three months? No, but I should have known considering the man who's my soon-to-be husband.

Husband.

Most would think going from meeting to married within eight months is crazy, but neither of us want to waste any more time. We've both been through so much this year, and if it's taught us anything, it's to never take life for granted.

So here we are, back where we met and getting ready to get married tomorrow.

We kept it an intimate affair, only having the girls and their husbands along with Sydney, Pierce's assistant, here for the wedding. Sydney and I have become fast friends since working on the foundation together, so although she's working at the moment, she won't be tomorrow.

I'm currently speed walking to the lobby hoping to catch Sydney because I'm freaking the fuck out.

I skid to a halt when I see Sydney behind the front desk talking to my fiancé. Her eyes meet mine and I jerk my head to the side telling her silently I need to talk to her.

I pivot on my heel and walk around the corner out of view waiting for her to come talk to me.

"What is going on? Are you having cold feet?" she asks in a whisper.

"No! God no! I need your help, and I don't want Pierce to know yet."

"If you get me fired, I'm going to be really pissed."

I roll my eyes. "He's never going to fire you."

"What do you need?" She ignores me.

"I need a ..." I lean closer to her. "I need a pregnancy test, but I have no idea where to find one on this tiny ass island, and I don't want anyone to know yet in case I'm wrong, and I'm freaking out a little bit, but I need your help!" I ramble.

"Holy shit!" She yells.

"Shh! Geez! What part of I don't want anyone to know missed your brain?"

"Sorry! I just wasn't expecting this at all. I can get you one, but I have to dodge Pierce in order to get it."

"Okay ... Okay, here's what we're going to do. I'll go distract him, you go get it and leave it somewhere ..." I spin around looking for something and find a potted plant close to us. "Here! Leave it in the pot, and I'll grab it on my way out."

She looks at me with awe in her eyes. "You really think you're pregnant?" she whispers.

"I'm not one hundred percent sure, but I have a hunch."

"Oh my god I'm so happy for you!" She squeals.

"Shh!"

"Sorry, sorry! I won't say a word." She mimes zipping her lips shut, and I have to laugh.

"Go so I can figure out if I need to freak out or not!"

She gives me a hug and pulls back. "I'm so happy for you both, regardless of the outcome of the test." And then she spins away from me and marches back into the lobby like the badass she is.

I casually walk up to Pierce and hook my arm into his.

"I thought you were trying to not work on this trip." I give him a hard time, but the amount he's accomplished in such a short amount of time is still mind boggling.

He presses a kiss to my hairline. "Miss me, love?"

"Always."

"I was just talking to Sydney making sure everything was set up the way we wanted. I know she has it handled. I just want everything to be perfect for you."

"I'm just happy to marry you, you know that." I peek around his shoulder and see Sydney walking back from the agreed upon pot.

"I know and I love you for it. Well, I'll be in the villa but take your time." I press up on my tiptoes to kiss him.

Walking as calmly as I can, I walk out of the lobby and grab the stack of four tests Sydney left me. I laugh out loud at the fact she knew one wouldn't be enough for me. Looking behind me to make sure I didn't alert Pierce; I find nothing so I run to the villa to prevent him seeing me before I can know for sure.

Inside the villa, I go to the bathroom and close the door behind me. My heart is pounding and I'm so nervous.

Pierce doesn't even know I'm off my birth control. I had my IUD taken out two months ago in hopes my hormones would level out by the wedding and increase our chances of getting pregnant quickly after the wedding. Jokes on me apparently.

I finally get the courage and go do my business, opening all the sticks up and dipping them.

I'm sitting on the edge of the tub with my timer set for three minutes. I don't hear Pierce come in until I his voice pulls me out of my daze.

"Love ..."

My timer goes off, and I swipe it away before looking at Pierce.

"I don't know for sure yet," my voice cracks.

"How is this even possible?" There's awe in his voice, but I can tell he doesn't want to get his hopes up yet.

"I wanted it to be a surprise for tonight. Tell you I was ready to start trying if you were. Everything I've read says it'll take you a little time after getting off of hormonal birth control to get pregnant. What they don't tell you is it's a freaking crap shoot and anything can happen."

The corner of his lip lifts up as he comes and sits next to me.

"When do we look?"

"Now. That was the timer for it. But I'm nervous."

"Do you want me to look?"

I look at him then, and see he'll do anything I want him to do. I also see sheer want in his eyes. He wants this, wants a baby and my heart is about to combust.

"Yes, please."

He grabs one of the digital tests off of the counter and stares at it. He has no inflection on his face, and I can't figure out why he's taking so long to tell me. I mean he can't be confused right? It's a digital test it literally says pregnant or not pregnant on it.

"If it's negative just tell me. It'll be okay. We'll just keep trying," I finally say. I tell myself it's not a big deal, but the truth is I want this so bad. I want little Pierce's running around the farmhouse. I want to fill the rooms we have empty upstairs.

Pierce's hands on my cheeks pull me from my thoughts and I see the stunning smile on his face.

"Holy shit," I whisper. "It's positive?"

"We're having a baby," he murmurs before kissing me hard.

Crawling into his lap, I burrow my head into his chest and let out all the emotions I'm feeling.

When I calm down a little, Pierce's hand running up and down my back soothingly, I pull back.

"Are you happy?" I ask him.

"Fucking ecstatic. I put my baby in you." He grins.

"Such a caveman." I roll my eyes.

"Are we telling everyone tomorrow?"

"I think we should keep it to ourselves for a little while."

"Done. Now let me take you to bed *Mrs. Almost Vanstone*, we need to celebrate." The salacious smile on his face makes me giddy as hell to see what he has in store for me.

And we thought life couldn't get any better.

It's finally here. The day I marry the love of my life.

From the very beginning of planning, we decided we wanted to do things our way and not even think about tradition. We slept together last night, although now that we know we have a third party involved, you wouldn't have been able to keep Pierce away from me. We've spent the entire morning together, enjoying brunch with our friends and just soaking in the day until it was time to get ready.

And now that time is here.

I kept things simple, much to Pierce's chagrin. My dress is a simple satin sheath but it's ridiculously flattering, and I feel amazing in it. The girls are wearing whatever they want to because we're not doing bridesmaids and groomsmen. It's actually a lot like Pen's wedding not so long ago.

Speaking of Pen, Pierce and I wanted to do something special for her and Andy since they're wedding was the only reason we met. So, Pierce is bringing Andy over here before we have to head out to the beach. Bea and Larkin are already there helping Sydney with last minute things, even though there is nothing to be done. I know my soon-to-be husband wouldn't stand for them working today.

The men finally show up and I nod at Pierce, letting him know this is his show.

"So, Jane and I wanted to do something special for you two. As a thank you for unknowingly bringing us together." He smiles over at me.

"We literally didn't do anything, man." Andy claps him on the back.

Watching Pierce fit in with my best friends and their husbands has been one of the highlights of the last few months. He's never had a true friend group before, and I come with a built in one.

"Yeah, I'm going to need you just accept the gift." Pierce chuckles.

Andy bows his head for him to continue.

"We want to gift you an anniversary trip every year. Whether that's here, or at another one of my resorts, it's your choice."

"Pierce, that's way too much," Pen says.

"It's really not. This isn't a lot for me, I promise, so just take it and enjoy a week or two every year on us."

"Thank you, man, that's beyond generous." Andy wisely accepts the offer. They all know getting Pierce to budge is not a thing that happens.

"Now, if you don't mind, I just want a minute with my fiancée one last time before we head out to get married." He grins at me.

They walk out, leaving us alone together.

"We shouldn't keep them waiting," I tell him.

"I just have one thing to give you first." He reaches into the pocket in this suit jacket and pulls out a letter.

It's become something of a thing with us. We both leave letters for each other around the house, telling each other how happy we are, how much we love each other, what we want to do to the other in bed later.

I snatch it from him, eager to see what words he wanted to tell me before we got married.

"I had a different one ... Before last night. This one felt better," he says as I pull out the letter.

My love,
Every single dream I had given up on has come true because of you. I love
you with every beat of my heart, every child we feed from the farm, every
baby we make.
I never thought this could be my life.
So, thank you, for letting me be the one you call husband.
Let's go get married, love.

I look up at him with nothing but excitement.

"Let's go get married!" I grab his hand and drag him to the door.

———◆———

Our ceremony is short and sweet, and now we're all eating our weight in incredible food and laughing until we cry.

"I'm so glad you didn't have that baby during the wedding," Pen says to Bea.

"God, me too, but I still have like seven weeks left, and I don't know how I have any room left for this kid," Bea says.

"Well as long as we get you back to Austin with no labor, I'll be happy," Riggs says. We almost had the wedding at the farm so Bea could be there, but she's just on the edge of not being able to fly, and her doctor approved it.

"You know, pretty soon our brunches are going to look a whole lot different," Larkin says.

"How so?" I ask.

"I mean, if the pattern holds, we're all going to be popping out kids soon. And then brunch will just be playdates with the kids and being responsible parents."

"Number one, I'm not following suit on this one, sorry guys, Andy and I are absolutely fine being the cool aunt and uncle," Pen says as Andy nods his head. "And two, we have husbands for a reason. Let them manage the playdates while we go to brunch. They can handle it."

"Amen!"

"Sold."

"I'll definitely take the baby so you can brunch with the girls, little bee," Riggs adds with a smile on his face.

"Same. I mean Gavin's pretty chill but if we grow our family, I'd be happy to stay and watch the kids while you guys go do brunch," Theo adds. Larkin turns and looks at him dreamily. "I like the sound of that," she says.

"So, the men will have the playdates, and we'll still get girl time then," Bea says to the group.

"We can take them to a park, right? Wear them out?" Riggs asks to the group, and we all laugh at his sweet innocence. It'll change in just a few short weeks but I know he's incredibly excited.

"How are you doing, love?" Pierce's voice sounds right next to me as he sits down.

"So good. We were just talking about how if we all have babies, minus Pen, the men will take the kiddos so we can still brunch."

We share a pointed look and a sly grin spreads over his face.

"Sounds like a great idea." He presses a kiss to my temple, and I fall in love all over again with him.

I've always dreamed of my life being a romance novel, but never in my wildest thoughts did I think it would come to fruition.

Pierce is my real-life book boyfriend come to life, and I'm holding on with both hands and never letting go.

THE END

Acknowledgments

I'm going to keep this one short and sweet because I'm too emotional that this is the end of the series.

Michelle- I couldn't ask for a better friend. Thank you for helping me, pushing me, and just being here for me every single day.

Tori- Thank you for constantly pushing me. For helping me make each book the best and pushing to make me a better writer

The Husband- You're the best. Every day you ask me what I need. If I need a break, or quiet time to write, you make it happen. I love you forever.

To my readers- Thank you will never be enough. You give me inspiration, hope, and so much love. I am not the author I am without you.

The Beginning
Meet the women of The Catalyst Series a decade before the series takes place!

The Detour
Bea and Riggs

The List
Penelope and Andy

The Vacation
Larkin and Theo

Be sure to join my newsletter to stay up to date on new releases and all other things me!

http://www.samanthamthomas.com

Made in the USA
Monee, IL
10 August 2023

40724007R00187